BEYOND ANDROMEDA

PETER TIRANT-JAMES

CHAPTER 1

ENCOUNTER

JORDAN AWOKE SUDDENLY, his senses immediately aroused as his awareness was so attuned to the sound that was reverberating through his ears, and indeed through his whole body. He sat bolt upright catching his breath and aware that his heart was racing. Could this be them? Could it really be happening?

Within a moment he was pulling on clothes and trying to be very quiet as he didn't want to raise suspicion with his older brother or his younger sister. He slipped his jumper on and moved his feet in an effort to locate his shoes, he couldn't risk turning on the light for fear of attracting more attention from the family. Finding his shoes, he made his way stealthily down the stairs and emerged into the living room before heading to the kitchen and out the back door. The knob seemed to take an eternity before it responded to his grasp, it finally yielded, but not before making the usual squeaking sound that so many doors do when they need some maintenance.

Within a moment he was outside in the semi-moonlit night and catching his breath in the cool night air. He was so glad he had donned his jumper given how cold he suddenly felt and of course he had just left a nice warm bed.

He quickly made his way to the shed where the familiar sound was coming from. What he hadn't realised at that moment was that his younger sister, Melissa had also been awoken but Jordan had no idea about this and was blissfully unaware of her presence.

He continued in pursuit of the sound and being careful not to make serious noise so that he would not lose the element of surprise. His breathing was quite measured now, and he moved slowly to where the sound continued to emanate from. The closer he came the brighter the light emerged from the place of the sound. Suddenly he was confronted by the sheer brilliance of the light and his eyes closed attempting to protect himself from its piercing invasion upon his senses. Instinctively he held his hand up in order to protect himself from the brightness and at the same time to look at what he had stumbled upon. He gave a sudden gasp as he realised that this was indeed what he had intuitively felt was always going to happen. Eventually he was able to look with steady gaze and begin to take in the enormity of what he was witnessing. He could scarcely believe his eyes. It was undoubtedly a craft from another world, that was his first thought. The craft was quite different from anything he had ever seen. Its oval shaped appearance and its clean lines made it like something he could not even imagine. He stopped in his tracks and watched at what he thought was both a safe and respectful distance. He stood completely and utterly mesmerised; he couldn't take his eyes off the craft completely absorbed and wondered if it really was from beyond the stars or just another product from some country's attempt at hoaxing the people. He watched intently listening to the sound and noticing that the pitch kept rising and falling and simultaneously emitting a variety of differing coloured lights. His curiosity was increasing as he began to edge his way closer. Eventually he was able to see it in more detail and noticed just how seamless it really was. He stood motionless transfixed by the sheer beauty of the craft.

Suddenly and without warning a panel in the craft opened and he could actually see inside. He peered through the light straining every part of his body to get a better look. He remembered his sister's words about being nosey,

"Gee your nose won't get rusty," and smiled to himself.

He could no longer help himself, he pushed forward no longer captivated by his fear but more compelled by his curiosity. By now he was at the entrance and looking inside. It was not very big at all. Suddenly a voice seemed to come from nowhere. Perhaps he was hearing things because it sounded like it was coming from inside his head. Was he hearing things? He shook his head in disbelief only to hear the sounds again. What was going on? He could see no one inside, it appeared quite empty. His breathing had become elevated and he could feel his heart beating even more audibly than before. It was then he became aware of somebody else's presence and he quickly looked around. He gasped as he took in the full view of his sister Melissa. Before he could ask any questions, she calmly volunteered that she had heard the sound too and had followed him, whilst keeping a safe distance. Jordan's mouth just gaped and for a moment he was lost for words. He looked at his sister almost in disbelief. Melissa seemed neither afraid nor overawed by the sight of this craft, but almost treating like it was usual to find this in one's back yard. She then asked out loud, "I wonder where it has come from?" Before she had finished her question there appeared to be an answer right inside her head. Her eyes visibly widened, and she caught Jordan's vision who was looking equally stunned! "We are from a planet far, far away and it is not visible from your planet you call Earth." Melissa caught herself wondering how it was possible for them to answer in this way and before she knew it the voice was explaining that formal speech was an older form of communication and that they had long been able to communicate telepathically. She gasped as it dawned upon her that her own thoughts were no longer private, and her cheeks began to colour quickly.

"Do you read everybody's thoughts?" she asked impatiently. "No," was the swift reply. "Only when we are seeking to make contact and build links of friendship."

Melissa breathed a sigh of relief. Now she could allow herself to think about some of those girlie things that she often daydreamed about.

She then questioned further, "You say from beyond our solar system but in what direction?" Immediately the response was forthcoming,

"We are beyond your star system of Andromeda and for now that is all you need to know." Melissa felt satisfied for the moment.

Jordan had listened to the whole conversation and was still trying to come to terms with what he was hearing and witnessing. His mind was racing with so many questions pushing into his consciousness.

"How long have you been coming to our planet? Why haven't you made contact before? Why have you come to us and what do you want by coming?" The questions kept tumbling out. Now there was only silence; suddenly the gravity of the moment began to dawn on this young mind.

There was something of high importance with their presence and Jordan and Melissa were seemingly part of this plan! Was there a plan? Jordan couldn't stop his mind from jumping ahead. What was really going on? He looked at Melissa wondering what it was that they had stumbled across? How would this event impact upon their lives? Still more questions surfaced, and no answers were forthcoming from these visitors from a distant galaxy!

Then as if by magic the craft's open hatch closed and within a second it lifted ever so gently and was gone. Jordan and Melissa looked at each other in total disbelief. Had it all been a dream? No, it couldn't have been, because where the craft had landed there was a distinct mark and an unusual silvery trail by the spot where the hatch opened. They looked around the site again and again searching for more evidence of their Extra-Terrestrial visitors. But no more traces were to be uncovered in the night light.

Then they both decided that nothing more could be achieved so they made their way back to the house. They made a pact that they wouldn't share their story with anyone else, especially members of their immediate family. Somehow this strange encounter had brought this brother and sister closer together. They began to realize they had a very special bond. This bond was going to develop some amazing gifts in the future, of which they had no idea.

Slowly they made their way back to the house pondering why the craft had disappeared so suddenly? Both stood nonplussed. As they reached Melissa's bedroom Jordan did something he had never done in his life before. He reached out and drew his sister closer and held her close giving her a huge hug. She was taken by surprise but didn't resist at all and in fact it felt so good. She began smiling all over her body giving her a warm glow inside. For the first time in her life she felt totally accepted by her elder brother, as though she really belonged.

She then opened the door to her bedroom looked at Jordan and smiled saying, "I don't really feel tired, do you want to come in for a chat?"

He nodded sensing that there were some things that they needed to discuss in more detail. With that Melissa slipped off her coat and still in her PJs, slipped under the covers and propped herself up with pillows. Jordan made himself comfortable on the end of the bed.

He began, "You know I don't think we can share any of this with the rest of the family." She nodded in agreement. Jordan continued, "They would only laugh at us especially David our older brother." "What, and did you see little green men as well and did they offer to take you for a ride?"

It was decided emphatically, no sharing not with anyone. Melissa then looked at Jordan and said,

"There is something more I need to tell you; I haven't told you the whole story, but I feel I must say this now. It is true that I heard you getting up but that is not what awakened me, I was already wide awake."

"How come?" questioned Jordan.

"Well," replied Melissa "I had the strangest feeling as though there was somebody in my room. I woke up looking all around and as I did, I caught a glimpse of this figure disappearing as though it went straight through the walls," she paused for a moment waiting for Jordan's response. He sat there motionless for what seemed ages and then said,

"I really don't know what to make of it, but I certainly believe you, in fact, I do accept what you are saying." Melissa had felt right to trust him, and the hug now seemed more important than ever.

"I wonder how they do it?" mused Jordan. "I mean walk through walls." Jordan was already an avid student of quantum physics and read anything that would increase his understanding of one of his favourite subjects.

Suddenly the door opened and in the dim light of the passageway stood Mum.

"What on earth are you two doing at this time of the night?" There was a stony silence for a moment and then Melissa confessed.

"I was having a bad dream and Jordan had heard me and had come in to see if I was ok." That was not out of the question as their bedrooms were next to each other and Jordan was the more sensitive of her two brothers.

"Are you ok, honey?" asked Mum looking concerned regarding her daughter's confession. Melissa looked up her face now shining brightly and affirmed that she was fine, and Jordan had been 'ace'. Mum then admonished them that it was time for bed and that Jordan needed to get back to his own room. He nodded acknowledging that he had heard Mum.

The door closed as suddenly as it opened, and Mum returned to her bedroom. Jordan looked lovingly at his sister and said,

"I really do have a lot to thank you for." She beamed back at him and said,

"I'm sure I will think of a way you can pay me back," and with that comment Jordan returned to his room.

What neither of them realized was that they had begun an incredible journey which was going to change their lives forever and many other lives as well.

The next morning the breakfast table was very quiet, Melissa and Jordan could hardly exchange glances. Mum looked on with curious interest, as no mention was made of the night disturbance for Melissa and Jordan's rendered assistance. Mum felt it was best left unspoken and it would heal more quickly.

Jordan was already finishing his cereal and getting ready for his day. Melissa asked casually, "What have you planned for the day?"

He responded by saying, "Basically I will be taking myself off to the science museum and doing some research on the planetary system," Melissa responded,

"That sounds interesting and would you mind if I tagged along with you?" He thought for a moment and nodded in the affirmative.

"I would enjoy the company."

David who had now finished his breakfast and was moving over to the sink threw a glance over at his kid sister indicating complete surprise at her interest in science. He then couldn't help himself and chided "Girls should stick to domestic science and not involve themselves in such disciplines." His Mum then stepped in and reminded him that in fact she had a science degree and had spent many hours in research work in a laboratory. David's face reddened and Mum recognized that he felt suitably chastised.

The morning air was fresh as the two of them made their way to the museum. What interested Melissa was the way Jordan had planned to get there. Instead of going down the lane and catching the bus he had chosen to go through the woods. Melissa immediately questioned his choice of routes to which he readily replied,

"I thought this way would give us privacy and more time to discuss the events of last night." Melissa smiled and nodded in agreement saying,

"This was good thinking."

Jordan began by asking, "What really stood out for you about last night?" There was a long pause and eventually she began to speak,

"Well the appearance of the figure in my room has left me wondering just why they wanted to contact me or us and why it disappeared when I awoke. It all seems a mystery to me and there doesn't seem to be any ready answers, nothing seems to fit." Jordan then chipped in and suggested,

"The suddenness and speed with which the craft sped off didn't add up either!" Neither of them could make any sense of their encounter. They continued in silence for a little while until they came to a clearing in the wood. Melissa decided to sit for a moment and just reflect on the events breathing in the clear morning air. Then Melissa began thinking out loud,

"I wonder if they just want us to be curious about who they are and what they are doing here?" Jordan responded, "Yes, but why us?"

Again, there was more silence and more bewilderment on both their faces. Then Melissa spoke again,

"I wonder whether they will make contact again?" "Well we will have to wait until tonight I expect or maybe some time in the future," said Jordan rather matter-of-factly, but there was no conviction in his voice.

"I guess we will just have to wait and see. And if there is a next time, we need to have all our questions ready in our mind," Melissa reflected.

Jordan jumped up quickly, "Melissa that's brilliant, let's get to work now and prepare our list of questions."

They both continued to make their way to the museum and after arriving placed themselves in two seats with plenty of writing space. They continued writing and exchanging their questions and there were many of them!

Primarily, "Why us two?" and "Why did they disappear so quickly?" and "Why wouldn't they share the name of their home planet with us!" more questions arose as they sat there. Lunch time had come and gone, and they had both gone off to do their own research. Melissa had found the curator and was asking him about systems beyond Andromeda. Somehow this became important to her. There was a deep nagging feeling that somehow, she was linked to this planet! How could this be since she knew that she was born in a local hospital and had often talked about her birth with her Mum.

She recalled some of those earlier conversations now. Suddenly they began to take on a whole new meaning! Mum had shared with her,

"Your birth was not only very easy but also very fast," and as though her daughter had signaled before the usual means that it was time for her to arrive. No labour pains, no back ache just this almost telepathic message. It was time for me to be born. It set her wondering how come she was able to communicate this to her Mum. Melissa had developed a strong sense of herself and her self-worth and struggled hugely with people who displayed characteristics of dishonesty and false modesty. Maybe that is why she had always got on so well with Jordan and struggled with both her Dad and David, not that they were dishonest but not always the easiest to communicate with.

She was always challenging her eldest brother who often became both defensive and aggressive. For her part she seldom enjoyed these exchanges and had learned to disrespect her brother because of it. Her Dad was different again. He often dismissed her and put her attitude of self-confidence and intuitiveness down to her immature years. This didn't go down well with Melissa, but she had dealt with in a most mature manner. Anyway, Dad was mostly at work and even on the weekends she had more than enough interests to keep her out of his way. She was reflecting on her Dad and wondered how she might get closer to him?

Suddenly she came back into the room and focused on the business in hand. The curator was now showing her the very latest research made available to the museum around new discoveries in the solar system and beyond, alas there was nothing appearing beyond Andromeda that looked remotely like a planetary system that would support life.

She returned to her seat only to find Jordan packed up and ready to make for home. "We must get going," he said hurriedly, "It has already started to get dark and we won't make the woods before it does so!" Melissa recognized the urgency. She immediately packed her backpack and left the building after a grateful goodbye to the curator.

The night air was already chilly as they made their way to the woods, the first part of the journey had already taken them some 15 minutes and by now it was quite dark as they entered the woods. However, they had both done this before so there was no real fear for either of them. They continued to chat excitedly, Melissa sharing her research around the possibility of a life support system beyond Andromeda. She expressed her dismay about her results but then said something that stopped Jordan in his tracks.

"You know I feel like the planet from which our visitors have come from is somehow known to me, almost as though I have been there. I seem to be getting these hazy images of the planet,"

Jordan now began to wonder if his little sister was going too far in her imagination. He eventually replied,

"How could you possibly know this, what evidence could you have to support this?" Before she could answer he reflected out loud,

"I know this is your intuition!" He had not meant it as a criticism more like an afterthought.

Melissa responded,

"Oh, not you too, it's bad enough having Dad going at me about this and now you." Jordan was perceptive enough to know that he had touched a sore spot and immediately tried to retrieve the situation with his rejoinder,

"No, I do respect your intuition and more than ever how it has guided you." With that comment Melissa felt somewhat reassured and went on to explain, as best she could about the images that had come to her conscious level.

Suddenly from seemingly out of nowhere a man appeared and grabbed Melissa, put his arms around her, preventing her from escaping, but he hadn't counted on her letting out the most ear piercing of screams. Jordan turned around in a flash and seeing the man and his attempt to take his sister leapt fearlessly onto his back putting both hands over his eyes and digging his fingers right into his eyes. This was more than enough for him to release Melissa and concentrate on his assailant. At that point Jordan shouted,

"Run Mel, I'll be OK."

Melissa needed no second invitation and took off, the next moment something happened that took them both by surprise. Melissa had burst into the clearing to find the spacecraft right in front of her and before she knew it, she was somehow magically inside and sitting next to her was Jordan. He looked at her completely dazed. What had just happened stunned them both. The door was already closed and they both had this wonderful feeling of safety.

What about their attacker was their immediate question? Before they could draw breath, they were hearing,

"It's all ok he is just stunned and when he comes around, he will have no memory of you or this craft, we will have erased it from his consciousness."

By now their respective breathing had settled and the heart rate was subsiding to something like normal. They simply sat for a moment just allowing for the events of the last few minutes to sink in.

Clearly Melissa was aware that her anxiety levels were still very high, and she needed some more time, Jordan then did something else he had never done before. He put his arm firmly around her and just held Melissa. As he did this he noticed something he had never witnessed before, Melissa began to relax almost as though the fear which had gripped her body was now leaving, her breathing had completely normalized and her body had become soft to hold, the stiffness had dissipated. She looked at him and smiled with a warm response which had thank you all over.

"You really are a good brother and back there you showed how much you really care, I'm so glad I chose this family to be born into."

Jordan simply smiled but was still trying to take in her last comment but had decided that this was not the time ask for clarification about her choice of families. His wisdom already developed beyond his years.

In the next moment it dawned on them just where they were, immediately the questions came. "How did you know where to come and how did you get us into the craft so quickly?"

"My you really are good with the questions and some of them will have to wait especially all those you planned for us at the museum today. It is especially important for us to know you are safe, therefore we intervened to ensure your safety. Beyond that we will not interfere with your normal life until we have helped you to understand your mission and our part in that mission. We let the man go because your own system needs to take care of him, and that will be your decision. We are not yet ready to elaborate on your future, and yes Melissa you are correct in that you have memories of your origin. These memories belong to our system and let us assure you that your insight serves you well." They both looked at each other as they took in the comments, it took them completely by surprise.

How could it be that they were to have this special mission and what could it mean and what could it be? No more answers were forthcoming regarding their latest questions, but one question was answered. "The reason we left in such a hurry last night was due to our scanners being alerted to surveillance in the area. We don't wish to attract unnecessary attention at this stage. As you become more aware you will understand most governments are suspicious and controlling, neither which serves your world's best interests".

"When will we see you again?" There was a long pause and eventually they were being told, "Your development will be continually guided and supported and that whenever it becomes necessary for us to visit, we will find you, like we did tonight." "When does our mission begin?" they both asked simultaneously.

"When you are ready," came the swift reply. Again, "How long will that be?" The question asked by them simultaneously. This time the answer was more puzzling.

"Your last question tells us that you are indeed close." They both looked at each other stunned, "Whatever does that mean?"

At this point the hatch opened and they were outside without any movement on their part. The craft disappeared in the same manner of the previous night and they were left standing in the cool night air. Suddenly Jordan looked at his watch realized that it was late, and they needed to be home.

They had a brief look around the site but there were no tell-tale signs of evidence of their Extra-Terrestrial friends. This time they knew beyond any doubt that they were really friends because of their intervention to save them both.

Now it was clear that none of this could be disclosed to the family least of all David or Dad. They talked most animatedly all the way home and focused on their final comment regarding the final answer given by the Extra-Terrestrial. "Your last question tells us you are very close to begin your mission." It was this answer that would haunt them in the coming weeks.

As they approached home, they realized that they needed to tell their parents why they were so late. Melissa was ok to disclose her attack by this horrible man in the woods and of course Jordan would have no difficulty in backing it up. It was agreed.

They burst in through the back door only to be greeted by a very anxious Mum with, "Where on earth have you been?"

They both sat down together and told the story of the attacker in the woods and how brave Jordan had been to come to the rescue of his sister. Once the story had been told, father was informed, and it was decided that a statement needed to be made to the police.

After tea was served and the two were then taken down to the local police station where the reports and statements were made. Both Melissa and Jordan looked at what seemed endless mugshots of villains. Eventually, they found a picture of the man they both recognised as being the person who had attacked them. That being done they were both taken home. They showered and were ushered off to bed.

It had been a day filled with all kinds of adventure, including excitement and fear but now they were home in their own safe world, and it felt very safe indeed.

CHAPTER 2

THE MISSION BEGINS

TWO FULL WEEKS had elapsed and there had been no more contact. Jordan and Melissa had not been idle. They were spending more time together than ever before, and it hadn't gone unnoticed by the rest of the family.

Janet had been warmed by the closeness that had developed for her two youngest and she had spent more time than usual reflecting on their pasts. Ironing was her reflection time and there had been a lot of it lately and it had given her more opportunity for this reflection. She had always known that Jordan was a gifted child and from an early age he had shown aptitude in areas of science she had barely touched upon whilst doing her degree. From an early age he had used his computer time to continue to research everything he could on quantum physics. She would always remember the occasion when, at the age of seven he came in and announced that the world's greatest brain the late Dr Albert Einstein had not only never fitted in at school. Furthermore, he struggled to come to terms with the world of quantum physics. He declared boldly to his mum,

"I know that he considered the subject spooky indicating I believe that he didn't quite understand it, pretty amazing hey Mum from such an eminent scientist?" He looked at his mum and said, "How come our greatest brain in the last century didn't get it?"

His mum could see the bewilderment written all over his face and then responded knowingly and simply saying,

"I guess the world was waiting for someone like you to come along and tell us how it all works." Her answer took him a little by surprise but certainly gave him more impetus to continue pursuing this field. He wasn't like some other boys his age for he was honest and troubled by the double standards he found wherever he looked in the world. His experience of school left him confused. The acceptance of and lack of interest in making the world a better place. People were regularly bored by class and lessons were often aimed at the lowest common denominator. The brighter kids in his class constantly played up because they saw no challenge in the work. Jordan became increasingly frustrated by the whole enterprise. On one occasion his parents had been summoned to the school to see what could be done about his errant behaviour. George his father had spoken sternly to him admonishing him to toe the line and fit in. Janet, his mum knew that that would never work. She recognized that Jordan saw the sham in the system. Janet had tried to speak with George about what she saw in their son and how gifted he was, but it was always going to be a difficult decision for his parents to agree. Especially since George was not so academically inclined. Nevertheless, George could see the value of learning and continued to support Jordan's pursuit into expanding his horizons. This included his avid interest into the world of quantum mechanics. She continued to reflect on her son's compassion for other people, and this had really developed in the last few weeks in relation to his sister. She was so admiring of the way he had supported her with the incident in the woods and how much genuine affection he had for her going and sitting with her after the bad dream. Now she had observed him reaching out and giving her hand a squeeze in a most supportive way. There was never any competition in their relationship. He was so ready to acknowledge her own giftedness, especially with her intuition. Janet felt reassured by their mutual support for each other and could see them nurturing each other in a way that gave her so much pleasure as a mum. It also gave her hope for the future of the planet especially if it was in the hands of people like these two. Little did she know that it was going to be the case. This was going to unfold even in her lifetime. There was both an air of contentment and an air of apprehension when she reflected upon the world they were inheriting, a world that she and her generation had helped to create.

Suddenly her reflection was shattered as her three adult children arrived home. Two at high school and one in her fourth year who was just beginning to find her feet in life. They all landed home together. David was now happily enrolled in his second year at university and clearly enjoying the freedom and challenge of being the master of his own destiny. However, on arriving home David's first stop was the fridge.

"Mum I'm starving what's to eat?" Before she could answer him, he was already scooping the ice cream into a bowl and getting into the stewed fruit which just happened to be his favourite, apple and rhubarb. Having consumed that in no time at all he made his way to the bread box to make another sandwich with lettuce cold meat tomato and mayo. Having managed to put it on a plate he plonked in front of the T.V. and proceeded to find a program to his liking.

Jordan was very much into his food but for Melissa it was not so important, but they still made their way into the kitchen to engage with Mum.

"So how was your day today Mum? What was your highlight?" Janet smiled and said, "You would be really surprised." They both chimed in together,

"Then surprise us!" Tears welled up her eyes as she looked lovingly into their eyes one and the then other.

"Oh, Mum nothing horrible has happened tell us please," they responded together. She sat down so completely overwhelmed by these two beautiful young adults she had helped create and raise.

"No nothing like that at all. These are tears of joy and are due in no small measure from my family and especially our beautiful children." Both Melissa and Jordan paused for a moment looking at her intently, they were suddenly aware that this was a very poignant moment and nothing more needed to be said. Janet looked at them both and stood up and hugged them both, holding them ever so close and tightly. It was going to be one of those family moments which would be forever etched in their memories for years to come, and from which enormous strength could be drawn.

Just at that moment David appeared and watched with interest and intrigued at what was happening. His remarks reflected his age as much as anything else when he simply said,

"Oh, it's group hug time is it?" and shrugged and walked out.

Mum called after him, "You are welcome to join us the more the merrier" For a moment he stopped, turned and walked over and reached out to his sister, brother and his Mother and felt the warmth of his family. For an instant he felt relaxed and welcomed in a way he had not experienced for an awfully long time. He looked at his Mum and smiled and somehow words were no longer important.

David went back to his television whilst the others went off to their various pursuits.

Within moments of them reaching their bedrooms Melissa burst into Jordan's bedroom saying, "I think I understand what they meant when they said, "Your last question is the key." Jordan looked puzzled, "How so?"

"You know what just happened out there when we both asked Mum the same question at the same time and the impact that had on Mum? Remember when we were in the spacecraft, we did exactly the same thing. We both asked the very same question at the same time." Jordan looked at her for a full moment realizing that yet again his younger sister had this incredible insight which had opened another door. His own intuition was now kicking in and something inside him was resonating in his whole body telling him that this was another step in their journey. He reached out and hugged her and danced with her round and round. Eventually the excitement abated, and they sat and talked about the future. They were already both aware that they would be contacted very shortly and this time there were going to be some important developments.

They both went to their lockers to retrieve their list of questions prepared what seemed an eternity ago at the museum. Jordan ventured the next question, "How is it possible that we know we are going to be contacted soon?" What happened next just blew them away.

"It is because you have recognized your joint strength and have continued to support each other in ways that will enhance your mission here on this planet." The voice came from within.

"You are also aware that your roots are not just in this planet, but you have what we call dual citizenship. Yes, we are telling you that you have some intelligence from another source and that is from our planet."

There was a long pause as Melissa and Jordan tried to take this in. "How did this happen?" they chimed in together.

"We will explain this to you at a later date and soon it will all make sense."

Just at that moment Mum's voice sounded announcing that tea was ready. They looked at each other and could scarcely take it in, and now they were going to eat unable to contain their heightened emotions and wondered just how this was going to affect their lovely family. Would it ever be the same again?

Tea was most enjoyable, and the chatter was bright and breezy, but of course nothing was said of the previous conversation they had encountered just before the call for tea. Much of the conversation focused on the good feelings within the family. David spoke about how good it was for all the family to be at one, and this really surprised both Melissa and Jordan. It also encouraged them to embrace their brother more thoroughly.

Tea was over and the Melissa and Jordan returned to Jordan's bedrooms and once the door closed, they began to revise their questions in readiness of their next encounter. Hardly had they entered the room when it became clear they needed to return to the woods and the opening where they had initially been in the spacecraft. Their immediate problem was how would we leave the house without causing disturbance and concern for the rest of the family. It had been a long day and Melissa had decided that it was an early night for her. She took herself off to her bedroom, bidding everyone goodnight. She gave her mum a long hug and said her personal goodnight. Janet was surprised but put it down to the early show of affection with the rest of her siblings.

The house quietened down and slowly but surely, the two slipped out without being detected. It was only about twenty to twenty-five minutes' walk and they would be in the clearing. They arrived just to see the craft landing noiselessly. They looked at each other and could hardly believe that this was happening to them. The hatch was now open, and they made their way inside. They could hear their instructions being given. There was another smaller area where they were directed to. There were small benches whereby they were invited to lay and be strapped in. When this was effected smoothly, the hatch closed, and the craft rose as noiselessly as it arrived and within a moment was miles above the earth's circle. They were still strapped in and instructed to remain there until the craft had docked in the larger craft.

Eventually the straps were released, and they got up and were able to stretch their legs. It was hard to believe they had reached such a distance in only minutes, and immediately it was explained that the process of propulsion was vastly different from that which earth people used to go into space.

"Our process is more efficient and much safer, faster and therefore better."

"Now it is time to begin your training and tell you why you are here and why you were chosen. But first we need you to come aboard our main support vessel which has been out of view of your earth community." The words resounding in their minds still took some getting used too. Jordan immediately thought of Star Wars and the huge ships appearing in the movie and was quickly questioned about Star Wars. He was happy enough to share his view on the movie and explained it in the following way 'making special mention of the force.'

"Well they certainly weren't far from the truth and yes there is precisely this kind of energy throughout the galaxy."

Jordan smiled to himself knowing that he was right all along and the kids at school mostly had not really understood how much energy there was available in the world and beyond.

They were standing gazing on one of the viewing platforms at the earth watching it intently. Jordan's vision was fixed on what he could see as being a mixture of dark grey and black spots enveloping large areas of the planet. He was musing to himself and looked again and again. What was happening to the planet? Before he could mouth his own conclusion, he heard the message loud and clear.

"Yes, you are already a long way down the track to destroying your beautiful planet and only a concerted effort will repair it."

Jordan felt a cold chill run up his spine. How could we be so blind, how is it that we haven't seen the signs? He gradually began to realize that at least part of his life's mission had to do with challenging the ever-increasing problem of pollution and its many impacts. His face became grave and his whole manner took on a much more sombre stance. His mind began working overtime on how he might begin to challenge the vast waste that so many of the developed countries had embarked upon which continued to threaten the health of the planet. Yet he was aware enough that simply stopping all production would have catastrophic results for everyone, jobs would go, families would be destroyed in the wake of unemployment. What about the civil unrest? his mind was racing and then he noticed Melissa whose face just shone in the light of the craft. She stood there silently, and he noticed the tears just streaming down her ashen face. Could she be upset about what impacted upon Jordan? It was as though she was transfixed her eyes focused on earth never flinching for a moment but processing this incredible grief and still the tears flowed ever so gently and consistently. Finally, Jordan had to know what was so sad for his sister.

"What are you seeing?" he questioned insistently.

She looked at him for the first time since they were in space and began describing just what she was seeing. "Jordan, I see this intense energy all over the earth and in places it is just so dark that the people who are surrounded by it are losing their way." She paused for a moment and then made a profound statement; declaring that humanity was in the grip of a dreadful cancer epidemic. Jordan looked at her thinking immediately that she was speaking about a huge medical catastrophe. Jordan continued looking at her intently.

"How can you be so sure, what medical training have you had which allows you to reach that conclusion?" he questioned further.

Melissa fixed her gaze upon him and just said.

"We are all human aren't we and really belong together needing to support each other and help each other to reach our true potential and develop our giftedness." She continued, "Yet here we are plotting to control, to kill, to exploit, is that not what cancer is when one organism turns on anther and seeks to destroy it!" Jordan was stunned by both the simplicity and the eloquence of her comment, and he nodded in agreement, he had never looked at it like that before. He then had to ask,

"How is it that you can see that from all the way up here?" Melissa thought for a moment and then replied, "I'm not really sure but it is as though I can see this concentration of energy around certain people all over the planet and I have only become aware of it since coming to outer space. This energy feels destructive and it is characterized by fear, revenge and hate." At that moment her talking was interrupted by their hosts. They both heard the remarks that yes this would be part of their work and that there was much to learn and to research and other contacts to be made.

Suddenly they looked at their watches and realized they had been gone some time and needed to be home. Before they could express their thoughts, they were transported to their smaller craft, strapped back into their seats and gliding effortlessly to their special part of the woods.

Melissa was already thinking about the vibrational level of the people who had caught her attention and was wondering how she could find out more.

The craft gently rested on the soft earth and before they knew it the hatch was open, and they were on their way home.

Suddenly Jordan froze, he was conscious of some people close by and immediately cautioned Melissa to be quiet. Instantly she obeyed but it was too late and Jordan's worst nightmare was upon them. It was none other than the gang from school who delighted in pushing him around and generally bullying him whenever the opportunity presented. Terry the leader stood up close and right in his face ready to throw the first punch, then he stopped for a moment and turned his attention to Melissa. The rest of the gang had now made a circle around them both so there was no escaping. Terry eyed off Melissa and spoke softly and deliberately,

"Let's have some fun with her, she's old enough for us to have some fun with."

With those words ringing in his ears, Jordan's fury knew no bounds and his fist found its way right into the solar plexus of Terry. Terry was immediately winded and fell to the ground writhing in pain. For a moment there was confusion and Jordan reached for Melissa's hand and pulled her along with him through the woods. The plan was to escape but it was short lived as the rest of the gang had now gathered its wits and held the two tightly and as much as they struggled there was no escape. Terry had started to recover by now and was eyeing off Jordan menacingly. He walked all around him whilst he was being held and made ready to really punch him up. Jordan now had nothing to lose, so he baited Terry taunting him,

"Can't even fight your own battles you have to have your mates to hold your victims, you really are just a big coward."

That was more than Terry could take and he motioned to his minions to release Jordan so he could prove his superior strength once and for all. Jordan now having been freed seemed to get a new strength and was shaping up to the challenge No one could have anticipated what happened next. Terry and his gang were laid out flat each member was lying on his back as though he had been totally knocked out cold. Jordan could scarcely believe his eyes and continued to scrutinize the bodies lying motionlessly on the ground. They seemed to be breathing ok but almost in a deep state of unconsciousness.

They both turned their attention to the craft which was now clearly in view.

"They will not trouble you further. We have not hurt them but simply how would you put it 'disabled them' for the time being and when they wake up, they will have no memory of this whole experience." They both uttered their profound thanks to their friends knowing that they were always going to be safe with them and their trust had been further reinforced.

Jordan and Melissa now turned for home quite shaken from their ordeal but highly relieved that this whole experience would never be raised again by Terry and his gang and they would certainly not be raising it.

Melissa looked thoughtfully in Jordan's direction and mused,

"You certainly gave him something to go on with," and with those words took his hand and gave it a big squeeze. He smiled for a moment feeling proud that he had defended his sister's honour. Then they discussed what had happened and were amazed at the way their new friends had come to their rescue and how they had not wanted to harm Terry or his gang. Terry was not so caring he would have been happy if they had been roughed up. This incident challenged Jordan at many levels and he was going to revisit it more than once. He couldn't quite get his head around this level of aggression, but he knew it was an important lesson as too how he might deal with this type of behaviour in the future.

It really was quite late by now and they would have to get into the house without being seen and this was no easy matter. They needed a plan as to the best way of achieving this. Melissa was thoughtful for a moment and then she smiled knowingly.

"Why don't we use some of the branches to cover ourselves and sneak up to the house quietly so that we will not be seen or be obvious?"

It seemed like a good idea at the time and Jordan certainly hadn't thought of anything else, so they began to effect their camouflage. They could at least enter the house through the back gate which meant they need not be caught up in the glare of the streetlights. The gate creaked a little as they began making their way up the path, but it seemed that they had been heard as a light went on in the back almost catching them in its glow. They both stopped and the bushes that covered them seemed to give them protection for the moment. Suddenly the shadowy figure of Mum emerged and in her hand was a flashlight streaking eerily up and down the path. Nothing had caught her attention and she had decided that there was nothing untoward happening so the light went out and the door closed quietly. Now how were they going to get into the house whilst Mum was still awake? This was really going to be a challenge as Mum was such a light sleeper and she was already awake. It was quite cold now and neither of them wanted to spend any more time out in the cold than was necessary. Melissa's mind was working overtime. Could their alien friends work some more magic? Hardly had she thought about it. when she became aware of their presence and feeling amazingly comfortable. She began disrobing her camouflage. "What are you doing?' whispered Jordan.

"Mum will be out again and then we'll be for it!"

"No, it's ok I have spoken to our friends and they have assured me that Mum will be fast asleep, and we will be safe to go in without being seen." Melissa replied in hushed tones. Jordan (who had not picked up on the communication) looked fondly at his sister and began disrobing. They quietly made their way to their respective bedrooms and lay wondering what lay ahead for them. There were so many questions that continued to exercise their minds, not the least being just what two people could really do to change the world for the better? And indeed, what was for the better? What about progress? What about technology? How could they possibly keep coming and going from the house without being spotted? Eventually the questions ceased to rumble around the corridors of their minds, and they drifted off into a deep sleep.

The next morning arrived all too soon and the two space travellers managed to get to breakfast at the same time. David was already down as he had decided to go to see if he could find some work during the long university vacation. He decided to look for work before he took himself off for more preparatory study at university. He was really enjoying his bacon eggs tomatoes and hash brown breakfast when he looked up and saw his two younger siblings come down. He smiled and nodded as they sat down but couldn't speak whilst he was still enjoying what looked like his last mouthful of food.

"What are you guys doing today?" he enquired Melissa threw a quick glance towards Jordan and nonchalantly said,

"I think I am off to the library." David looked thoughtful for a moment and then ventured. "Is my little sister really starting to become an academic?" Melissa smiled and simply said,

"I have some research to do on the computer and hopefully there would be some books I can access as well." David was visibly impressed and was really encouraging as he commented,

"I am really proud of you and I wish you well." Melissa smiled and said,

"Thanks."

She was not used to receiving compliments from her eldest brother. She realised that he wouldn't be so proud of her if he knew what she was researching but Melissa was content to accept the support and took it in the spirit it was given. Melissa paused for a moment looking more intently at David whilst he was not engaging with her. Her face became quite soft and she seemed to be quite curious about what she was observing.

Jordan immediately picked up on her demeanour but decided that now was not the time to ask what was going on. David was oblivious to it all and by now had finished his coffee and was pushing his chair under the table and making off to the job centre. He left but couldn't help himself and had to have a parting shot at Jordan.

"I don't suppose that you will be taking a leaf out of your sister's book and do some serious academic work?"

Jordan simply smiled and offered no response; it would be better to say nothing and not arouse any suspicion regarding their space travel. Now that David had left Jordan had to ask what Melissa had seen whilst gazing at David? Now he was met with that similar look which he had observed whilst she engaged with David. He paused and looked inquiringly at his sister until he could contain himself no longer.

"What is it?"

By now Melissa was smiling and nodding and then broke her silence, "I can see all these amazing colours around you, and I could see them around David as well."

Jordan was taken by surprise when he heard these words from her and wondered what it meant.

Suddenly Melissa realized that there was another area of research she needed to work on. She pondered for a moment and then offered her response,

"I think it means I can see people's energy and how healthy or not they are!" Melissa suddenly became very quiet, just what does this mean for me? What kind of responsibility have I been given? More questions arose and she could hardly stop her heart from pounding. Now her mind was racing, and her breathing became shallow and she slumped quickly into the nearest chair. She had not asked for this, so why was it happening?

Her mind continued to race, and she immediately grabbed for a glass of water, Jordan watched quietly wondering what was going through Melissa's mind? He reached over the table and took her hand gently, sensing her disquiet and smiled in a gesture of understanding.

"Do you want to talk about what is happening for you now?" He enquired quietly. Melissa paused for a moment and then began to voice her deepest fears. "What if I can see everybody's health and what if I can see when they are close to dying?" Jordan suddenly saw the reality of her plight. He began to realize how deeply this would impact upon her life; it was certainly not something he would want to have any time soon. He was now very quiet and thoughtful, wondering if there was anything, he could say to his sister that would lighten her burden. Just at that moment Mum appeared and immediately changed the direction of the conversation with a breezy question about what they would like for breakfast. Melissa's response was swift and to the point.

"I'm not hungry so I think I'll skip breakfast."

Mum immediately cast a knowing look at her daughter and pursued her with a question.

"Ok what is going on are you feeling unwell?" She queried. Now Melissa was on the spot, knowing that she couldn't fake sickness with her mum but not wanting to share her unwanted gift at this stage. She looked thoughtfully at her mum and volunteered that she just wasn't that hungry and really wanted to get to the library sooner rather than later. Mum was not completely convinced but was able to trust Melissa. Whatever was going on she would speak to her when the time was right or decide that she could manage the matter anyway. Melissa picked up a juice drank it quickly gave her mum her customary kiss goodbye and headed off to her bedroom to get her backpack. Only a brief minute had elapsed and both in the kitchen heard the door closing and Melissa leaving for the library.

"So, what will you have for breakfast, As if I didn't already know?"asked Mum.

"Well what about bacon and eggs, hash browns and tomatoes," he ventured a wry smile at his mum. Mum, being Mum had anticipated his request and was well into the preparation. It wasn't very long before he was fortifying himself for what was going to be a long day although Jordan was unaware about future events.

"Now what might you be doing to-day?" Mum asked. "Well I am going to do some research on Global Warming, and I will be using my lap-top at home, but I might go to the library later." He replied. His mum countered immediately,

"If you are going to the library then keep an eye on your sister, I'm sure there is something worrying her."

"Of course, I will" he responded emphatically. Mum paused for a moment and then looked at Jordan very closely and said,

"You and Melissa seem to be very close these days and I have noticed just how sensitive you are around her. You don't know how good it makes me feel that you really do look out for your sister."

At that point she couldn't help herself and she looked directly at Jordan and asked,

"I don't suppose you know what is going on in her life?" Jordan was half anticipating the question and brushed it off saying,

"I don't really know but I imagine it's 'boy' trouble." Mum scowled for a split second and then remembered her own first flush of love and reminded herself that her daughter was transitioning to becoming a young woman. Perhaps I should speak to her voicing her concern out loud. Then Jordan piped up with his own wisdom,

"I think it might be wise to wait until she raises the subject with you." Mum looked at Jordan affectionately, and replied,

"You know you are absolutely right, and I need to trust her, and I know that she will make the right decision." With that Jordan wandered over to his Mum and gave her a hug and whispered ever so gently,

"You know Mum you are the best."

Her heart filled with joy as she reflected upon his comments and her whole being glowed inside. What a lovely family I have she thought to herself and what a great privilege it is to be a mum.

Janet would treasure this comment in the year ahead in a way she could hardly imagine.

"You know that if you need any help with your research, I am always happy to help especially as it is my field of work," volunteered Mum. The reply was instant,

"Gee thanks Mum, this is a huge issue and reckon I can use all the help I can get." With that final comment Jordan made his way to his bedroom and thus began his initial research. He was really looking forward to this, especially after he reflected upon their encounter last night, which now seemed ages ago. However, his mind went out to Melissa and just how she was processing her new gift and how he might help her. It had exercised his thinking for the entire morning since becoming aware of its power and responsibility. What could he do to share the load or assist his sister? Suddenly, a thought flashed through his mind. What if we spoke to our Extra-Terrestrial friends? I am sure they will have some wisdom they can offer. Now he felt a sense of relief because it appeared to be a solution to her dilemma. It felt so good that he thought he would go to the library immediately and offer this as a possible solution. He changed quickly into warmer clothes and headed off but not before telling his Mum that he had changed his mind and would be going to the library. She looked at him knowingly.

"This doesn't have anything to do with your sister does it?"

"Oh, I dare say I will see her, but I want to check out the literature on my subject as well, just to see what's available. Of course, I will walk her home if I'm still there," he replied. Jordan had already made up his mind that he would walk his sister home especially after their last brush with the gang.

He arrived at the library and immediately went in search of Melissa; it wasn't long before he came across her and seeing her beamed a big smile as he slid into the seat next to her. Melissa was still looking very sombre though she did brighten a little when she saw him.

"Hey sis, I think I might know someone who will be able to help you with your new gift," he began, and now she really did give him her undivided attention. "Well how about this, what about asking our Extra-Terrestrial friends for their wisdom?" Jordan watched her face as it visibly relaxed and softened.

"That's brilliant!" she exclaimed. Melissa knew intuitively that this would be the way to go and it would be a particularly good learning experience as well. The sense of relief was felt all over her body and she felt more ready to embrace her new gift.

Melissa suddenly became aware of just how hungry she had become and was already packing up her things. Jordan looked puzzled by her response, wondering what he had said to bring on this action. No longer able to contain his confusion he inquired "Was it something I said?" Melissa replied immediately,

"Yes, silly, I now feel so much better I could eat a horse and maybe the rider as well."

Jordan breathed a sigh of relief and followed her to the coffee shop. They were soon seated, and Melissa ordered her extremely late breakfast, but certainly not as large as Jordan had managed at home. He settled for raisin toast and coffee.

They then began to plan when to contact their special friends and knew instinctively that they would need to go to the woods again. There was a certain fear for them both, but they felt buoyed by the support they had already received, and this had given them both greater confidence to rendezvous at their familiar location.

Melissa had now finished her breakfast and was feeling much more contented. Just then she raised her eyes and who should walk through the door but the leader of the gang who had tried to jump them in the woods only a few nights ago. Melissa gasped and for a moment was quite still. Jordan, with his back to the entrance quickly turned around and followed her gaze. There was no mistaking it was Terry. Interestingly, he didn't even give them a second glance. Then they both looked at each other and were quite bemused by his total lack of response. It was then that Melissa leaned forward and whispered to her brother,

"I think he's in real danger I can't see any colours around him, this usually means, from what I was reading this morning, that he's not long for this world." Melissa felt suddenly compelled to get up and speak to him, and without a second thought she was standing in front of Terry and began asking him "Do you feel alright?" Terry was taken aback by such a direct approach and stammered. "Of course, I'm ok, why wouldn't I be?"

For a moment Melissa was stumped, she hadn't anticipated that response. Then she looked him right in the eye and said,

"Well you need to be very careful in whatever you do in the next few minutes." Both Terry and Jordan were speechless, and with that Terry turned tail and headed out of the door. The next moment he was crossing the road. Then he stopped for a split second only to be clipped by a speeding car. The impact was immediate, and Terry dropped like a sack of potatoes. His body lay motionless on the road. Within moments a small crowd had gathered around him, someone was already calling for an ambulance and by this time Jordan and Melissa were on the foot path observing the tragedy. Melissa pushed her way to the front and quickly picked up his limp hand and held it close to herself. Jordan was perplexed and confused by what had happened, he was trying to make sense of it all. By now everyone was aware of the proximity of the ambulance and the crowd, whilst still being interested was moving back. Meanwhile Melissa was still kneeling next to Terry and holding his hand. In the next moment the paramedics were there, and the ambulance trolley was being unloaded. The officer in charge came straight to Melissa and asked if she was a relative.

"No" was her clear reply, but then declared,

"I do know him and where he lives as he goes to our school." The officer quickly cast his eye about, checking with bystanders to see if anyone else could offer any closer connection, but none was forthcoming. The officer turned to Melissa again and she began to furnish the personal details he sought. That being done Melissa then asked,

"Do you think he will make it?". The officer looked at her carefully before saying that he was not at liberty to disclose what he had observed but suggested that she might like to visit the hospital. Melissa was encouraged by this comment and checked which hospital he was likely to be taken to. The commotion had all but subsided and the small crowd had dispersed but standing in the background was Jordan. He was still confused at what he had witnessed but was totally admiring of his sister who had shown a compassion and maturity well beyond her years.

It was well past midday by now and Jordan was still trying to piece together what he had witnessed. It was back to the library for them both and Jordan could hardly contain his questions, "What happened back there in the café? How come you could say he needed to be careful?" "I have to say what you did was pretty awesome." Melissa responded very clearly and simply stated,

"Well, being able to see colours does mean that you can see different levels of health, but when those colours are very dull or non-existent you know the person is in danger of dying. What made this a challenge was Terry's response, when he said he felt quite healthy. He is a young man, so I figured he was in danger in some other way and that he really needed to be careful."

"Wow" was Jordan's immediate response, and then he ventured,

"I guess you have really begun to answer some of those questions you have about your gift."

Melissa nodded in acknowledgement and it was clear that some of the fear had dissipated around her new gift. She ventured another of her fears was precisely around people who had very low energy and she could see them slipping away, and if they were people she knew, how could she tell them? Jordan was painfully aware but had no immediate solutions except that he hoped their special friends would know. They spent the rest of the afternoon in the library and Jordan had read Al Gore's latest findings on Climate Change, He came away feeling a little uplifted but some of the material was just too much to handle. He was so glad he had an ally in his Mum. Melissa on the other hand had gone looking for articles on reading auras and some of the great psychics in the present and past. She was busy reciting one of the late Edgar Cayce's story about the two men who died in the lift. He had observed the two men entering the lift and noticed that they had no aura at all. He mentioned this to some of his close friends who were in the area where the lift could be caught. No sooner had they entered the lift when the lift cable snapped, and the two men plunged to their death.

It was still light when they entered the woods and now, they knew that Terry the Gang's ringleader would not be there, so there was a great deal more assurance in their step. They reached their familiar clearing and waited patiently, within minutes their visitors appeared. It was unnecessary for them to mention the subject in hand, but they respected Melissa's concern and allowed her to speak. She immediately raised the issue of seeing someone whom she loved and deeply cared for and whom she knew was dying. How could she just stand by unable to do anything?

There was a long pause and Melissa was feeling quite uneasy by this time.

"Melissa your gift is given with the express purpose of redirecting humans along a spiritual journey. Do remember that we are first and foremost spiritual beings and that as We come from spirit and we return to spirit." She pondered these words for some time and finally responded,

"What about the people who don't believe in spirit?" "Well, the fact of believing, is in a sense, immaterial. Belief really makes the transition easier and more pleasant. Those people who die in faith look forward to the release from their human body, whereas those who don't believe, die in fear and often fight every step of the way. You will see this play out many, many, times. Your role is to assist their understanding and allow that transition. However it is only a small part of your work."

Melissa felt overwhelmed but had a sense that she was just beginning her real life's work.

"We are very pleased with the way you used your gift today. For not only did you save this young man, but you have possibly opened another door for him, and he may now gain a whole new purpose. Time will tell". Melissa could scarcely believe her ears, "Terry an agent for good, I don't think so." But they came back and simply said,

"Wait and see what comes out of all this. Please trust us." They reluctantly agreed but were filled with scepticism.

CHAPTER 3

A BRUTAL BAPTISM

I T WAS JUST on dark when they arrived home and the relief on Mum's face was obvious. "I was getting worried," she said.

"There are some rough characters out there especially, if you came from the woods."

"Well we did come through the woods, but it was light all the way and we were extremely careful," replied Jordan, "and I did say I would walk Melissa home."

Mum then suddenly changed the subject and said rather casually that she had a call from the manager of the café where Melissa had enjoyed a very sumptuous breakfast.

"Oh, what did he want? I'm sure we paid for everything." chimed in Melissa.

"He didn't ring about that but what he witnessed that took place between you and that young hooligan Terry Cross."

"Do you want to tell me about him my darling daughter?" Janet continued.

Melissa paused for a long moment and threw a sharp glance in Jordan's direction, how was she going to get out of this, she thought?

"Well, I don't know that there is that much to tell, I just said he should be careful," said Melissa drily.

"Well the manager seemed to add a whole lot more detail and it seems you could have been credited with saving his life!" Mum added.

"Mum I think that is really over dramatizing the whole incident." she retorted and hoping that would be an end to the matter, but then it only got worse.

"Well the manager said that you pushed your way to the front of the crowd and for while held his hand close to you," followed up Mum.

"Mum you can't be seriously suggesting that I have a romantic attachment to Terry Cross." She replied scornfully. Then Mum came out with one of her classics "Verily me thinketh thou doth protest too much," and added 'Shakespeare'. It was no use Mum was going to win this round and at that point the argument ceased, and a more light-hearted conversation emerged.

Jordan again reminded his mum of the earlier discussion on Climate Change and asked if they could set some time aside towards the weekend. Mum nodded in assent and that matter was dropped. Tea was nearly ready and as usual Mum had excelled with a most delicious shepherd's pie and a plateful of yummy vegetables.

Everyone was now home, and the table was set, and the meal was served up with Mum's usual finesse. Soon everyone was tucking in and there was minimum conversation, which indicated just how good the food was.

Dad was now nearing the end of his meal and was doing his check in with the family, and as usual began with his daughter. Melissa paused for a moment, threw a sharp glance to her Mum waiting for her approval and once given, commenced to tell Dad of the incident involving Terry Cross. Dad listened intently to the whole event and then paused whilst considering whether he needed to respond. "It would seem we have someone with clairvoyant skills in our midst," but Melissa knew from the tone of voice and her dad's take on that subject, that he was sceptical in the extreme, but this time she had misread him. Nevertheless, he decided that there was something going on in his daughter's life that he couldn't easily dismiss, and he left her feeling that there was more to this.

Melissa now decided to turn the tables and she began to check in on her dad. George was never big on sharing his work with the family.

"So, Dad what happened for you at work today?" she inquired. George was surprised by the question and paused for a considerable time composing himself as how he might answer this. What seemed a simple question was seemingly presenting their Dad with an enormous challenge. George began to speak in quite measured tones,

"Well we have just begun trials with this new battery technology that may yet prove to revolutionize the world's power supply and this information must remain in these four walls." There was a most pregnant silence as the family began to take it in. Jordan gasped for a moment realizing that they may well be witnessing one the most significant watersheds in the history of the world. Questions flowed quickly, but Dad simply put up his hand indicating that he was done with giving any more information.

Mum very quietly began clearing the dishes now but wondering just how much this family was contributing to the change in the world's paradigm.

Melissa and Jordan now returned to their bedrooms and a quiet but peaceful hush descended upon the Thomas household. Melissa began to process the events of the day, pondering just what impact her warning had upon Terry Cross. Could it be that in that split second, he had taken on board her comments and managed to minimize the impact. She went over and over thinking of all the possible scenarios but there were no definitive answers. Finally, she decided there was only one course of action, she would go to the hospital and check this out for herself. Having made the decision, she could now go to sleep, but then how was she going to explain the decision to her family? They were already suspecting her of having a soft spot for this obnoxious young thug.

Jordan was absolutely focused on what his dad had shared with them and couldn't shake it from his mind. He searched the internet looking up every possible lead on battery technology. The one name that stuck out for Jordan was Nikola Tesla, it seemed this man had made some amazing inventions, and somehow, they had never seen the light of day. Jordan was puzzled, how could this be? Why had the world not taken up such amazing inventions? His mind knew no rest that night and he would make his mission to find answers to these questions. He lay awake for a long time wondering what was going on, eventually he fell asleep.

Morning arrived abruptly in the Thomas household and everybody seemed in a rush at the breakfast table. Jordan was not going to be quietened by his Dad this time, and he weighed straight in.

"Dad, how much do you know about Nikola Tesla?" Jordan was insistent with his question. George looked long and hard at his son who still had all the idealism that comes with someone so young and largely unsullied by the cynicism of the world of commerce and big business. George measured his answer thoughtfully not wanting to dampen or discourage his son, who he knew was so passionate about making the world a better place. How could he share all his years of experience without prejudicing Jordan's idealism?

"Yes, we know about Nikola Tesla. There would hardly be a person who works in our industry who doesn't." George paused for a moment and then continued,

"In many ways he was a man born before his time, not unlike Jules Verne, and sadly the world was not able to cope with such brilliance."

Jordan could see and hear the pain in his Father's eyes and voice, Jordan's voice was now considerably more measured as he spoke,

"Well Dad I tell you this man will not be forgotten if I can help it, the world will know of his genius."

George looked fondly at his son knowing that he had not only stalled his cynicism but had kindled a flame that would stay alight for many years to come. George put his hand on his son's shoulder and gently whispered in his ear.

"There will be many challenges ahead for you, especially if you take up this man's cause. Just remember, always stay true to yourself and owe no man."

Jordan found the words strange from his father and their significance would not become evident for some years. Jordan then turned and smiled at his dad and sat down for breakfast, whilst his dad made for the front door ready for work. Just at that moment Melissa and David came to the breakfast table and took their seats.

Melissa looked deep in thought but was jolted out of her thoughts when David began to tease her.

"Well are we off to hospital today to see our newfound friend?" He inquired. For a brief moment Melissa blushed but David was not paying attention so missed an opportunity to press home his point. However, it was not lost on Jordan, but his discretion was assured and there was no chiding from him. David continued his banter to Melissa, but she was used to him by now and was happy to let most of it pass over her head, until David really crossed the line.

"Well it will be interesting to have a little thug like Terry as a prospective brother-in-law." Melissa could no longer help herself and she let loose,

"I suppose that you have never done anything wrong in your life have you Mr. Perfect?" chided Melissa. At that moment a hush came over the table and even Melissa was surprised by the level of passion she had displayed. David now moved in for the kill,

"Oh, we have touched a raw nerve, haven't we?" gloated David and it showed all over his face. By now Melissa was close to tears and her face was visibly shaken. At that point Mum intervened and said sternly to David,

"Enough David, there will be no more comment on the subject." For the moment David looked suitably chastised and continued his breakfast quietly. Jordan simply observed but was concerned for his sister. Surely, he thought, she couldn't have feelings for this thug who only a little while ago had tried to harm her? Jordan was confused but later when it was safe, he would raise the matter with her. Breakfast concluded without further ado and they all went off to their various tasks. As it happened Jordan and Melissa were heading off to the library. They had chosen to walk and as had become their custom, they walked together and through the woods. Jordan offered his support by saying that she shouldn't let David get to her and she nodded appreciatively.

"Yes, he did get to me, but he can be such a pain at times," she offered hesitantly.

"You don't have to convince me, I know only too well just how many times he has set me up," said Jordan ruefully.

You know Jordan I really could see Terry's colours, or his aura and I tell you when I told him to be careful, I noticed a slight colour change.

"What are you telling me?" asked Jordan. "Well," began Melissa "When he walked into the shop his colours were quite dark and fading rapidly then I told him to be careful it seemed like they became a little lighter and started to return," she offered curiously.

"I need to find out what actually happened, and I want to visit him, but I couldn't stand it if David were to find out." Jordan could understand that and simply said,

"Well he won't find out from me." She smiled as she knew she could count on him for support.

"I still don't see why it is so important to see him. What are you looking for?" he inquired inquisitively.

"Well you see I really have to be confident in this gift and maybe I can speak to Terry and check what really went through his mind when I told him to be careful," she replied.

"Yes, that's providing he would tell you the truth, which I really doubt, imagine what he would look like in front of his other gang members," Jordan proffered.

"Hmm, I suppose you're right, but I must try," responded Melissa.

Jordan nodded in agreement now he understood more clearly her reasons for making contact.

By now they were standing at the entrance of the library ready for more research.

Jordan could hardly contain his excitement in following up on Tesla and Melissa was equally excited to continue her research into vibrational energy. As usual they would meet for a light lunch at their favourite café and share notes on the mornings research.

Lunch time came around so quickly and neither was quite ready to give up their research time, but Melissa had made up her mind. Today she would visit Terry in hospital to see if her understanding was correct. They walked to the café together, Melissa eager to share her findings of the morning began with her findings referring to Dr. David Hawkins and his vibrational energy scale.

"Did you know this man has designed a scale which tell us at what level people are living. Emotions like resentment, fear and shame resonate at a level of 20 which is lowest possible level we can operate."

Jordan wasn't quite sure what this meant for him and of course others around him and raised this with Melissa.

"Well," she said. "It means that if you hold onto angry, shameful and fearful emotions, you are operating at a very low level and will be unhappy and hard to get along with."

Jordan looked thoughtful for a moment and then volunteered, "I suppose if you take someone like Terry, it is likely that he will have many angry and shameful experiences."

"Yes, you have grasped it very clearly and that will be very interesting when I go to see Terry this afternoon," responded Melissa happily.

Jordan glanced at her looking quite concerned that she was putting herself in harm's way. He was beginning to see a new side of his sister and he liked and admired this growth in her.

The light lunch consumed Melissa made her way to the hospital and Jordan returned to his research at the library.

Now that Melissa had reached the hospital, she noticed that her anxiety levels had risen a little, but she pressed on knowing she needed to see this to the end. After enquiring at the main desk, she made her way to the ward where Terry was and eventually came to his ward. She then enquired at the Nurses station and was immediately directed to his room. Nurse Scott had volunteered to show her just where to go.

"Well I think he will be pleased to see you because as far as I know he hasn't had one visitor since his admission two days ago."

Melissa went in and greeted Terry. He looked up and immediately began his tirade. "What the F>>> are you doing here?" he belted out angrily.

Melissa was taken aback, and it showed, so Terry continued to attack her with even more venom. She just listened and tried desperately to let it flow over her head and what she had learned this morning helped her to let go of these extremely destructive outbursts. Eventually Terry stopped, and that gave Melissa her opportunity to ask,

"Terry what I wanted to know from you was when I said to you to be careful, did that influence you when you walked onto the road?"

Terry was caught off guard for a moment but then went back into his aggressive stance,

"You are wasting your time now get out and don't come back, can you imagine what my gang would be saying if they knew that you of all people had been to visit me?"

Melissa turned and walked out choking back her tears, but she was not going to let Terry know what he had done. Just then Nurse Scott appeared, and she had a most determined look on her face. She stormed into Terry's room and began to give him one almighty serve. She tore strips of him, and Terry just lay there. He had never had anyone tell him off quite like that,

"How dare you speak to the one visitor you have had since you arrived." "What gives you the right to speak to another human being like that? This young woman was good enough to take some time out of her day she didn't raise her voice and you behaved like a monster. You need to get a grip on your life and definitely need to make an apology to her," Nurse Scott bellowed straight at him.

Terry gasped audibly "Apologise," he sneered "I would be the laughingstock of my gang and that is not going to happen," he barked right back. That only moved Nurse Scott into another gear and for the first time in his life he felt ashamed about his behaviour. It all went quiet and Nurse Scott retreated to the corridor to allow Terry to lick his wounds and reflect on his appalling behaviour. At that moment she caught sight of Melissa who had undoubtedly listened to the whole saga. She smiled at Nurse Scott and nodded appreciatively.

"I'm not sure that it will sink in, but I do have some time on my side, and he doesn't seem to have any of his so-called fiends calling on him, we will have to wait and see," she offered.

Melissa looked thoughtful for a moment and then made her way back to Terry's room. She cautiously peeked around the door and checked to see if he was looking in her direction, but he was not. She breathed a quiet sigh of relief and fixed her gaze on him for a full twenty seconds looking intently around his head and then quietly moved away. Nurse Scott was intrigued by her behaviour and could contain her curiosity no longer.

"What on earth were you looking for?" she asked in her almost matronly manner. Melissa looked at her for a moment and then volunteered,

"I don't think you would understand,"

Nurse Scott was not to be put off and countered immediately,

"Try me honey you will be surprised what this old woman knows. There aren't too many things that have gotten by me."

Melissa hesitated for a moment and looked intently into her kind face and then almost on cue Nurse Scott said,

"Your secret will be safe with me." Melissa's face visibly relaxed as she felt the anxiety slip from her body,

"Well you see I can see colours around people and their colours tell me how healthy they are," Melissa said matter of factly,

"So, what did you see when you looked at Terry?" Melissa paused for a moment and then replied,

"To be honest I'm not certain, it was a puzzling picture and I still need some time and even maybe some help to understand what I was seeing."

Melissa had made up her mind where to go to obtain help and said a very warm. "Thank you" to Nurse Scott for her support, and immediately headed back to the library. Once she arrived, she went straight to the physics section and began her quest to look more carefully at auras. She had already decided that she would search the Net once she got home. What Melissa saw left her overly concerned. They were not the bright colours of red and blue, yellow and green which she saw in most people. Terry's were dark brown and black and very little colour besides. As she continued to pour over her references it was becoming more obvious that Terry was a troubled young man and that his energy field was operating at a very low vibrational state. Melissa instinctively thought back to the time when he walked into the café, she recalled seeing very little colour at all and the absence of colour could mean only one thing. Terry was maybe about to lose his life, the energy field around him was already fading giving weight to the fact that he was about to die. Melissa reflected on what she had read and was now picturing this young man living in a place of hopelessness and futility. It was not her task to rescue him but, knowing what she knew did she have a role to play in assisting him into a better space? Just as she was pondering this matter and deep in thought, Jordan appeared and immediately asked, "What's up sis?"

Melissa then related all the events of the last three hours leaving nothing out, especially the part where Nurse Scott had put Terry in his place in no uncertain manner.

Jordan then posed the question that Melissa had been mulling over in her mind for the last little while. "What do you think is your role in all this?" he inquired.

Melissa looked up at him and just blurted out.

"I don't know, and I am beginning to think and feel this gift is a curse and not a blessing."

Jordan looked on, stumped for words. Who could help her to make sense of what was happening? He was not at all sure though he did think the Extra-Terrestrials would have some wisdom to offer, and maybe the walk home through the woods might prove useful at this time.

They had now packed up and were leaving the library and making their way to the woods. It wasn't long before they came to the clearing where the craft would usually land, so they sat and waited. Half an hour had passed and nothing, Melissa looked at Jordan anxiously, another fifteen minutes passed and still no sign and none of the usual telepathic contact. Jordan motioned that maybe it was time to head home as it would be getting dark soon and they promised Mum, they would be home before dark. Melissa felt quite flat as they opened the front door to home. Why hadn't they come and how do I work through this she thought to herself?

As usual Mum was busy preparing the evening meal and upon their arrival greeted them cheerily, pausing for a moment and catching Melissa's mood. Janet was quite amazing at reading her children and without a second thought she stopped what she was doing and promptly put her arms around her daughter and gave her a warm hug and just held her for some considerable time. Melissa melted into her arms and straightway began feeling better. Melissa looked into her Mum's eyes and words were superfluous to convey her gratitude to her mum. Jordan watched and learned; how come he couldn't have done that?

Just at that moment David burst into the kitchen looked straight at Melissa and began to tease her about her thug 'boyfriend'. Janet only needed to give him the coldest and iciest stare and he stopped in mid-sentence; it was so cold that David was momentarily frozen to the spot.

Jordan now chimed in,

"Back off David. Didn't you learn anything from this morning?" Jordan's words were scathing and suddenly David felt quite lonely, his face was already red, and he looked away rather sheepishly. A quiet hush descended upon the kitchen and David was about to make himself scarce, when Mum reminded him that dinner was ready, and he needed to set the table. This was done so they could all eat together, as was their family ritual at Mum's insistence. It had become a forum to share many things and even resolve other things as well. Tonight, was going to be no exception and before they sat down David without any prompting went over to Melissa and quietly apologized. Melissa readily and happily acknowledged his apology and they both sat down for their evening meal. By now George was home and had taken his place at his usual spot.

There was not a lot of conversation until the meal was concluded and then Melissa looked straight at her dad and inquired,

"How was work today and what kind of progress did you make with your tests?" I am happy to report that,

"It was an exciting day and without going into detail we have made some progress, but it will be a long time before it will be released for use to the general public." Now it was Jordan's opportunity to show off his newly acquired knowledge,

"Dad has your technology been influenced by any of Tesla's work," he inquired eagerly.

"But of course," was his quick response, "No one person has influenced electrical theory and practice as much as Tesla."

"Which aspect of Tesla's work does the technology draw from?" rejoined Jordan. At that point Dad held up his hands and clearly indicated there was no more information to be shared.

Chairs were pushed in. washing up duties taken up for those whose turn it was and everyone else returned to the lounge or to their respective bedrooms. Quietness descended upon the house and Melissa eventually made her way to her bedroom having completed her washing up duties. Melissa now began to feel the stress of the day, her time at the hospital was now being felt, she was replaying the scene again and feeling the rejection and being treated as totally unimportant. Melissa decided that she would do more research on aura's, so she sat herself in bed with her tablet firmly placed on her knees. One minute she was quite focused and the next her eyes closed, and her chin slumped forward, and she was off in the land of nod. It was not long before Mum came in to check on her daughter only to find her already fast asleep. She removed the tablet and couldn't help noticing the site which Melissa had been accessing. The light was now turned off and the usual kiss goodnight given. Mum closed the door quietly.

Jordan had more stamina and of course he had not endured the experience of the encounter with Terry, so he was still very much awake. Mum just popped her head around his door and found him sitting up in bed laptop held firmly on his knees. Mum reached down and gave him a gentle kiss goodnight and then left him to turn his light out. Mum was wise enough not to mention what she had seen on Melissa's tablet. Mum was just closing the door when Jordan gently called,

"Mum".

She paused and poked her head around the door again.

"Mum, you did say you would help me get my head around Climate Change?" he quizzed. "What is your concern?" Mum inquired,

"Well," began Jordan, "there are so many viewpoints and they all seem so convincing, who do I believe?" Mum looked at him fondly, what could she say?

"Well you have to weigh up all the evidence and check each source and the calibre of the person offering their evidence. There is no easy solution for this kind of hard work. It is what science is about. You do have to sift through all the evidence", sighed Mum heavily.

"I think I have done that, but I would like you to hear me and check my reasoning," pleaded Jordan "But of course," Mum responded.

"I believe that the weight of evidence is clearly in favour of Global Warming and that we need to act as a people sooner rather than later." Jordan said with conviction.

"Yes, I hear your conviction but now I need to hear the evidence."

"Carbon Dioxide levels have risen, and the measurements indicate just that. We have significant evidence of this from Hawaii and other places around the world. This is the hard evidence said Jordan."

"Australia is another piece in the evidence chain. The continent continues to heat up each year and this evidence has been collected over the last 40 years." He continued.

Janet put up her hand and simply smiled.

"Yes, you are on the right track and I am proud of you, but you must also counter the evidence to the contrary as well."

Jordan smiled right back, acknowledging his mum's comment and feeling both relieved and pleased with their conversation. The door closed quietly, and he happily turned out the light. The house was bathed in darkness and a peacefulness seemed to descend upon the area as Janet climbed into bed after a kiss goodnight to George.

The next morning came around quickly and everyone was down for breakfast early. Jordan was positively beaming, still thinking about their conversation last night, but now he had something more to add.

"Mum why don't we have a holiday in Australia this year and we could spend some time with our cousins, where do they call it, you know the outback," his face was lit up with enthusiasm. Dad looked across at his wife and their eyes met with a synergy that was obvious.

"It sounds like a plan to me," George volunteered "Let's start looking at dates to see what will work." David was the least enthusiastic as he hated the wide-open spaces where their cousins lived. He knew it was going to be dull and boring. What could he possibly do? But he knew it was pointless to protest as everybody else was already totally sold on the idea.

Today was going to be their last free day as it was back to school next week. This was going to be a significant change for Melissa and Jordan. It was customary for them to advance to the next year after the long holiday break. So now they needed to make the very most of the little time they had left, as the next year would be especially important for them both. Jordan was in his final year and Melissa in her penultimate year. They were off to the library yet again with more research to complete.

Mum and Dad were off to work so the house would be empty. They walked in silence for much of the way but again chose to go through the wood which was becoming more familiar with each visit.

Upon entering the clearing, they paused for a moment as if to check whether their space friends had been, but everything looked the same. The sun was shining handsomely through the trees and filling the air with a stimulating energy and they sat for a moment as if to recharge their batteries. Silence filled the air and they became aware of just how powerful the silence was. Suddenly Jordan reached out and grabbed Melissa's arm, the stillness was shattered by the voices of a group of noisy boys. Jordan now led the way to a place to hide sensing, that danger was imminent. They were now a safe distance from the clearing observing some of Terry's gang at work. Melissa watched in silence gasping at what she was seeing. There were darker and greyer colours, it could only mean one thing. They were looking for trouble and hurting people was always part of the plan. Jordan and Melissa sat motionless hardly daring to breath, the memory of a few nights ago firmly fixed in their minds. They waited for what seemed forever before the gang finally left and when the coast seemed clear they made their way out of the woods; little did they know that the gang was still hanging around as they emerged into the open space. Suddenly they were surrounded by the gang and Jordan and Melissa grew visibly pale. The gang was now starting to enjoy their prey circling and getting ever closer and taunting them. It was looking bleaker by the minute when seemingly from out of nowhere David and his friend appeared. Now both David and his friend were trained in martial arts and they were now able to demonstrate their ability because of the impending threat to someone in obvious distress. It only took two swift moves from the pair and the gang hightailed leaving Melissa and Jordan much relieved. Melissa looked gratefully at her eldest brother and gave him a big hug and said, "He was more than ok."

It was now quite late when they arrived at the library, and they made their way to the areas of research. By now the staff were becoming well acquainted with these new converts and smiled when they saw them. Melissa went immediately to her usual section only to be greeted by one of the staff. The librarian invited Melissa to sit down and began to talk to her about auras. Melissa could hardly believe her ears. Here was someone who could read auras and had been doing so for many years and was offering to help Melissa in a way she could not have dreamed. Melissa was so excited she squealed in delight forgetting for a moment that she was in the library. There were some stern looks and Melissa felt suitably rebuked, and quietness fell upon the space. They continued to speak in hushed tones and had now moved to a more secluded spot. Melissa looked at her watch and suggested that Judy, the librarian join them for lunch at their favourite café. That was not going to be possible on this occasion, as Judy had a previous engagement.

Melissa swiftly made her way to Jordan's space and the two happily chatted about the mornings adventures as they made their way to the café. They made their way to their usual spot and waited patiently to place their order. The next thing Melissa felt was a gentle hand resting on her shoulder, and quickly recognized Nurse Scott from the hospital. Both seemed equally surprised, and that being acknowledged Nurse Scott filled Melissa in on Terry's recent behaviour. Not a lot had changed, and he was still extremely aggressive to the staff and still no visitors. The exception was his dad who had popped in for just a few minutes to check on him. Melissa was really surprised as she had at least thought that his gang members would have found their way up there. Melissa pondered for a moment and then shared what had transpired earlier that morning just as they came out of the woods. Then with a twinkle in her eye she looked at Nurse Scott and said,

"You may like to share that with Terry, how his friends couldn't even spare a moment for him." Nurse Scott nodded but wasn't convinced that this was such a good idea but maybe she could use it in a different way. Lunch being over the two made their way back to the library and continued their research, sensing this would be their last opportunity for a long time. Melissa was now bubbling with excitement as they left the library. Auras now began making more sense, especially as she had really come to appreciate the work of David Hawkins. His scale was so important as it allowed her to assess which friendships would be in her best interests. She immediately began to think of her school friends and her teachers. What surprises were in store for her on her first day back, she could hardly wait.

The morning came around so quickly, and breakfast was over with little conversation. Melissa and Jordan were off to school, clearly eager to be punctual on their first day back. There was excitement to see the makeup of the new class. There was much chatter now as they approached the school yard and Melissa noticed some members of Terry's gang. They looked scornfully in her direction and sneered menacingly at them both. Melissa glanced at the group for some time and noticed that one member had an extremely dark aura completely enveloping him. Melissa gasped quietly for a moment and then turned away as if she had seen a ghost. Jordan saw it all and quickly inquired,

"What's wrong? What have you seen?"

"I can only guess that Alistair is really at risk but I'm not sure whether he is very, very, sick or is going to meet a deadly accident," she said hesitantly. Nothing more was said as they continued to make their way to class. Melissa was still in a state of shock, her focus entirely on what she had observed. What could she do to help this unfortunate young man? She was no longer excited about looking at her friends but entirely consumed with his plight. Her attention was elsewhere when the teacher entered the classroom. The custom was still strong in this school and within seconds everyone was on their feet and becoming quiet in preparation for their good morning greeting. Melissa was still in her own world and slowly began to rise, but before she was able to raise herself to her full height, her legs suddenly began to give way and the pain in her abdomen overcame her completely. The next moment she was on the floor writhing in pain and her classmates were gathering around. By now the teacher had caught up with the commotion and was making her way to where Melissa was still writhing on the floor. Ms Archer quickly summed up the situation and quickly dispatched a student of to the sick bay room to get the nurse and a stretcher. She then bent over Melissa inquiring as to where the pain was worst. She was grabbing just to the side of her groin and screwing up her face simultaneously. It was not long before the nurse and stretcher arrived, and Melissa was whisked away to sick bay.

Once arriving Melissa was settled in one of the beds and seemingly started to relax. The pain started to dissipate, and colour began to return to her cheeks. She now felt a whole lot calmer and began to concentrate on her breathing and was soon dozing off. It wasn't long before Janet made her way to the school and was by her daughter's bedside. She quietly took Melissa's hand and began stroking it ever so gently. Melissa opened her eyes for a moment and a fleeting smile danced across her face as she drifted off again. This drowsiness was only for brief moment for something caught her attention. Her eyes were on the bed next to her, she blinked and then took a second look. Was it really Alistair? Once again, she saw the darkness surrounding him and simultaneously starting to evaporate. His face contorted with pain. In an instant she was wide awake and searching for the nurse, Melissa couldn't help herself and she almost screamed.

"Nurse, Nurse!"

It was so loud that Mum backed away quickly. The next thing the nurse was by her bed. "What is it my child, what is wrong?" Melissa looked at her pleadingly and almost demanded that she get Alistair to the hospital immediately. The nurse looked puzzled for a moment.

"Why does he need to go?" she inquired patiently.

"I can't explain right now but you have to trust me he is very, very sick and his life is slipping away."

The colours had all but disappeared. The nurse began to humour Melissa. "There, there, he's ok and we will take good care of him," she said soothingly.

"No, no, he needs to go now," Melissa kept insisting. The nurse began to look at Alistair again. She moved over to his bed and took his pulse again and noticed that his breathing had become increasingly shallow. An instant later she was on the phone calling for an ambulance, she then returned to his bedside checking for his vital signs and looking more worried as the minutes ticked by. The nurse had so been taken up with Alistair that she had almost overlooked Melissa. She glanced over at Melissa and was relieved to find her sitting up and watching intently the drama unfold with Alistair. Her mum now seemed less concerned with her daughter's well-being and just watched on. Janet began to wonder just what it was that Melissa knew, she was deep in thought when the silence was broken by the unnerving and unmistakable sound of the ambulance. Within seconds the paramedics were in and Alistair was on the trolley and into the ambulance.

Janet was looking at her daughter in a way she had never done before, there was a faraway look in her eyes as she reflected upon what she had witnessed. Did she really know her? Melissa was now aware that her mum was somewhere else, her distant gaze, the quiet stance there was something in her eyes.

"Mum, where are you?" she asked.

Suddenly Janet came back into the present. "Oh, don't mind me I was just off with the fairies," she volunteered. Melissa looked her right in the eyes and said,

"Come on Mum you can tell me." Janet engaged with Melissa for a long time trying to choose her words carefully. She began stammering, this was so unlike her mum, she was always in control of her feelings and her speech, this was the first time she had seen her mum stumble awkwardly and now Melissa was feeling anxious sensing her mum's faltering stance. Even when mum began her fore into sex education and speaking about girls becoming women, she never showed this amount of discomfort. Now Melissa was wishing she had not pressed Mum into sharing.

Janet then began, "Melissa what happened in here today, how did you know that this young boy was so sick?" Melissa realized that this may be the time to share what had been happening to her over the last weeks.

"Well Mum," she began, once the room was quiet, "Please promise me that this is just between us and you tell no-one else certainly not David or even Dad, please, please, please."

"My darling I have never kept anything from your father, and I don't intend to start now!" Janet was emphatic.

"Well I want you, no I need you to make an exception this time," stated Melissa confidently.

Janet was surprised by Melissa's resolute determination and grudgingly agreed that this would be an exception. Melissa leaned over and gave Mum the biggest hug ever and then began.

"Well Mum it's like this, I can see auras and these colours are so clear to me that I know when people are well but especially when they are sick and I could see that Alistair was very sick. I still don't know whether he is going to be alright," she tumbled it out in relief.

"I saw it as soon as I arrived at school and Jordan knew that something was wrong when I looked over at some of Terry Cross's gang members. Then I saw Alistair next to me even his dark grey colour was fading which meant he was slipping away." Janet just stared at her daughter and could scarcely take it in, realizing that she had a very special child in the family. Janet paused for a few minutes recognizing that this could be an enormous burden for someone so young, in fact a burden for anyone.

Now it was mum's turn she leaned over the bed and held her daughter so tightly and whispered so gently in her ear,

"My darling I am so, so proud of you, you really are quite special, but I have to admit that I am also very concerned for you as well." She held her for such a long time that Melissa felt like her spirit would burst out of her chest.

Just at that moment the nurse came back to see how her other patient was doing, Melissa was now sitting up in bed fully awake and raring to leave and stating as much.

"Not so fast young lady we need to know what was going on with you and we need to conduct our usual tests," said the nurse. Melissa said,

"Well I am feeling fine now and there is no pain at all."

Nevertheless, "I will check your blood pressure, temperature and pulse and we will need to check for the pain. If I don't do it, I could lose my job and you wouldn't want that would you?" She asked knowingly.

"No," replied Melissa.

That being completed satisfactorily Melissa was then allowed to leave and they had decided that Melissa would spend the rest of the day at home and probably in bed. Before leaving she inquired as to how Alistair was, but the nurse could tell her nothing. Only his Mum could know, and she had been called. The nurse did say, "It was because of you he has a chance of making it! There is no doubt that it was touch and go for him."

"What about Jordan?" queried Melissa,

"Well he needs to stay at school so he will be ok," Mum replied.

"Oh, but he will wait for me and not know anything about what has happened," responded Melissa.

"Well I will speak with his teacher and let him know that you are ok and that you have come home with me, ok?" re-joined Mum. At that point the nurse stepped in indicating that she would personally deliver the message. Melissa was now satisfied. Nevertheless, she was still wanting to share her story with Jordan. Mum gave her one of those looks and Melissa volunteered,

"Yes, Jordan does know about me and has been really supportive all the time." Mum smiled knowingly and felt so pleased that her special daughter was being supported by her brother.

Then came another surprise.

"Mum can we go up to the hospital and check on Alistair please?" insisted Melissa. It was an unusual request given that both her children had expressed concern about Terry and his gang, but she agreed to go. It wasn't long before they arrived and quickly made their way to the Emergency Ward. They weren't family so they were unable to glean any information. The triage nurse went and checked with Alistair's mum and she was out in an instant. The deep furrows on her forehead said it all as she met their gaze but there was also a look of warmth. She looked straight at Melissa and said,

"I believe I have you to thank for his speedy arrival at the Emergency." Melissa nodded. "I am so grateful I don't know what I will do if I lost him and tears filled her eyes.

"His dad died six months ago, and he hasn't been the same since." Melissa couldn't contain herself,

"What do they think is wrong with him?" She questioned. His Mum didn't hesitate, for now she had found someone with whom she could share her grief and shock.

"Well they found that his appendix had ruptured, and he was developing peritonitis and now he is resting in the ICU. They are still uncertain as to whether he is going to pull through." she confided. Melissa looked at her mum quickly and asked if she might just go into the ward for a minute?

"I won't say anything but maybe just wish him well." By this time Alistair's mum had introduced herself and Sheila was more than happy for Melissa to visit, but only for a minute.

"Oh, that's fine," she re-joined "I only need a minute." Sheila was quite perplexed by Melissa's response and looked blankly at Janet.

Melissa made her way to the ICU and went straight over to where Alistair's motionless body was lying. She gazed for a full minute and noticed the colours surrounding him, the grey was still present but now there were other colours emerging as well, the signs were looking good. Then something happened that completely took her breath away. She became aware of their Extra- Terrestrial friends' presence; she just knew they were somehow in the room and it was as though for a moment that his body was bathed in this beautiful light. She just muttered under her breath saying,

"Thank you," turned around and headed for mum and Sheila. Mum needed no reassurance as to how Alistair was, she could see the quiet confidence written all over Melissa's face. Sheila was oblivious to it all but said,

"Thank you," to them both for their obvious care and concern. They turned for home and when they were out of earshot mum questioned saying.

"Ok what did you see?"

"Well there are still dark colours around him, but they are no longer faint as they were before, but there are other colours around him still faint, but I know he is going to make it."

Mum looked at her both in astonishment and with a certain kind of pride, saying openly.

"I am so proud of you." Suddenly all the heartache of the morning and worry about what she needed to do melted away completely. There would be many times in the future when Melissa would draw upon those lovely, healing words offered by her mum.

They arrived home without incident and Melissa plonked herself down in the lounge and in front of the TV and now she would maybe have some lunch and afternoon tea all rolled into one and just veg out for a while. It was no time at all before her mind slipped into gear, as she wondered why she had the sudden attack in school? It puzzled her how it just as suddenly appeared and then disappeared. Try as she might it would not leave her consciousness. She been reading somewhere that sometimes a person with her skills may mimic the symptoms of the victims. As she continued to turn this over in her mind, she became aware of another stream of thoughts imposing themselves in her consciousness. It was her alien friends, confirming her initial thinking that she did in fact empathetically feel the pain of the person she was observing. This was seemingly another aspect of her gift and not a part she really felt that comfortable with. Melissa was quite lost in her thoughts and paying no attention to what was going on around her. Mum came in ashen faced and speaking very quickly, "Oh dear, Jordan has been taken to the police station and has been involved in some kind of altercation." Melissa was snapped out of her daydream and wanted more detail.

"I don't know anymore, but I need to get down to the police station. Will you come?" Mum asked quickly. "Try and stop me," responded Melissa and she was up in a flash and putting her coat on and making her way to the car.

They were soon driving into the parking area at the police station and Janet had said nothing during the journey, although it was obvious from her demeanour that she was troubled. Jordan had never been in trouble before. Melissa was now watching her mum and noticing the colour changes in her aura, it was indeed a learning experience for her and contributing to her growth and experience.

Janet was now inside and speaking quickly to the desk sergeant who then took them to the interview room.

Jordan was sitting quietly, pale and visibly shaken, but his manner picked up upon his mum's arrival and when he saw Melissa his face positively lit up. A police officer sat with him and was writing busily. Janet moved to Jordan's side and gave him a big hug and as she did so, his body seemed to relax measurably. At that point the officer introduced himself as Detective Sergeant Brian Cluff stating that he would be conducting the enquiry and that Jordan had been cooperating very well to date. It all sounded overwhelming to Janet and she wondered whether she needed to have George present as well. "Is my son being charged?" asked Janet almost impatiently.

"No, Mrs. Thomas, your son is the victim of a crime perpetrated by a group of boys from his school. The reason we are involved is because it took place outside school grounds and a concerned citizen rang the emergency number."

Janet gave Jordan a quick glance as if to reassure herself, and then inquired, "Has he been injured and if so, does he require treatment?"

"Mrs. Thomas, we have taken care of his physical well-being and he has been treated by our doctor. We will be offering counselling when our interviewing has been completed. Jordan has been able to give us a list of most of the names of the boys who attacked him, but we haven't been able to establish a motive," Detective Sergeant Cluff stated clearly.

Melissa had now put the picture together and quickly informed the detective.

"They have been trying to hurt us for a long time and without success up until now." "But why?" re-joined Detective Cluff.

"Well I can't be sure, but my guess is, they are jealous and also very angry about life and they see us as having it all," Melissa suggested hesitantly. There was a long pause and eventually the detective responded, "You may well be right. We will be interviewing them all one by one." Detective Sergeant Cluff motioned to Janet indicating that she could take Jordan home unless he needed to speak to a counsellor. Jordan declined the offer all he needed was the support of his family and he would be fine. That being decided they all left and Detective Sergeant Cluff said he would be in touch if he required further information.

It wasn't long before they arrived home and the house was empty but it felt so good to be safe. Nothing had been said on the way home, it would need to wait until they reached a place where it would be safe to share. Mum went straight into the kitchen and put the kettle on to make a cuppa and prepare some afternoon tea. The kettle soon whistled, and the tea was made. Melissa had been busy making sure there was a variety of food ready for the table. They were all sitting down when the front door opened and in walked David. He smirked all over his face, looking like the cat who had just licked out the cream bowl. "Gee, my timing is impeccable, don't you think?" he said quizzically. His mum smiled acknowledging his timing. She then invited him to come and sit down and listen to some of the events of the last couple of hours. David recognised this was not a time for levity, so he took his seat whilst Jordan described the events before being taken to the police station. "I was leaving school after the last period and not really taking much notice. When I reached the school gates members of Terry's gang were waiting for me. They began telling me that they had you tied up in the wood. And if I wanted to see you again, I would need to follow them into the woods. My mind began to race as I hadn't seen you at all at school all day, I didn't know what to think let alone what to do." Mum looked stunned,

"I left a message with the nurse who promised you would be told. Your teacher should have been given the message. The nurse knew what had happened to Melissa and to let you know she was ok," offered Mum. Jordan looked taken aback,

"Well my teacher said nothing, I wondered if he had forgotten," but then Jordan remembered that his teacher had suddenly been called away for an urgent phone call.

"So, what did you do then?" asked Mum.

"Well," continued Jordan "I went with them of course, but I soon realised that they didn't really have you. Just as we got to the edge of the woods, I decided I would make a run for it, but I couldn't outrun them and that's when they started to beat me up. It was just so fortunate that the lady who lived in the last house saw what was happening and she must have called the police." The next thing I knew she was coming over, calling out to the gang,"

"Stop it!"

They stopped for a moment, and then turned their attack on her until she told them,

"The police were on their way," "Just at that moment I heard the wail of the police sirens,"

Jordan continued "The gang began to disperse quickly, however the police managed to pick up two of them. The next minute I was taken into one police car and the others were taken into another car. I didn't see if they interviewed the lady, but I guess they did because I'm sure she saw most of what went on."

David was scarcely taking this in. He had already had a run in with this gang and thought he had straightened them out, how wrong he had been. He realized that they were extremely dangerous. Little wonder the police had taken the call so seriously. Melissa's eyes had only grown wider as Jordan retold his story. At one stage she found herself holding her breath feeling more and more anxious as his story unfolded. Melissa now began to go inside herself. What was really going on for these boys? Their dark colours meant something more than she imagined. She recognized that she desperately needed more teaching.

"Well, it's been a day of high drama, but the good thing is that we are all safe," reflected Mum philosophically. Jordan knew that something else had gone on, but he needed to ask those questions out of David and Mum's hearing, so he would bide his time.

Jordan finished his tea and cake and then made his way to his bedroom to wash up before dinner. Melissa followed him upstairs and right behind him into his bedroom. She then disclosed the events of her day and how she had been able to effectively save Alistair. She looked at her brother as he could scarcely take in. Melissa paused momentarily realizing how harsh this would seem to him after his ordeal after school. She just walked up to him and held him so tightly, that for a moment that he found it hard to breath. Jordan felt his whole body relax and all the tension evaporated from his body. Melissa continued to hold him, just relaxing her hold until they were both more comfortable.

Jordan was so much more relaxed, and his breathing was rhythmic and even. He began to feel this incredible sense of peace throughout his entire, a sensation he had never felt before. He shared the experience with Melissa who began to reflect on the healing that took place when you gave someone a genuine hug. This was another part of her learning and she knew she would need to do some research on hugging.

Jordan was now ready to listen to Melissa's story. He could hardly believe what she was telling him. "Jordan I really do want to go back and see Alistair; I believe he needs help and I know his mum wants us to help him," she pleaded. Jordan knew instinctively that she was right, so he offered no argument only his support. Jordan checked with Melissa,

"So, Mum knows about your gifts and how they work?" Melissa nodded and simply added, "It feels really good that she is so supportive, and I feel we are all the stronger for it," Jordan nodded in agreement. "What about dad?" he added.

"No not yet, Mum has promised to keep it from Dad for a while," She said. They sat for another hour discussing Melissa's empathetic response and the power of the darkness exhibited by the gang. Melissa was also warmed by the intervention of the Extra-Terrestrials at the hospital. The next thing it was dinner time and they made their way down for the evening meal. By now dad was home and had been brought up to speed about Jordan's ordeal. He looked him over, noticing the bruising under his right eye and the grazing on his forehead. Dad put his arm fondly around his son and gave him a squeeze. Jordan smiled in appreciation and everybody sat down and enjoyed the evening meal of Lancashire Hot Pot. There was little talking as the meal was just so tasty.

CHAPTER 4

AN UNEXPECTED ALLY

THE NEXT MORNING everybody arrived for breakfast at the same time and the conversation flowed. Dad finished first and was soon gone for the day. More conversation followed about their cousins in Australia and just how soon they might plan their vacation. It was clear that they couldn't leave before Christmas and so planning would focus on five weeks very early in the New Year. Most of the discussion centred around how long they might spend there. Clearly five weeks found support among all the family though. David's concern was about how much it would take him out of his University Course. Maybe he was having second thoughts, he was very dedicated to his studies and he didn't want to miss any of his course. On reflection he really did enjoy the friendship of his cousins and it was hard to pass up a chance to visit Australia. He loved surfing, and there would be at least a couple of days when he could get to the beach. Slowly but surely, he was liking the idea of this vacation. Breakfast concluded Mum offered to take her two to school, but they both declined and preferred to walk. They left together and immediately began an animated conversation. Melissa after considerable reflection began,

"I am still not sure why the gang is so destructive, I suspect it has something to do with their collective energy, but I can't be sure."

Jordan nodded, he was unclear too, but his mind went back to when they were in the craft and Melissa was observing the clusters of dark energy from such a distance. It was true she could see the concentration of those dark spots but was not quite sure why they were there? Then Jordan offered this comment,

"Maybe just maybe when you have a concentration of energy it has a cumulative effect and it becomes more powerful."

Melissa was impressed with the reasoning and began to realize that in order to change that effect she would need to work on some of the individuals in the group. Her mind turned to Alistair, she needed to work on him. She then turned to Jordan and said,

"Will you come with me to the hospital later today after school?"

Jordan was quite deliberate with his response. "I'm not sure, I mean how will it look if the police find out I have been visiting a member of the gang?" Melissa could see his point.

"Well if you just come with me and wait in the lounge room that would be a help." That appeared to be a compromise which would work, and it was resolved to both their satisfaction. The school gates were now clearly in sight and so too were some of Terry's gang, but once Jordan appeared, they made themselves scarce.

It was now their second day back and there were still friends to catch up with and Melissa couldn't wait. Her eye caught Melanie her very best and closest friend. Melissa noticed her colours straight away and breathed such a sigh of relief. Her aura was huge and so full of blues and reds and all so healthy. They held hands together and headed off to the classroom, but Melanie really wanted to know what happened yesterday. There was no time to explain so Melissa just passed it off as a stomach pain. The day passed without incident and Jordan had opportunity to catch up with his best friend again. Much time was spent swopping information around their favourite subject, quantum mechanics. Tom was in the same class as Jordan and ever since Jordan came to secondary school, they had become firm friends.

School was done for the day and Melissa waited for Jordan and they quickly made their way to the hospital. It took a good thirty minutes, but they eventually arrived, and Melissa went straight to the desk asking for Alistair. She was really pleased to learn that he was no longer in the ICU and quickly made her way to his new ward. As she approached the nurses' station she asked if it would be ok if she could visit Alistair. The nurse nodded and indicated that he already had one visitor. Melissa approached the door cautiously and recognized his mother's voice. She poked her head around the door and caught Alistair's gaze. He half smiled and his mum turned around and her eyes lit up when she saw Melissa. There was a warm welcoming smile as she made her way to his bedside. Melissa was not prepared for what came next. Alistair looked at Melissa,

"I really want to say thank you for your part in saving my life. Mum tells me that you insisted that they take me to hospital without delay and then the doctors told me that had I arrived a second or two later I wouldn't be here. Melissa you really are a true friend and one I frankly don't deserve but thank you again."

By now Melissa was blushing wildly and words seemed to fail her. Sheila came over and gave her hand a big squeeze. Melissa was about to be even more surprised with Alistair's next question, "Could you find it in you to be my friend?" he asked hesitantly. This came so far out of left field that Melissa was speechless. Her thoughts raced,

"What about Terry and his gang?" she questioned. "Well I have talked this over with Mum and I think it's time for me to change direction. This has been a wakeup call for me." Mum stepped out for a moment and Alistair turned his full attention to Melissa. "Melissa when you were in the room when I was in the ICU, I had the strangest feeling. It is so hard to describe but it felt like someone else was in the room taking care of me and it was so reassuring and warm. Was there anyone else besides you?" he questioned Wow this really took Melissa by surprise and she had no idea how to respond, but she had considered his request for friendship and was quietly delighted to say yes,

"I would like that."

"Well I'm sure there was no other person in the room, so, I don't think I can be any more help," she said with a very straight face.

Melissa then changed subject, "Tell me about your dad?" Melissa enquired quietly. Alistair paused for a considerable time and Melissa noticed that his colours had changed, and not for the better. Had she made a mistake she thought quietly to herself. Alistair then confessed.

"I have never really spoken about my dad dying to anyone, and it is so painful that I would try and think of something else. I do feel very confused when I think about him," He paused for another minute. "I'm not sure what I would do in your shoes," she then volunteered. Then there was another long pause and Alistair eventually said,

"May we speak about something else?" Melissa nodded in assent and had noticed that his colours changed slightly for the better. At that moment his mum walked in and that was Melissa's cue to leave but before she did Alistair asked her if she would please come back and visit him again? Melissa said nothing but smiled and nodded.

Meanwhile Jordan was waiting patiently in the lounge when to his surprise Terry hobbled in. Jordan held his ground and just looked at Terry. Terry was not going to pass up an opportunity to have another crack at Jordan, but he was at a disadvantage being on crutches and not very steady. "Just wait until I get out of here, then we'll see what goes down. My gang will make mincemeat of you and your sister and your big brother won't be able to help you," Terry announced confidently. Jordan couldn't contain himself.

"Well, I don't know about your gang but most of them are being interviewed by the police so I am not sure just how strong they will be. I bet not one of them has called in to see you,"

Jordan boasted happily as he had already gleaned at school during the day that the gang couldn't really contact each other. Now they were facing charges. Terry stood in the door and was quite speechless. Jordan was right, no one had visited him, and he had no idea what was happening to his gang. Just at that moment Nurse Scott came to the door and saw Jordan.

"Oh, you have your first visitor. I hope he's not as objectionable as you," she added.

"He's no friend of mine nor is his sister" he re-joined. Jordan just sat quietly making no contribution. So, the nurse looked at him and asked, "Was that your sister who came in to see Terry about four days ago?" Jordan nodded. The nurse looked straight at Terry and declared, "Well you would be better off with friends like these than your present lot, who up to date, have not given you the time of day." Terry then made a hasty exit knowing that he was no match for Nurse Scott. She had already put him in his place at least three times. He hobbled back to his bed feeling very let down by his gang. He did reflect on their words and realized that this was not the first time he had been let down, but on all the other occasions, it had been by his mother. She had left the family when he was just seven years old. He was the eldest of three and he had so often had to look out for his younger brother and sister. Dad had such a tough job and found it a difficult balancing act since his wife left. He had desperately wanted someone else in his life but between work and caring for the children, there was never enough time.

Soon Melissa poked her head around the door her face positively alive, and from that Jordan knew that her time had been well spent. On their way home Melissa shared all that had transpired, Jordan listened quietly hardly able to take in what an amazing sister he had, and how she had won the heart of one of Terry's gang members. Alistair had made the decision to quit which surprised Jordan no end. Melissa couldn't wait to tell Mum; she was just so happy she thought she would explode with excitement before arriving home. Melissa burst through the door and went straight into the kitchen where she knew Mum would be busy.

"Well, I can see someone is happy." exclaimed Mum. "Mum Alistair is giving up the gang and has asked me to be his friend, and I have said yes," Melissa blurted out without drawing breath. Mum looked at her daughter with a look she saved for special people only, Melissa looked at mum. "What Mum?"

"I am so proud of you both, you continually make me so happy," tears running down her face. Jordan thought to himself just how much his sister had grown in the short time since they had their first encounter with the aliens. She had begun to effect change in such a dramatic way. "We now have Alistair as an unexpected ally."

There would be one more visit to the hospital and this time Jordan would come as well. They poked their heads around the door to find only Alistair sitting there quietly reading. He looked up and instinctively smiled upon seeing both Jordan and Melissa.

"I have to say, I'm very pleased to see you. I know that I was very quiet about my dad when you left the last time, but I was glad you asked me about him."

Alistair continued,

"I did speak with Mum the next time she came in and she commented that I had hardly spoken about him since his death. In fact, she went on to say, I had just shut down, become moody and angry. This had become a regular pattern for me, and I couldn't seem to break it," Alistair went on. "Mum and I talked for a very long time and I started to realize just how angry I had become; I just didn't understand my anger until Mum said to me. 'Your anger is because you're hurting at losing your dad'. Suddenly my behaviour started to make sense, at least to me anyway," he reflected. Jordan and Melissa listened quietly and nodded at the appropriate moments giving Alistair the support he needed. They both acknowledged that it made sense to them, and that they were delighted with Alistair's insight. Melissa then suggested that in the coming weeks and months, he might like to keep a book in which he would write all of his thoughts and feelings about his dad. Alistair looked at them both thoughtfully for a moment and then volunteered.

"That seems like a good idea, and I have to say I am feeling a little better in myself. You will be pleased to know that I will be discharged tomorrow and I'm really hoping that I can come around and meet the rest of your family." Alistair said quietly. Jordan and Melissa nodded in the affirmative and then added that they were expecting him. They then made their way quietly from his ward and took themselves off home. They had indeed found an unexpected ally.

CHAPTER 5

A HOLIDAY TO REMEMBER

WEEKS PASSED AND school went on with its usual ups and down. The gang had almost disintegrated but not quite and Alistair, Melissa and Jordan had now become close friends. Furthermore, Alistair was a regular guest at the Thomas family home. Sheila had also found a friend in Janet and this had been such joy for them both. Sheila had learned so much about parenting and watched just how close the family worked together. There had been no direct contact between our unlikely heroes and our Extra-Terrestrials. Life had seemingly returned to pre-Extra-Terrestrial times as they had experienced no further contact. Melissa had become much more adept at understanding and using her gift, she now knew that she would often take on the symptoms of the person she was observing. She had read widely and knew that animals would sometimes mimic the pathology of their owners which supported her understanding of vibrational energy. Melissa had continued to learn and grow. The other part which had puzzled Melissa was the intensity of the gang's dark colours. It was now becoming clearer that their dark energy had a cumulative effect, and each member contributed which compounded that energy.

It would always continue to grow because they fed off each other. It also dawned on her as it worked that way for the dark side, so it would for the light! This thought never left her and was a constant source of encouragement. She was still to learn how important it would be in the future. Her own background in faith was also helpful. She remembered reading that where two or three were gathered in the spirit of Christ the power was immeasurable. She had often wondered about those words, but now in the light of a new experience they made exciting sense and she pondered just how this would work.

It was now approaching the time when they needed to start packing in readiness for their Australian trip. The tickets had been booked for some time and Melissa had packed and unpacked at least three times. Everybody else was nearly packed and David had decided it was too good an opportunity to miss. His lecturers enthusiastically encouraged him to make the trip.

Even Dad was excited, especially as it was his last week at work. He was pleased to have a break because it seemed that so many blocks and so much red tape had been placed on the project and he was becoming increasingly frustrated. He had watched Government bureaucrats come and go and each time the project was either stopped or put on hold. It just didn't make sense unless someone was trying to sabotage the project.

The weekend came all too soon and their flight was leaving early on Saturday morning. It was dark when they awoke, and the house was filled with artificial light as they prepared for their departure. There was so much excitement and the chatter went on nonstop. Suddenly there was a toot out the front and the sensor light switched on with the cab driver waiting at the door. The luggage was all ready and soon enough they were on their way to the airport at Gatwick. Check in went off without a hitch and the wait in the lounge was pleasant enough, Melissa had worked out that it 3.00pm in Eastern Australia where they were heading. She took out her mobile phone and called her cousin Emma. Within a minute Emma picked up and squealed in delight when she heard Melissa's distinct accent. They talked for at least ten minutes and began to make plans for when they met at Melbourne. Just as the call finished the boarding call was made and slowly, they made their way onto the aircraft and they were all eventually seated. It seemed to take ages for them to become airborne and they settled back for the first leg of the long flight. Melissa had brought a great deal of music on her iPod. She now closed her eyes and decided it was a golden opportunity to catch up on some sleep. The next minute Melissa was asleep and Jordan sitting next to her was busy playing games He soon became bored and decided it was an opportunity to complete some more research. The time seemed to accelerate as he worked. The next thing Jordan became both anxious and alert, for he could feel the presence of their friends. He looked at Melissa sleeping peacefully and decided to wake her. Within seconds she was wide awake looking out into the bright morning sunlight and knowing that they were close by. She whispered,

"Have you seen them at all? I can't believe they would show themselves in broad daylight." Jordan replied ever so quietly,

"No, not a sign," but they both knew they were being shadowed; it was a reassuring experience.

The flight seemed to drag on forever and Jordan jokingly suggested that they should have got a lift with their friends. Melissa nodded in agreement and then said, "It would have been cheaper, and we would be there by now." They both chuckled in agreement. It was now time for their evening meal and Jordan was already indicating just how hungry he was. He was still hungry after his meal and spoke very politely to the stewardess seeking more food. She smiled at him and said,

"I'll see what I can do." In just a minute she was back with another meal and Jordan positively beamed, no formal thank you was necessary his look said it all. Nevertheless, Jordan polite as ever, thanked her warmly.

David had watched all this play out and was looking enviously at Jordan's new meal. He was sitting just one seat away, in the middle isle. David waited to attract the stewardess's attention and when he had managed, he very politely questioned as to whether he could have more. The stewardess looked at him for a moment,

"Are you two related," motioning to Jordan. David was somewhat taken aback by the question, "Well yes," he stammered hesitantly.

"He is my younger brother," The stewardess smiled warmly at David and mentioned how polite he was.

"Yes, there is more food, but it will be a few minutes away." David was delighted with this news and was already looking forward to more food. After all, he thought, I am still growing. It was now getting dark and a few people were turning out their lights and reclining their seats in readiness for some sleep. David had now finished his second meal and was focused on doing some more work on his assignment. It wasn't long before most of the lights were out and quietness descended on the, as most of the passengers were trying for some shut eye.

Melissa was now whispering quietly to Jordan wondering where their friends could be. They were both so aware of their presence and as more time elapsed, they both noticed how much more sensitive they had become.

"I wonder whether they will meet us when we arrive in Australia?" and before the question had been completed, they had their answer.

"It is part of the plan. Your cousins will also be part of the mission. Don't worry it will all work out." They looked at each other in sheer incredulity, their eyes sparkling. This was going to be an amazing holiday. They continued to talk quietly until conversation waned and both finally drifted off to sleep.

The next thing they knew was the plane was preparing to descend and the seat belt sign was on and they were both rubbing their eyes. Jordan looked up at the screen only to see the flight path heading to Singapore, and the ETA was 35 minutes. It was soon going to be light and they could vaguely make out building shapes as the plane continued its descent. Finally, the descent was complete, and the plane made its way to the terminal. Jordan looked over at David who was very much awake and chatting to the stewardess.

"Do we change planes here?" Jordan asked, and before David could respond, the stewardess nodded in the affirmative. "How long will we be in Singapore?" questioned Jordan further. "We have about a two and a half hours wait before we board for Australia and Melbourne in particular," reported David.

Eventually the plane came to a halt and everybody was pleased to stretch their legs and move from the confined space of the aircraft and into the spaciousness of the airport. Melissa was excited and ready to explore skipping happily through passageways filled with the most beautiful orchids. She paused regularly noticing the delicate shapes of orchids and just how exquisite they were. Their beauty struck her just as their individuality did. Melissa simply marvelled at their beauty and reflected as to how could something be created which were so intricate and different.

In the meantime, David and Jordan had found some interesting and different food stalls and were eyeing off a selection of dishes. Meanwhile

Mum and Dad were content to walk around checking out some of the duty-free shops and thinking what they may take to their hosts in country Victoria. Time slipped by easily and it was soon time to take themselves to their next departure lounge. Melissa was already waiting. There were still twenty-five minutes before boarding. A brief conversation took place, but the boys were nowhere to be seen. Mum was looking around anxiously wondering where they could be? The plan had been to assemble at least thirty minutes before boarding so where were they? She looked with great anxiety at George, but he could offer no explanation that would account for their lateness. Janet sprang into action. She spoke briefly to George about staying in one place just in case they showed up and then she was off. Janet had all the passports, so she was able to go to security and ask them for advice as to how to find them. Passport photos were duplicated and sent to every station in the airport, this was a difficult task and time was evaporating so quickly. The network of communication was amazing and within five minutes, reports were feeding back into the central command post, but no sign of the two boys. Panic was now setting in and both Mum and Dad were beside themselves. Melissa was surprising calm, and this didn't go unnoticed by her mum. Janet looked at her daughter and couldn't help wondering if she was tapping into one her gifts to locate her brothers. Melissa was suddenly aware that her Mum was looking at her.

"What are you looking at me like that for?" questioned Melissa earnestly.

"Darling are you able to use your gifts to maybe help find your brothers?" pleaded her mother. Melissa thought for a moment and smiled to herself. Yes, they were here, and she could feel that her brothers were now safe. She looked at her mum and smiled knowing that it was going to be okay and her mum was at ease straightaway. As if on cue, the boys arrived but looked very shaken. Both parents looked concerned and relieved at the same time. By now it was the last call for their flight so there was no time for explanations. They boarded the plane for the last leg of the journey and gradually made their way to their seats. By now mum was wanting to know what happened and leaned over to the boys with her 'please explain look'. It was up to David to share their harrowing experience. "Well Mum you won't believe this, but we were eating our meal in this little alcove and the next minute a few of the family members came out of the kitchen and surrounded us. There was no one else in the restaurant and they had knives and they were threatening us," David said in hushed tones. Mum's eyes grew visibly wider.

"How could this happen in such a busy airport?" David nodded in agreement,

"How indeed? I think they were wanting to see if we would be missed and it appeared that were motioning at our bodies. I did just wonder if they were looking for body parts. We were completely mystified! We couldn't understand anything they were saying," Mum looked perplexed and stunned she could scarcely take it all in.

"Well how come they let you go?" she questioned further. David replied,

"We are not sure, but it seemed that our disappearance was causing quite a stir with security staff running everywhere, waving pictures of us and asking people if they had seen us. It seems as though someone who was in the restaurant noticed us and the security officers came in and started asking questions"

"The next thing we knew we were pushed out of their kitchen into the dining area," David continued,

"Then the security staff brought us straight here. They had already put the plane on alert that there may be a delay."

"We still don't really know what they planned to do with us, but anyway we're here now, and finally on our way."

It was now time to relax and get some rest. Melissa leaned forward and gently took Jordan's hand and gave it a squeeze. She was so pleased to have him back safe and sound. Then she began,

"What do you think was going on in that food place?" quizzed Melissa.

"Well I am certain they were members of a gang because they all had tattoos on their forearms. I'm not even sure that they even owned the restaurant. Maybe they were there to collect protection money and just tied up the family and took over. They didn't know much about food." observed Jordan.

"It was unusual though the way they let us go, I mean one minute they were getting ready to put us in a kind of bag and take us right out the back. Then the guy who appeared to be the leader came back in, his face as white as a sheet and was telling them to undo the ties and get rid of us," continued Jordan.

"It was our friends wasn't it?" suggested Melissa knowingly. Jordan nodded confirming her insight, as they continued to be aware that they were not alone.

The next meal was served, and Jordan began to think more deeply about the incident at the airport knowing that there was more going on. They weren't interviewed by the police, nor were any statements taken, there were so many unanswered questions. He ate his meal slowly and quietly which was most out of character.

The afternoon passed without further incident and it was an opportunity for more rest and relaxation. They had been travelling now for what seemed to be forever. In another thirty minutes they would hit the west coast of Australia, and then the end was in sight. Only another four hours to go and they would be in Melbourne and their family would be there to greet them.

They both looked at each other in anticipation and excitement, this was going to be a holiday they would never forget. Little did they know it was going to change the course of human history, and there were huge surprises in store for them.

Time slipped by quickly and they were soon descending into Melbourne Airport. Now the excitement was palpable and the whole family was now preparing to meet their cousins. There had been so many animated conversations over the last six weeks. They were going to be in Victoria for at least five weeks and there was so much to see and do. They were looking forward to doing the touristy thing. The plane had finally landed and had come to a standstill at the disembarkation platform. The whole family was ready and gradually made their way forward. There were no holdups at customs and the family was soon in the main lounge and before they knew it, they were surrounded by their cousins, and aunty and uncle. Next, they were warmly welcomed and embraced. Ken and Nancy were so delighted to see their English cousins and Ken immediately began telling them about the plans. Nancy gently put her hand on her husband's arm restraining him and suggesting with the gesture that it might be a little too soon to be making plans. What really mattered was the Thomas's needed rest and Ken was now encouraging everyone to follow him into the car park. Emma was holding hands with Melissa and chatting excitedly about what things they could be getting up to in the coming weeks. They eventually came to the car. However, it wasn't exactly a car, it was a large people mover and could comfortably carry up to ten people with room to spare. Luggage was loaded and off they went towards the city. Ken and Nancy had organized a couple of nights at an hotel in Russel Street, right in the centre of the city. They had two apartments with three separate bedrooms and each with a self- contained kitchen. Nancy was describing it happily as they made their way into the city. Janet was warming to the idea with each descriptive feature and was looking forward to finally putting her head on a pillow and being able to fully stretch out. By now the traffic had dispersed and the journey to the city was both fast and smooth. It was evening and the only thought for the Thomas family was a hot shower, a brief bite to eat and then bed.

The next morning arrived in bright sunshine and all the young people were up, Andy, Emma's brother was marshalling the others and suggesting they head off to the Victoria Markets and get some food at the many stalls. This was greeted with great enthusiasm, and everyone was down the stairs and in the street in a flash. Everyone that is except the adults, they were enjoying a lengthy sleep in after such a tiring journey.

The adults made their way down to breakfast and were sitting back enjoying bacon and eggs when the young people bounced into the dining room, looking entirely satisfied and ready for whatever the day had in store. Everyone was ready for the briefing as breakfast was now over. Ken was suggesting that the boys, all five of them should go to visit the MCG to watch England and Australia face off in a one day international. There was excitement a plenty at that suggestion and they were to meet in ten minutes in the foyer, catch a tram and make their way to the 'G' as it was known. Meanwhile Nancy was suggesting a shopping trip for the girls visiting the Carlton strip where all the factory outlets were located and many of the 'seconds' could be found. That being agreed upon and received happily they located the tram they needed and headed off for the day. It was a very warm day and enjoyable and Andy treated Jordan and David to the famous Pie and Sauce at the 'G' saying jokingly. "Well mate you're real Aussies now!" It was a great match going right down to the wire, with England winning by the narrowest of margins with only a couple of balls to go.

Everyone thoroughly enjoyed the day's outing. They arrived back at the hotel to find the girls resting in Nancy and Ken's room, having walked for miles up and down the Carlton strip. They had a fantastic shopping experience the only problem was how were they going to fit all this gear in their suitcases on the way home.

Chinese was the food of choice and the men went out and ordered and came back with two roast ducks, all prepared roast pork fried rice and Chinese vegetables. Everyone agreed it was a fabulous meal to finish of a memorable day. The holiday had really got off to a flying start. Tomorrow would see them head off to the country and to the family farm, the other side of Stawell. It was going to be over a three-hour journey but there was no way it would be boring, there was so much to catch up with and still some interesting things to see.

It was another warm day and breakfast being over and check out effected the families began their homeward journey. An hour and three quarters later they reached the famous city of Ballarat stopping briefly for a toilet break and a cuppa. No-one looked for a soft drink, so it was an easy break. Nancy always prepared food and the melting moments were way better than any cake shop quality. There was some discussion about whether they would visit some of the more notable tourist attractions, but the consensus was. "Lets head home and see the farm." It was just after two o'clock as they passed through Stawell and the end of the journey was now in sight. Another twenty minutes and they would hit the little township of Glenorchy and from there it was just a couple of kilometres to the farm.

Ken had grown up in this part of the world and the Talbot name was well known throughout the farming community, Nancy had met Ken later in an exchange program and the relationship had blossomed from there.

It had gradually become warmer as they headed inland, and everybody had begun to shed some of the layers. After passing through the very small town the van began to slow down to turn in through the farm gate. No-one needed to open it as it was a cattle grid entrance.

"Why all the steel bars at the entrance?" queried Jordan. "Well," explained Andy,

"It saves us having to get out every time we come and go, it also keeps the animals in the paddock. You see they can't really walk on the rails."

Jordan had had his first lesson about farming in Australia and he was already acknowledging the ingenuity he had just witnessed.

The vehicle came to a gentle stop and everybody piled out. It was now mid-afternoon and of course everyone was looking for afternoon tea.

Just at that moment there was a loud bleating sound and the lambs recognized that Emma was home and they also were looking for their milk. Emma ran over to them and Melissa needed no second bidding, she was right behind. The lambs were now in full voice and demanding a feed. Emma patted them affectionately and spoke to them kindly. They would have to wait at least ten minutes until they had made up and heated their bottles. That explanation fell on deaf ears as they bleated all the more. Soon everyone was in and sorted to their various rooms. Emma had now prepared three bottles for the three lambs. Armed with the bottles Emma and Melissa made their way to the pen and began the task of feeding them. The bleating stopped and the tails wagged incessantly. Melissa was thrilled to help and to see the result. That being completed the girls made their way back to the house and were happy to join the others for a cup of tea and more cakes and homemade biscuits.

The boys were not actually in part of the main house. They had a large room joined to the house by a covered in veranda. David thought this was 'ace' as they could do a whole lot of things without being disturbed. Andy had turned nineteen and was a very competent driver having driven all the farm vehicles for many years now. He had passed the silly stage of doing donuts and wheelies and was content to drive carefully and responsibly. He said to his dad.

"How about I show the family the farm?"

"Of course," re-joined his dad. That settled, George and his two boys along with Melissa and Emma headed out to the vehicle. The farm was just over two thousand hectares and was quite a substantial holding for these parts. It was also diverse, having sheep for wool and a small number of fat lambs. There were cattle mainly beef and two milking cows which always needed to be milked for the family's milk supply, but no pigs. Each year there were paddocks sown down with crops and these were usually wheat, but latterly some to canola. This was all explained as Andy drove from paddock to paddock and was of course always mindful of leaving gates as they were found. Everybody nodded about the importance of keeping everything as they found it. "The beef cattle were in prime condition and would soon be off to the sale yards, but they would all be steers. Most of the cows were with calf and ready to drop in a couple of months when winter food would be available. The planning was meticulous," Andy explained. Melissa looked at the herd thoughtfully and began to realize that her gift extended to animals as well and she was astounded about what she saw. Now there was a real dilemma, how could she help her cousins without exposing her gift? For the moment she would need to keep it to herself and maybe speak with Jordan about it later.

They were heading back to the homestead and everyone was starting to feel hungry. The thought and smell of food was already wafting in their direction. Andy knew the aroma of one of Mum's lamb roasts. They were all out of the vehicle now and the smell of food was amazing. Nancy had always cooked in the Weber outside because it kept the smells out of the kitchen and meant no regular cleaning of the oven. It all made good sense and the lamb was always beautiful and tender. The evening meal was a blast according to David and there was so much good food. He had consumed so much of the food, everyone including David wondered where he had put it all. Everybody helped with clearing the table and washing up and then some more conversation and eventually bed. Melissa had managed to catch Jordan's attention and the two had found a moment alone for Melissa to share more of her insights. There was no advice given but at least Jordan had become a good listener and that was always helpful.

Just as they were about to go back inside, Jordan looked at Melissa showing some real consternation. She sensed what he was about to say and began,

"I don't know what we can do about the others, but I know our friends from outer space are here and they really want to meet with us." Jordan smiled,

"Of course, you would know what was on my mind. They have been communicating with us since we arrived in Australia, and more so now we are on the farm," then Melissa said reassuringly,

"It's going to be ok. Think back to how they took care of Mum when we had to sneak back into the house." Jordan nodded acknowledging how well it had all worked out.

Returning to the house they found everybody moving into their bedrooms but not before Melissa had gone up to Nancy, put her arms around her and given her the biggest hug imaginable and said,

"That was a beautiful meal and I won't ever want to leave." Nancy smiled happily responding with,

"We are so delighted to have you stay and you never know one day we might get over to your part of the world." Nancy replied.

"That would be awesome," replied Melissa "Especially if you can bring roast lamb like that," smiling all over her face. Another brief hug and then one for Mum and Dad and Melissa was off to bed. The whole house was soon plunged into darkness and the night air seemed perfectly still. Then Melissa who had been in a deep sleep suddenly woke up. She instantly knew their friends were here and wanting to meet. She had enough forethought to have some night clothes ready along with her pencil like LED torch. She was dressed in a flash and quietly making her way through the lounge to the hall and the front door. Within moments she was striding through the bush where they had driven earlier in the day whilst looking over the whole farm. She was confident that Jordan would have got the message and would be making his way to the same spot. Sure enough there he was, flashlight in hand walking in the same direction. What happened next surprised them until they recalled the communication that had taken place on the plane! Andy and Emma were just in front of them but totally in the dark. Andy began,

"What took you so long? our friends have been waiting nearly five minutes?" he joked.

"We must have needed more sleep than you guys," Jordan responded and then they all laughed.

"Our friends have been preparing us for this meeting for the last few days. They knew you were coming, and they gave us messages to indicate when they would be here," Emma said confidently. Jordan and Melissa stopped momentarily recognizing just how important this trip would be. Indeed, their friends from another planet had skilfully orchestrated it. They could see the craft behind Andy and Emma, and then the importance began to dawn on them both. They stood motionless for a moment and the excitement was effusive. Just as they were coming to terms with this event another burst in upon them which was totally unexpected. David arrived and was already asking,

"What on earth is going on?" and before anyone could answer his question, he caught sight of the space craft, and froze on the spot. They all looked at him for what seemed forever, but his speech had deserted him, eventually he managed to stammer,

"What is that thing behind you?" Jordan and Andy both responded at the same time and with the same words,

"Come and see, they are not hostile they are our friends." David visibly gulped for air, still dumbstruck, he just couldn't take it in. Firstly, he didn't believe in 'little green men' and how could they know they are friendly?

The next instant the four moved towards the craft whilst David not only kept a very respectful distance but urged the others to be very careful. His warning had no impact as the four made their way right up to it, the hatch then opened, and they went in. David watched in total disbelief and then was completely blown away. He heard as plain as day a voice saying to him,

"It's ok David we know you are sceptical, but your family is very safe, and we mean you no harm. Do come in and take your place." David looked all around, who was speaking to him? He could see no-one. He just couldn't take it all in. His entire world had been turned upside down in the space of five minutes. By now the others were watching and listening to all this play out. They were so sympathetic to his predicament. Jordan alighted from the craft and simply put his arm around his older brother and reassured him everything was ok. They had done this a few times before. David looked at him in total disbelief and said,

"You must be mad to even think about going in this thing, whatever it is." It was clear David could not be consoled or convinced to come on board. At that point Emma hopped out and put her arm firmly around her cousin and said,

"It's perfectly ok, you will be safe, I promise you." David had already decided that Emma was an ok chick and being his cousin, he was all the fonder of her, but he was still reluctant to board.

There was only one course of action left and the four realized that David was not going to be coerced into coming on board. With that decision made the craft closed its door and within a split second had slipped silently and like a well-oiled streak of lightening sped off into the night sky. David watched it spellbound for a minute and then it totally disappeared. He still couldn't take it in. For a moment he literally pinched himself, it had to be a dream this could not be happening. He stood there transfixed to the spot watching and now beginning to wonder whether he would see his siblings and cousins again. Hardly had the thought formed in his mind when he was reassured that they were perfectly safe. Furthermore, they would soon return. Just as quickly as they had disappeared, they were back and as silently and noiselessly, the craft landed on solid ground.

David just stood there with his mouth open, the hatch opened, and everyone jumped out. "Come on David, come and see what we have just seen." they chimed in unison, but he was still apprehensive. "No," he thought, "If I do get in then they will take us all to some distant planet and we will never see our family again!"

His thoughts were challenged by this voice he was now becoming accustomed to.

"David had we wanted to take you by force we could have done so easily, but we need you to trust us. We need you to know without any doubt at all in your mind, we are not just on your side. We want to work with you to help save your world for your sake and for future generations."

"How can you force me to get in?" he said defiantly. Jordan looked over quickly and assured David that they could do so easily and swiftly. "But would they?" "No, they need you to trust them." There seemed nothing more to be gained from the ongoing communication and the spacecraft closed its door and was gone.

The five stood around for some time sharing their experience whilst David still tried to get his head around what he had just witnessed. Eventually they made their way back to the house and back to their own bedrooms. Melissa gave Emma a big hug and said, "It's really great having like an older sister." Emma was quite chuffed and was happy to take on that mantle. Melissa looked at her seeing her colours standing out so brilliantly that she knew she was in very safe hands.

The boys went into their bedroom and couldn't stop talking; however, David was largely silent. He was still reflecting on what he had seen and what he had heard. It was just too much for him to take in and he just kept shaking his head in disbelief.

"Be careful David, if you keep that up, it's likely to fall off," quipped Jordan facetiously. The comment was lost on David, he was too steeped in his own thoughts.

Could it have really happened the way it had unfolded, he was lost in his own world of thought. He then realized Jordan and Andy were looking straight at him, asking him a direct question. He was suddenly aware of them for the first time since the craft took off.

"Where were you?" Andy asked jokingly. However, Jordan knew his older brother only too well and knew just how much he would be struggling with what he had witnessed.

"Will they be back?" asked David hesitantly.

"But of course," said Jordan and Andy in unison. David looked stunned the way they both answered together with exactly the same words. By now the boys had become used to this process but it still did take them by surprise.

"Will you come with us next time David?" inquired Andy. David was hesitant, "To be honest I'm not sure, I still have some more thinking to do. It is really a matter of trust," he concluded.

Jordan then chimed in,

"Take your time bro. I am sure you will make the decision that suits you." David was impressed with Jordan's maturity and felt very reassured.

Meanwhile the girls had continued to have a most animated discussion, regarding how long the visitors had been coming and just what they had shared with each of the girls. Their excitement was obvious, and they chatted into the wee small hours, eventually falling asleep.

The next day came around so quickly and everybody was woken by the rooster, whose duty it was to awaken all the sleepers. He was completely self-appointed, but nobody seemed to object. It was amazing, the sun was shining, and the birds were singing, and the Thomas family was taken by this incredible sound of this one type of bird or at least its song. Melissa who was soon dressed had stepped outside soon realized what type of bird it was. Black and white with highly defined markings. She figured that the birds with strongly marked colours on their backs were the males and the females were quite bland,

"Isn't that the way of it all?" she mused to herself.

David was also outside wandering about looking rather thoughtful and quite pensive. His quietness was not lost on Melissa and she just sidled up to him and said, "It takes a bit of getting used to doesn't it?" Again, David was taken by surprise at her comment, suddenly aware how mature his siblings were. He nodded and then they both heard the call for breakfast, and David needed no second bidding.

He couldn't believe his eyes when he saw what was laid out, stewed fruit, muesli, cereal, yogurt and then there was bacon eggs, tomatoes, mushrooms and eggplant as well as has hash- browns. Wow where would he start? His uncle was nearly finished, so he encouraged David to sit down and tuck in. David needed no second invitation. Soon the rest of the family had arrived and were seated amid lots of animated chatter.

Nancy was in her element preparing food, popping toast, lashings of home-made butter and quite the best marmalade and strawberry jam anyone had ever tasted. Breakfast was soon over and there was no hesitation with volunteering to do the dishes. The boys were first in line with David at the head of the queue. Emma noted this with interest and stood by him and ever so unobtrusively slipped her hand in his and gave it a big squeeze. David immediately felt quite special and his whole body warmed at her touch. He wasn't quite sure why, but he felt very close to her and really enjoyed her company. Maybe it was the kind of work she did and what she had planned for herself in the future. He reflected further, yes, he admitted, he did find her attractive and he was so glad he came.

Ken was now busy organizing the day so that the farm work could continue running smoothly. This was now moving into a hectic time of the year. There were crops to strip, headers and field bins to organize and trucks to hire for grain carting. As usual, Ken's machinery was serviced and ready to go. It would simply be a matter of assessing the crop's readiness for harvest.

Ken, George and Andy piled into the farm ute and headed off. It would be a couple of hours before they would return. The remainder of the family completed some of the routine chores around the farm, including collecting wood for the fire, baking scones, and whipping fresh cream.

"Gee you sure eat well on the farm, and there is so much good food, I could easily live here," David affirmed happily.

Emma was busy baking strips of puff pastry ready to be filled with jam and cream. Nancy and Janet were busy baking biscuits and more especially melting moments, which just happened to be favourites of both Melissa and Jordan. Nancy had also decided to make a large fruit cake so there would be plenty of afternoon tea on hand, for the future. Being away for two or three days, stocks had run low and this was a good opportunity to replenish supplies. It was now 1.00pm and the men arrived back after their stint in the paddocks, assessing the readiness of the crops. Lunch was ready when they arrived, and soon everyone was sitting down to cold lamb, tomatoes, salad, and freshly baked bread. Most of the conversation centred around farming and particularly the business at hand in the next few weeks. Andy David and Jordan had been allocated fire duties: which meant quite a challenging number of tasks, including servicing the motor on the truck, checking all the fittings and couplings and then testing for leaks. This would take care of the afternoon and some, so once lunch was over, they went to work. This time the girls tidied the dining room and kitchen in preparation for the evening meal. Suddenly there was an enormous shriek from the kitchen and everybody in the house responded straight away. The cause of the shriek soon became obvious. A large Tiger Snake had found its way into the kitchen, in search of whatever food and water was available. Melissa was the last to arrive but the first to respond to the crisis. The snake was very sick, and she could see the colours evaporating by the second, but what to do next didn't come quite so easily. She paused for a moment and then looked to her aunt and said calmly, "Do you have a long stick or handle we can use lift it out of the kitchen?" and then added, much to everyone's surprise, "It just needs to be helped out of the kitchen and left to die in peace." No-one quite understood how Melissa could know this, but the priority was the stick and Nancy had such a tool for the occasion. Emma was onto this and had positioned herself nicely, and without any more fuss, soon had the reptile in its natural habitat. The snake moved away slowly. Nothing more was said until the evening when the men came home from the machinery shed. Ken then observed,

"I see we had a visitor today, so who was the brave soul who killed it?" "Nobody killed it Dad," Emma volunteered,

"But I did remove it and it was alive and well when I did it must have died since then."

Then there were strange looks all round as Melissa's words came back to everyone. Ken and George looked at each other in bewilderment with no notion of what had just transpired. It was then up to Emma to explain Melissa's prophetic utterance regarding the snake's health or lack of it. Then all eyes focused on Melissa. Melissa handled herself with aplomb saying very clearly,

"Well, I think I have this kind of sixth sense which tells me how healthy some animals are, and I felt sure the snake was nearing the end of its days."

"Well," said Ken half joking, "We could certainly use that kind of knowledge on the farm. We may be able to save a small fortune on vet's bills." Everybody laughed and the subject was dropped for the moment, but Emma was waiting for the opportune moment to check out her prophetic cousin.

It had been a busy day for everyone, and bed was beckoning. It wasn't long before the house was shrouded in darkness and everybody was sleeping peacefully. Suddenly Melissa and Emma were awake, and they knew instinctively their visitors had arrived. They had prepared for the event and even though the evening was still warm their clothes were all ready to don. Quietly they slipped out, without a sound and just as soon as they had cleared the house, they began a conversation. Emma could contain her curiosity no longer,

"How do you know when an animal is sick?" she inquired insistently. Melissa explained it thus,

"Well each animal has an energy field and that field is full of colour, but when it is sick the colours start to diminish. When it is really sick it just has this dark cloud around it. The darker the aura the closer to death the animal is. The snake was almost black, so I wasn't surprised that it died shortly after you took it outside. There was no point in killing it, death was so close". Emma looked on admiringly.

"I knew there was something special about you. Our visitors told me that you had an important contribution to make to the team," she said knowingly. Melissa stopped for a moment and put her arms around Emma and the hug said it all. They continued to the spot where their visitors would be, only to find the boys already there. Even David was waiting but keeping his distance and trying to keep out of sight. He was still pondering the comments they had made to him the previous night. If they wanted, they could place him in the craft without any effort at all. Hardly had the thought crossed his mind and he was in the craft, already strapped in. David was stunned he couldn't believe what had just happened, and now he was sweating and felt totally out of control and was way out of his comfort zone. He struggled for a minute or two without success, and his breathing stifled and constricted, his face getter redder by the second. Just as quickly as he was in, he was out, sprawled on the ground by the other boys. His breathing had now settled, and he was back on his feet.

"How did they do that?" the bemused look on his face said it all.

"We just wanted to demonstrate to you that if we wanted, we could compel you to join the others. We know that you need to be here by your own choice." The words kept echoing in his brain. By now the others were in the craft and strapped in, and now they were hopeful of David joining them. David was still resistant and still wanted more time and the visitors knew it and respected David's reticence.

"Take your time," came the words crashing through his mind. He couldn't get his head around it at all. When he looked up again the craft had gone, and he had no idea where. He didn't panic now; it did mean he had more time to process what was going on.

Meanwhile the four were being transported across the world and within a few minutes had covered an incredible distance.

"Where are you taking us?" The question was formed but not asked audibly.

"You are needed somewhere, and you will see when you arrive why you are the best people to do this." Just as silently as they had taken off, they landed. Immediately they stepped out Melissa and Jordan recognised the surroundings. "We are back home," they exclaimed together, "But why?" Suddenly it all became clear. They could hear shouting and fighting. Melissa could now make out the figures and one of them was Alistair. The remainder were Terry's gang, she gasped, she could now see what was happening. She motioned to the boys and Emma and they speedily came over. Melissa explained what was happening and within a minute Andy, Jordan and Emma were in the thick of it. Andy was very well built for his nineteen years and the very sight of him struck terror into the gang. Emma was no slouch when it came to being physical. She had to learn from an early age how to throw a hay bale around and in her mind, this was not dissimilar. There was no real need to become physical for the gang was already dispersing.

Alistair instantly recognized Jordan and was so glad he showed up when he did. Then Jordan introduced Andy and Emma to Alistair. Alistair looked quite puzzled at the introductions as he was clearly aware that their accents were quite different and certainly not familiar at all.

"Where are you from?" inquired Alistair. Andy soon volunteered that they were Australians, and they were visiting their cousins, Jordan and Melissa. Melissa had managed to keep out of sight and was happy for it to stay that way.

"How long are you staying then?" inquired Alistair. "Not long, I expect we will be leaving very soon." Then it dawned on Alistair, he hadn't seen Melissa and wondered where she might be. He turned to Jordan and inquired.

"Where is Melissa? You know I think a lot of your sister, she is definitely ok." Melissa blushed at the comment and acknowledged to herself that he was not a bad sort either. The woods were now quiet, and Alistair was able to confirm that he had left the gang, but they were trying to bully him back into it.

"If you hadn't shown up when you did things could have got ugly," said Alistair. They nodded and agreed, it all happened just at the right time.

"Say hi to Melissa when you see her," called Alistair as he made his way home. Within an instant they were back in the craft and winging their way home.

In no time at all they were back in the paddock where David was still sitting pondering what he had seen again. He looked up in surprise and found them all piling out and before he could utter a word the craft was gone.

They were already full of news about where they had been but David 'flat out' didn't believe them. So, then Andy described some features of the woods and just two members of Terry's gang in some detail. David stood open mouthed, Emma then confirmed everything Andy had said and somehow it was easier to believe it from Emma.

Then Jordan couldn't resist it, "Guess who's got the hots for Melissa?" David couldn't begin to imagine. Meanwhile Emma was trying to distract

Jordan so he wouldn't embarrass Melissa, but Jordan wasn't going to be side-tracked.

"What about blonde Alistair we met in the woods? He's not a bad looker either," continued Jordan. Melissa was now bright red but luckily no one could see her cheeks in the darkness of the night. More conversations about their escapade in the woods and now David was feeling more relaxed. Emma and David stayed back a little and spoke at length. More and more David felt secure with Emma and her judgement and was keen to experience their next space adventure.

It was still before midnight as they made their way back into the house, and they were more than ready for bed.

The morning arrived, the day when the crop had to stripped and that meant all hands-on deck.

Everyone had been primed for this event and everybody had their special task allocated, so it was going to be plain sailing. Ken and George would be in the header, Andy and David would be driving the grain truck alongside the header. Jordan and Emma would be in the fire truck ready for any emergency resplendent with a brand-new water tank just made for the vehicle. Melissa would be in the house on the CB radio checking any messages from the local fire control officer, and of course the most important members of the team were in the kitchen preparing food for the workers, Nancy and Janet.

The first day went off without incident and everybody fulfilled their roles admirably. It had been an incredibly long day and only finished as the sun was setting and it was becoming too cold for the grain to strip properly. It was exhausting being in the heat and the flies were always present.

It was so good to be inside in the cool and away from the pesky flies. By the time everybody had washed up and sat down it was quite late and quite dark. Dinner was soon over and washing up done and there was no evening to speak of. Tomorrow would be another long day, so everybody was more than ready for bed. The house was soon enveloped in darkness and there would be no visitors tonight, simply because their alien friends were aware of the work needing to be completed.

Morning arrived punctually but far too soon for most of the family. They had hardly gone to bed it seemed and here was another hot day and work just beckoning to be done. David certainly had not managed enough sleep and whenever that occurred, he was grumpy. The sun was indeed heralding a new day rapidly ascending to a place of authority in the clear sky. It was going to be a scorcher. Nancy and Janet had arrived in the kitchen before sunup and commenced their breakfast routine. Soon all the bodies were sitting at the table, ready to consume more fuel for the long day ahead, everyone except Melissa. She was diligently at her post speaking to the Fire Control Officer checking out whether it might be a total fire ban day. It was going to be okay and that meant another busy day.

Another day passed without a hitch and nearly a quarter of the crop was off and on the way to the silo. David and Andy had made a great team ensuring grain delivery at the nearest major silo, St. Arnaud. They had taken it in turns to drive and reduce the stress, but both the boys were careful drivers and very watchful on the road and both had obtained special licenses for the grain season. The first twelve days had already come and gone and there was only a day's grain left to strip. The atmosphere in the house was becoming quite tense largely due to the pressure of work everyone was experiencing. Ken and Nancy were so grateful for the help of their cousins. This year the crop would be finished, and all processed because of the extra help available. This year the crop had been heavy but was off in a record time and the risk of fire had now abated. The day was over, and bed was a happy thought.

Breakfast was more leisurely and at a more reasonable hour as the end of stripping was now in sight. The mood was much lighter, and conversation was matching. There was friendly rivalry as to who would take the last grain to the silo, and what prizes might be expected for finishing well ahead of schedule. Breakfast over, Ken cleared his throat, and everyone was stilled. Ken began, "We have not only got the crop off in record time, and we are receiving a very good price, so I would like to propose as a treat that we all have a couple of days in Ballarat visiting some of the tourist attractions, like Kryal Castle and Sovereign Hill. We can stay at a motel or hotel of our choosing, and enjoy some well-earned R and R."

There was instant applause from everybody around the table. What a lovely way to spend a couple of days after a gruelling thirteen days of work. There were other attractions in Ballarat as well. Melissa could hardly contain her excitement as she had spent a lot of time talking to her newfound friend the Fire Control Officer about a great many subjects. Up until now Jake was only a voice on the end of the radio, but soon she was going to be able to meet him. Melissa had set up a meeting after speaking with her Uncle Ken. He had confirmed that Jake was a very safe person to be around, so now she really felt comfortable to see him in the flesh. Melissa was off to Stawell as soon as harvest was over.

The last day of harvest lived up to expectations. All the grain was off and delivered to the silo, and the fire truck not required now, finally put away safely, but always at the ready. It was late afternoon and for the first-time stillness overtook the farm, the first time in thirteen days. There was a great afternoon tea spread out in the kitchen and soon everyone was sitting down, not only full of chat but ready to eat a horse. Fruit cake, chocolate eclairs, scones and cream, David looked at his Mum and said very cheekily, "Well Mum, food was never like this back home." Janet nodded in agreement, stating,

"Well, I have to agree I have never been much of a baker and Nancy has always been talented in the kitchen." David suddenly felt awful, he had never meant to hurt his Mum. Janet knew that guilty look on David's face and straight away reassured him that it was ok, her gifts lay in other directions and she was more than content with who she was.

Melissa now changed the subject,

"Who is going to take me to meet Jake tomorrow?" she inquired. Nancy then volunteered, "Well, I will be heading off to Stawell in the morning, so if you like to arrange a time with Jake, we can work around that time frame." That sounded great and Melissa was more than happy to accept the offer. Then after suggesting a time to meet, she went off to the radio to see if she could arrange the time with Jake. It was a few minutes later when she returned beaming with excitement. Looking straight at her parents she asked, "Jake has asked if I could stay over one night at their house at Halls Gap. He would like me to meet the family and especially his daughter, Sally who is my age."

"Please, please?" pleaded Melissa earnestly. There was quite a period of silence before any conversation was forthcoming. Ken looked at Janet and George and said.

"There is no urgency to book our accommodation at Ballarat, I'm sure Melissa will have a great time at the 'Gap' and we could go there at some time ourselves." That was settled and everyone was feeling very relaxed and pleased that the harvest was finally over.

Emma looked at David and offered to take him down to the milking stand and show him how to milk a cow. David jumped at the opportunity as it allowed him more time with Emma. They went off quickly and Jordan wasn't sure whether he should go as well, after all Emma had only invited David. He looked at Emma for a moment and she caught his glance and quite spontaneously invited him as well. Melissa was not going to be left out either, so she was happy to tag along.

Three of them watched as Emma brought the cow into the stall and fed her. She then used the warm water in the bucket to wash the cow's udder and teats, then produced another larger bucket and small stool and began to milk her. It all seemed a little strange to see the milk gradually filling the bottom of the bucket and milk frothing up. David thought it all looked pretty easy and suggested he might try his hand. Emma was only too pleased and vacated the stool happily. David tried but nothing came out He was sure he'd watched Emma carefully, so was surprised when nothing happened. Emma knelt alongside him, taking the teat in her hand and showed him just how to grasp it and at the same time squeeze with rhythm and pull down at the same time. Eventually, a small stream of milk emerged and there were muffled cheers. Emma had warned them that they needed to be quiet as sudden noise could spook the cow and she would either kick or move quickly and someone could be hurt. David eventually got the hang of it but recognized that his wrists were beginning to get sore and so he gave the task back to Emma. By the time Emma had finished the bucket was a good two thirds full. The cow was released back into the paddock and the group were happily making their way back to the house.

It was now dinner time and an unusually light meal was served, largely due to the late afternoon tea enjoyed by everyone, and especially David. The dishes were soon done and put away and someone suggested playing cards. There were enough volunteers for a game whilst others decided TV would be an option.

It had still been a long and busy day and gradually each family member drifted off to bed except the card players, but even they were feeling tired and eventually they turned in.

It was quite late when the last light was turned off and only the sound of the animals could be heard with an occasional moo or bleating of sheep. The air was both warm and still, with little breeze and the promise of another hot day. The Thomas family had so enjoyed the warm weather, after leaving the cooler climate of England.

The new day was announced yet again by the rooster crowing with an unusual zest. It seemed he took his duty seriously and hardly drew breath in between his crowing, it was after all his role. And he did it so proudly and when in view, with huge swagger.

Melissa was first at the breakfast table announcing proudly that she had packed her overnight bag and was ready for her trip to Halls Gap. Soon everyone was down except Emma. Nancy inquired about her only to be told that she wasn't feeling very well and had decided to stay in bed. Andy looked in David's direction, "How would you like to take over the milking duties for the morning?" he asked teasingly. David responded most enthusiastically,

"But of course, I'll give it my best shot." "Good on you, I admire someone who will have ago" Ken chipped in.

Breakfast completed and Nancy, Janet and Melissa headed for the car and off into town. Melissa was dying to put a face to the voice. She had pictured what Jake might look like because she had been warmed by his soft well spoken voice, which seemed so different to the usual Aussie accent she had become accustomed to. They arrived at the town centre in no time at all and there waiting to greet them was Jake. Nancy had already pointed him out to Janet and Melissa. Jake was smiling warmly as he opened the door for the two ladies to get out. Introductions were made, and greetings exchanged and within minutes Melissa was in the car heading off to the 'Gap.' Janet was greatly reassured after meeting Jake and was sure that her very special daughter was in safe hands. Melissa looked out at the brown fields and was not surprised to see the occasional kangaroo but was really hoping to see a live Koala Bear. Melissa was full of questions about how long Jake and his family had lived at the Gap, she already knew that he had three children and Sally was the youngest. She knew that his other job was that of a ranger and that there were times when it was quite dangerous. There were times when he needed to be on the mountain range to help rescue tourist and search parties to look for people who had become lost or disorientated. His calming voice was so reassuring that he seemed perfect for the job. The twenty-five-minute drive soon passed, and they were driving into the Gap at a much- reduced speed. It already seemed cooler and Melissa remarked on just that.

Jake nodded in agreement and stating that was usually the case, the car was now slowing right down and came to a gentle stop in front of what was obviously Jake's house. There was excitement aplenty as Sally came out to welcome Melissa. Her Dad had already told her heaps about Melissa and how she had assisted in the stripping of the crop out at the farm.

It seemed that Sally and Melissa hit it off immediately, Sally was already showing Melissa her bedroom and the view from her window. Melissa was won over by the view alone, but she just knew that she was really going to get along with Sally. The next hour plus was spent chatting about music school and boys. Sally's interest was piqued when she learned about Jordan, Melissa's older brother, and the more Melissa described him the more Sally couldn't wait to meet him. There was no stopping the chatter and it wasn't long before midday meal was ready, and they sat down happily to draw breath and eat. Melissa then finally met Sally's brother who was much older and had left school some years ago. Bruce introduced himself and encouraged everybody to enjoy the meal as it was his own preparation. Jake now took his place at the head of the table and the meal began in earnest. Melissa had learned through her many conversations with Jake that he became a single parent some years before. Melissa had never heard how it all happened except that Sally's mum had left when Sally was only 6 years old, and since then there had been little contact and Jake had never found another partner. This was a deliberate decision by Jake because he wanted to make sure that he gave all his attention to his children. The girls had shared so much about their families and the bond between them continued to grow. Melissa was enjoying her time so much. The afternoon was spent with Jake and Sally as they headed off to Silverband Falls. The air was so clear around the falls and the sound of the water danced on the rocks as to almost mesmerize the family. Melissa seemed entranced by the stillness which was only broken by an occasional bird calling and darting among the many trees. Her thoughts turned to home as she pondered the different experiences of beauty. The magpies really caught her attention with their beautiful corralling, together with the black jays cheekily darting in and around them. Suddenly it was time to move and they headed off to Lake Bellfield to take a closer look at the Dam. Jake suggested some fishing, but the girls were too busy talking and the thought of sitting still and being quiet did not appeal at all. Melissa was constantly on the lookout for Koalas as they walked around, sadly it was not to be. As they made their way home the only wildlife they saw were the kangaroos dotted everywhere in the paddocks. Jake needed to be home to check in his fire control duties and prepare for the evening meal.

The girls straightway made a beeline for the bedroom with more chat about school, music, and Sally kept asking about Jordan even more.

Dinner was now being served and soon everyone was seated and still the chat continued but slackened considerably when the food was served. Spaghetti Bolognaise was one of Jakes standby dishes and a clear favourite with the family. Jake had even excelled and prepared a fresh fruit salad with ice cream and cream. Tonight, the dishes would be loaded in the dishwasher and the family could relax and chat.

Without even a hint of interest hitherto Jake began on the matter of UFO'S. Even his own family were taken by surprise by the subject coming from their dad.

"Well what do you think?" asked dad rather bluntly, "Are we being visited by other people?" Sally wasn't sure but Bruce was adamant.

"There is no life out there and if there was, we'd have heard about it by now." Jake wasn't deterred by his son's response and said rather quietly,

"I think I might have seen something unusual in the night sky just over a week ago." Melissa began thinking to herself, could that have been our friends from Andromeda, it would certainly be close to their trip back to UK. Melissa couldn't contain herself, "What did it look like?" She asked eagerly. Jake described something quite large with a silvery coating but beyond he was unclear except it was very long. Bruce then suggested that it may be good for dad to get his eyes tested, but his tongue was firmly in his cheek. Then Melissa spoke and with such certainty that she had everybody's attention.

"I believe there is intelligent life form on other heavenly bodies, and they are contenting themselves by simply observing how we live together, and how we manage our resources." It was said with such conviction that nobody was about to challenge her view. Bruce looked thoughtful for a moment and then offered this comment,

"I have a friend whose father used to fly all over the world and he often spoke about seeing alien craft and on one occasion they were flanked by these craft on a regular but short route to New Zealand." Everybody paused for a moment to reflect and draw breath. This appeared to be in distinct contrast to his original denial. Melissa went on,

"I think it's kind of reassuring to think that there are some beings looking out for us and I can't imagine they mean us harm given they have such technology to move through space as fast as they do." Jake looked with direct interest at Melissa sensing that there was much going on under the surface and for the moment it would have to stay there. It seemed for the moment the topic was exhausted, and cricket inevitably surfaced with the recent one-day match in Melbourne.

It had been a full day with lots of walking and chatting and both girls were tired. Bed seemed like a good idea and Jake had a big day ahead of him, so he was soon off as well. The house was soon cloaked in darkness and the stillness was welcomed.

Melissa awoke first and was peering out through the window looking at the imposing mountains. There were no views like this at home and her eyes continued to search the range fascinated by their sheer ruggedness and strength. The sun was already illuminating noticeable aspects of the Grampians and her vision was suddenly attracted to a light glinting in the sun. At first it seemed quite still but after a while it began to move almost as though it was transmitting some form of signal. Melissa's attention was quite fixed, she couldn't take her eyes of it, then as if on cue Sally appeared and came right over, and she too became engrossed. Sally then called her dad who had been preparing the breakfast. It wasn't long before Jake realized that this was quite unusual and that maybe he would call the police.

Breakfast was light and culminated with toast and jam, but Sally insisted that Melissa try some vegemite! Melissa was not impressed but had the good sense only to put it on a small corner of her toast. She managed to get it down whilst drowning it in a cup of tea. Melissa then went back to her room and packed her few things and was ready to head off back to the farm. Goodbyes were said and hugs given, and Sally promised that she would come and visit before they returned to the UK. Even Bruce stood in line for a hug and it was obvious that Melissa had made an impression on him. The journey passed almost without incident, but Jake was more than thoughtful, and he raised the question of UFO's again. This time he was quite pointed with his enquiry, asking Melissa if she had seen one. Her answer was swift, of course "Haven't most people? But they don't talk about for fear of being branded crackpots and nobody is prepared to do that." Jake nodded in agreement.

"Are you able to talk about your encounter?" was Jakes next question. This time there was a considerable pause and Melissa was searching for the right words without betraying any confidences. Jake with one eye on the road and the other on Melissa, could sense her reluctance and apologized for the intrusion. Melissa then volunteered some details of their sightings in the UK but none of their actual encounter details. Those would always need to be confidential. Jake then offered one final comment,

"I feel as though there is more you are not saying but I'm sure it's okay and you are not in any danger." Melissa answered him with a wan smile but made no further comment. The matter was now at an end and Melissa volunteered that she had really enjoyed her time at the 'Gap' and would very much like to return and spend more time searching the whole area. Jake nodded acknowledging the whole family had enjoyed her company and Sally had made a friend for life. Melissa confirmed the solidarity of the friendship and suggested Sally might like to come to the UK for a holiday in the future. They were now in Stawell and Melissa was busy thanking Jake yet again for her brief stay at the Grampians. The vehicle finally stopped at the fire station and there was Andy ready and waiting. Before hopping out Melissa did say hastily that she would love for Sally to come and stay at the farm but would need to check to see if it was okay and check some dates. Jake nodded and recognized that this would need to happen. A final hug from Melissa and Jake was on his way to Ballarat for his regional meeting.

All the necessary supplies were on board and it was back to the farm. Andy enquired just how Melissa liked the Grampians and she said it was 'super' but sadly bemoaned the fact that there had been no koala sightings, but lots of other wildlife including deer.

Once back on the farm Melissa began sharing all her stories including Jake's questions around UFO's. Andy looked a little apprehensive for the moment, but she was able to put his mind at rest. There had been no activity on that front for a while now but all that was soon to change.

Melissa was delighted to speak to Jordan and couldn't wait to tease him about Sally being interested in him. Jordan initially brushed it off but was quietly looking forward to meeting her. Melissa wasted no time in speaking with her parents and then her aunt about Sally's possible visit, it was soon all arranged. Melissa spoke to Sally and she would come for a whole weekend hopefully, and after the families had been on their stay at Ballarat. Jordan quickly filled her in on the details and they were going to be off in the morning.

CHAPTER 6

SERENDIPITOUS FRIENDS

THE REST OF the day was filled with sharing the plans for the couple of days in Ballarat. Emma and Andy were not nearly so excited as they had been to all the sights before. Nevertheless, they were looking forward to sharing their experiences with Jordan, Melissa and David and of course Janet and George. Melissa also shared the incident of the flashing light and had heard nothing more, but she had a gut feeling there was more to the story and it would unfold one day. Melissa went with Andy again as they did a stock check and of course everybody was interested to hear Melissa's report on their general wellbeing. She watched all the animals carefully and made sure she had them in a single stance otherwise they could influence or even mislead the reading. Andy was totally blown away by her gift and kept checking as to the state of the stock. Happily, there was nothing to report and when they arrived back, she delivered her findings. Ken was over the moon. Andy, now began to have an insight into Melissa's gift and could recognize that each one of us had this field of energy, but sadly couldn't read as well as Melissa. He looked at her rather cheekily and said,

"Well 'cous' how healthy am I?" she smiled right back at him replying,

"You are as healthy as a Mallee bull but I'm not sure how dangerous you are." They laughed together, and Andy then quipped,

"We'll make an Aussie out of you yet!" Melissa was flattered by the compliment and just felt her self-confidence growing by the minute. This had been an amazing holiday and it was not over yet. Lunch was now being served and it was cold lamb and salad which had become a good stand by as well as a healthy lunch.

Ken had now finalized all the accommodation and packed the car ready for an early start tomorrow. As usual there was a big cooler yet to be filled and boxes of homemade biscuits and cakes. They were never going to be hungry. David was now a proficient milker and the strength in his wrist had developed incredibly, at first, they had ached but now he was able to milk and strip the cow like the best of them.

Since there was little work to do on the farm that afternoon a game of backyard cricket was on the agenda. There was lots of shouting and lots of umpiring and even more laughter. The adults sat in the shade and looked on with interest and admiration. George turned to them and said,

"You know our world is in safe hands if it is left to these young people," and that would turn out to be so prophetic, but George would never know. The afternoon continued to melt away and the family was able to enjoy each other's company. There was so much excitement and fun that afternoon tea wasn't even missed, and the enjoyment continued to until near on dark. Soon everyone was inside and washed for the evening meal. As usual Nancy and Janet had prepared another great feed and true to form David commented on just how good it was whilst not missing an opportunity to remind Mum about learning from her sister.

"I notice how thin and anemic you are young man I can see that your mother doesn't feed you enough!" chided Nancy.

Everybody laughed including David who now felt put in his place. Bed was early tonight, and everybody needed to be packed ready for an early start, so there was no sitting around. All the young people tidied away the dishes and were off to their rooms Little did they know that it was going to be an interrupted night's sleep.

The house was bathed in moonlight and just the slightest of gentle breezes caressed the house as its occupants slept peacefully. Everybody was sound asleep until the young people were roused by the now familiar sound and vibration of the alien craft which was becoming anything but alien. Emma and Melissa awoke instantly, and it wasn't long before the boys were stirring as well. They moved stealthily from the house and were at the usual rendezvous and there before them were their visitors.

"Yes, we know that you are away tomorrow and that is why we needed to speak with you, and it is important that you listen carefully. It is going to be a little strange for you from now on. You will be walking through some crowded places and you will notice a kind of kinship with some young people who you have never met before. They may look at you or you at them and you will sense a connection to them. Do not be either afraid or alarmed, because what you are sensing is some alien genetic origin. Put another way these people are not entirely human they have downloaded some alien DNA. We are sure you have already sensed this as part of your family here and it has only grown stronger as you have spent more time together. It is no accident that you all get on so well." "David, we have to say to you that you do not have any alien DNA but in time that will change. You will develop a skill set that will be very important for the health of the planet."

"We will not take you anywhere tonight as you need to get your rest." And their mind oration came to an abrupt conclusion. No words were spoken but everybody heard everything they needed to hear and that being done the craft was gone. Melissa was visibly disappointed as she had some questions arising from her visit to Halls Gap. They would have to wait. They all looked at each other and there was an overwhelming sense of humility growing in the family. Here they were in the back blocks of a small country town being groomed for a role that would help to reshape the course of history. Not a lot was said as they made their way back to the house. It was still bathed in the pale moonlight and the breeze was almost non-existent.

The morning came around all too soon and the family, or at least the younger members had scored little sleep given what had been shared with them. Andy appeared to be the most relaxed, but David looked anything but relaxed. The girls were able to take most things in their stride and Jordan was much his usual self but with just less sleep. It was already 8.am as they headed off the farm and Ken had a neighbour to keep an eye on the property, so he was well relaxed. Within no time they were in Stawell and in another twenty-five minutes they were in Ararat. However, from here on in the truck traffic became heavier and the road was still narrow in so many places. They would be in Ballarat by11.am which would give them a good start to their sightseeing.

The trip was largely uneventful, and they pulled in well before eleven as they had made very good time. It was decided that they would have a picnic lunch at the Botanical Gardens. Before they sat down for their lunch a walk was in order and they enjoyed seeing the blooms in the glass houses. The layout of all the busts of the past Australian Prime Ministers was quite interesting from an adult perspective, Ken referred to it affectionately as Rogues Gallery.

Lunch was amazing especially from David's perspective he enjoyed every mouthful and the cream cakes after the meal were awesome, Emma watched on with interest and commented,

"Gee we know how to please you," David nodded in agreement,

"What else is there in life? Not a lot if you're twenty and nearly twenty-one and still growing," he mused thoughtfully. Nancy always said that she liked cooking for anyone who enjoys their food so David would always be welcome. He reciprocated with a warm smile.

Lunch over and the next stop would be Kryal Castle out of Ballarat. It was a slice of old England and the hosts felt it would help their homesickness, not that this subject had ever come up. They spent all the afternoon visiting the variety of exhibits and watching the jousting. It was going to be a long night as they had booked in for the evening meal which was served in a traditional way and food to match. All the staff dressed in period costumes and the serving wenches were indeed very buxom. The entertainment continued and there was much merrymaking. It had been a long day, and everyone was ready for the motel. The boys shared a room as did the girls and the adults each had their own room. Upon entering David's first thought was to order breakfast but then he realized that there could well be a dining room and he wanted to check which was the best option. It was clear that he would prefer eating in the dining room as that was buffet style, so he was all geared up to attend in the morning,

Breakfast bar was opened early and David was the first in and the last to leave, the remaining family members came in like Brown's cows and the girls were the last to appear. They had spent some considerable time speaking about the night before and the visit from their friends. Nothing stood out for them whilst at Kryal Castle. Not one person seemed to attract their attention, maybe today would be different.

The day was planned and most of the day would be spent at Sovereign Hill depicting some of the early gold rush days. If time permitted, they would go and visit the Eureka Stockade. They filed through the turnstiles at Sovereign Hill and the ladies were attracted immediately to the old shopping mall. Everybody who was part of the staff was dressed in period costumes, it really was a walk into history. They moved from shop to shop and the girls were busy buying old style jewellery and even some articles of clothing. Suddenly without any warning Melissa and Emma looked around together and felt this huge sense of connection to this very young boy. He too looked up and smiled as if to acknowledge the connection. They sensed an alien presence, it took them both by surprise, but it was exactly as their friends had said two nights ago. It seemed uncanny, but on further reflection it made sense. Telepathic communication was certainly built into their DNA so why not this other connection. They couldn't wait to find the boys who by now had gone to try their luck at panning for gold.

Eventually they found them literally prancing about excitedly as though they had found the crown jewels. Of course, they hadn't, but they had been panning for gold and had some strong colours, which delighted them no end. They were intrigued as to why the girls had sought them out and thrilled to learn of their encounter. They admitted that nothing had happened so far, but they had really enjoyed their experience so far, especially panning for gold.

It was now nearing lunch time and the girls wanted to share their experience in more detail. They described the feelings they both experienced. It was like a tingling sensation and it was coming from another person. When we looked and located him, we saw it was emanating from this much younger boy. At that moment our eyes met, he acknowledged us with a smile as though somehow, we were related. It was truly uncanny because we both felt the same thing." Both Andy and Jordan acknowledged their feelings and then made another interesting comment. "We have always felt a strong connection to you guys in England and likewise Australia," and they both said it simultaneously. Jordan looked straight at Melissa and smiled, and then offered.

"We noticed we started to speak the same words so often and we could finish each other's sentences." David had been quiet throughout the whole discussion as he did not share any alien DNA.

Nevertheless, he was still very thoughtful. Suddenly everybody realized that David had said nothing. They became aware of his quietness and they all directed their attention towards him. Happily, David had become more comfortable in his own skin and just volunteered that he knew something of his role in their future together. What he wasn't clear about was just what his role would be in the scheme of things. In the meantime, they eagerly devoured all the sandwiches which proved to be a more than adequate fare. With lunch over the girls went off on their own and continued to explore the history section whilst the boys went to look at the assaying process and pouring gold. It was now becoming late and telepathic connectivity allowed them to meet at an agreed time. This time it was Andy and Jordan's turn to share their experience of becoming aware of another person with some alien DNA. However, the boys had taken their encounter one step further, they had spoken with their contact and exchanged names and addresses. The feeling of Andy and Jordan was quite indescribable. It took some time for them to realize that they were part of a much larger and welcoming family. This was so exciting and now they had internet connection they could really share so much more. Melissa was ever increasingly wide eyed as she began to realize more clearly how her role was unfolding. Her whole understanding of energy development and its force was becoming clearer by the week. She stood there musing to herself, her excitement couldn't be contained, and it was showing. Even David was aware that something momentous was happening before their eyes. Melissa could contain herself no longer.

You all know about the 'Maharishi Effect'. She was met with silent blank stares.

"Well," she began "It is when a group of people come together with a common purpose and focus energetically on a number of selected outcomes. This group is able to shape and significantly impact on the behaviour of large sections of the population, whole cities in fact," Melissa continued, "There have been studies completed which indicate this process really works."

They could begin to see how important this would be for the wellbeing and growth for the planet. It took some time for this to sink in, but their excitement was obvious and infectious. Melissa continued to speak about some of the references she had unearthed. Her intention was to grasp the importance of energetic vibration. The most powerful energies people need to access are, compassion, peace and joy and these lead to changing behavioural patterns. Once again Dr. David Hawkins name came up and his energetic scale. Melissa had found it so helpful to realise how energy either helps or hinders our level of vibration and consciousness. It was at this point their parents arrived and could see that all their young people were clearly excited about something, and immediately enquired what was so interesting. Jordan, Andy and David began to describe just how much fun it had been to find your own gold.

That being settled they made their way back to the motel, cleaned up and eventually went out for tea. It has been a long day and it was not long before they were all back at the motel and in bed.

Melissa was still excited about what had become so important and she continued to talk about it with Emma. Eventually the talk ceased, and the chatter gave way to sleep.

The next morning arrived and over breakfast they mapped out the day. The ladies definitely wanted to have a look in the shopping centre and so it was agreed that shopping would be done at some part of the day. A trip to the Eureka Stockade and a visit to the wildlife sanctuary was included in the day's activities. It was another full day and again one very special surprise. It came in the late afternoon when everybody was in the shopping complex at the mall. This time it involved the five younger members of the family. It happened as they were walking down the mall and they all turned as one person, looking at two girls. The look was reciprocated, and they began to walk towards each other, the boys of course had an added attraction as they were two girls both of a dating age. Introductions were eagerly exchanged and specifically where they may have experienced alien DNA. The girls who turned out to be twins, were holidaying from the Sunshine Coast. Melissa looked more closely at one of the twins and her concern became evident as she continued to focus her attention on her auric body. Amid all the chatter and exchanging of views Melissa had managed to take Lucy to one side and was checking what her gift was indicating. Lucy listened intently knowing that Melissa had identified there was something going on in her body. Melissa was able to be more specific this time telling her that there was a serious infection in her kidneys, and she needed to have it attended to straightaway. The next instant Lucy was slumping to the ground and Melissa was bending over her and just gently humming whilst at the same moment holding her hands over the kidney area. Melissa could feel this incredible energy pouring from her hands accompanied by a flux of heat and Lucy was experiencing a warm sensation around the kidney area. It all happened within a couple of minutes, Lucy was now much more relaxed, and more colour had returned to her face, and her auric body. It was at this point Lyn her twin had seen her slump and began to panic. Lyn immediately checked on Lucy's condition,

"Has this thing flared up again?" inquired Lyn. Lucy nodded, "We need to get you to hospital."

Before anyone could say anything, Lyn was ringing triple zero. Lucy then spoke out,

"No, I don't need them, I'm okay, Melissa has worked a miracle, I know I am healed." The phone call was aborted for a moment whilst everybody tried to process what had just happened including Melissa. Lyn now stepped in and ordered an ambulance; she knew only too well Lucy's condition and she wasn't taking any chances. Lucy was quite convinced she was completely healed.

The next ten minutes were chaotic, Lucy was now lying down and Lyn was holding her head and gently caressing her hand. The family were all gathered around them both and keeping others at bay. Several minutes had now elapsed and the sirens were getting closer. The crowd continued to assemble and made it difficult to get to the patient. The ambulance was able to pull up alongside Lucy and within seconds the paramedics had her comfortably inside. Lyn then began to explain Lucy's condition. She was waiting for a kidney transplant and that each seizure made her condition more perilous. It was not long before they reached the hospital and Lucy was taken straight to the ICU. Lyn had always feared this moment but was so prepared armed with her medical records and specialist reports from her Queensland Doctors. Lyn loved her sister and had become fiercely protective of her since she received her diagnosis. Lucy was now comfortable in the ICU sitting up and feeling very well indeed. She insisted to Lyn that she had never felt better. Lyn had to agree Lucy did look very well. Lyn had decided that she would stay with her all night and would wait for the results of the ultrasound and CAT scans.

The family had returned to the motel, it was going to be their last night in Ballarat and they had really had an amazing day. The girls talked a great deal more after the evening meal, Emma was still pondering just what she had witnessed that afternoon.

"How did you do it?" Emma mused thoughtfully, but Melissa had no answer. It was as though the power just flowed through her hands. It was a warm feeling and she didn't even need to touch Lucy. Eventually they drifted off to sleep.

Everybody was out of bed early and off to the restaurant ready for breakfast and it was as if by magic they all arrived at the same time. Emma was still talking about Lucy and what had happened the previous evening, Nancy couldn't help but pick up snippets of the conversation and had become quite intrigued with what she was hearing. Melissa was trying to play it down. The boys were somewhat baffled by it all but had now began to focus on the day at hand. It was decided that they would take a trip out to the animal park and then head for home. Melissa and Emma had made a case for visiting Lucy in hospital and that was agreed to by both families, especially as the two girls been so involved.

They quickly packed their bags and made their way to the hospital. Emma and Melissa then met Lyn at the front desk who had been contacted on her mobile. Lyn was still amazed by her sister's recovery and just how well she looked. Lyn was now waiting for the results of the Cat and ultrasound scans.

When they arrived at Lucy's room, they were met by an entourage of medical staff who were busy speaking in tones of bewilderment and incredulity. Lucy was looking extremely pleased with herself and sensing that she had made a miraculous recovery. Lyn was first to ask just what the new findings had uncovered. The Consulting Physician began,

"Well we can find no trace at all of your sister's condition, there is not even scar tissue to say that the kidneys were breaking down. We don't understand because the scans you supplied indicate that another major incident would mean immediate dialysis, then hopefully a transplant sooner rather than later. We have rung her doctor in Queensland, and he confirmed that these were indeed Lucy's scans," he continued. "We just need to do another set of tests to make doubly sure that there have been no glitches in our equipment. In all our collective experience we have never seen such a dramatic change in such a short space of time." The doctor continued to look puzzled and continued shaking her head. Eventually they left the room and Lyn gave her such a big hug that she felt all the air leave her and was gasping for breath. Lucy then turned her attention to Melissa and tears welled up in her eyes,

"I don't know what you did but the moment your hands stretched over my body I felt this warmth and tingling sensation throughout my whole body and an overwhelming sense of peace. This feeling is still with me, almost like I am walking in divine light." Melissa beamed with excitement and thought to herself, of course this was divine light, and she too began to experience a deep sense of peace. They had now exchanged Facebook details and promised faithfully to stay friends forever. Laughter filled the room, there were hugs all round and with that Melissa and Emma made their way back to the main entrance where the family was waiting for them in the car park. The boys quickly asked about Lucy and Emma and Melissa spoke simultaneously.

"She is doing fine and will make a complete recovery." It almost felt they had rehearsed their answer but that was obviously not the case as the moment they finished speaking they looked at each other in amazement. Everything was quiet for some time until they reached the animal sanctuary. The place was bursting at the seams which wasn't entirely surprising since it was school holidays anyway. They all piled out and were soon inside enjoying the many different enclosures. The animals and birds were housed in their natural habitat as much as was humanly possible. David, Jordan and Melissa for the first time were close enough to reach out and touch koalas, although they were not encouraged to do so. Melissa was fascinated by the snakes and spent more time there learning about the intensity of their poisons and their habitats. She was totally surprised just how many there were in Australia in the top twenty most deadly snakes in the world. As she looked at each, she realized just how dangerous the snake was she had encountered on the farm. Momentarily she shuddered as she thought how much worse the it could have turned out. Then she began to recognize how she was being taken care of. It was something she would carry for the rest of her life, especially when she or her family was threatened in some way. This reinforced her sense of trust that continued to develop with their alien friends. Melissa chose to share this with Jordan and even with him it took some time for him to recognise that trust was still being built.

It was now well past lunch time and they had agreed to meet at the Barbeque area for their lunch before heading home. There was still no real talk about Lucy and Melissa was very happy that this had transpired this way. It had exercised her thinking for most of the morning and she was still trying to process what had happened and to make sense of it. Both families were now happy to be heading home and it was now quite late in the afternoon. There was continual chatter in the people mover now and both families had enjoyed renewing the strong bond that had been there for many years. It was soon going to come to an end as they needed to return to the UK. It was very clear to the young people that they had a great deal in common and that there would be increased communication between them. David was quite excited about this as he and Emma had already swapped Facebook details. Both sets of parents were so pleased that the young people had gotten on so well and noticed there had not been any tension between them at all. It had made for a remarkable holiday and Janet was so impressed with David and his response to Melissa, it seemed as though he had really come to appreciate his younger sister, though Janet wasn't sure why.

It was now just after five thirty as they turned into the farm gate, and everything seemed to be fine. David was the first to hop out and quickly made his way to the laundry where the milking bucket was kept. He was on his way before everyone was out of the vehicle and happy to continue practising his skills. Emma and Andy were more than happy as it gave them a break.

Everybody turned out to help with the evening meal, the men had volunteered to cook on the barbeque, and they were busily preparing all the meat and sausages and of course lots of onions. The smell was wafting everywhere with each wind change and it all felt very welcoming. Soon all the salads arrived, and the women folk had a spread fit for royalty. Soon everyone had assembled, and the meal began in earnest. There were some questions about Lucy and her progress from all the adults. No one had shared much detail of the event, but the parents were still both interested and concerned. Emma was able to speak now and described the outcomes quite excitedly. She was able to disclose that the initial tests conducted by the various medical interventions had given Lucy a clean bill of health. Surprise was written all over their faces and they looked at each other quizzically. It seemed that Emma's disclosure had raised more questions than it answered, however, Janet had thought quietly all along that Melissa was gifted in a very unusual manner. Janet had not been taken completely by surprise as much as the others. It was becoming clearer to Janet that her daughter did have a special mission in life. She was continuing to notice a level of maturity well beyond her years which both excited her and frightened her. Her greatest fear was that she would be used by others for their own ends. Indeed, would Melissa have the wisdom or insight to be able to discern what was in her best interest? There was a danger she would burn out long before her years. Janet had already made a note that it was important for her to support her daughter with some self-care strategies. Furthermore she would look for times to share those. Janet was so aware that her beautiful daughter also needed to be a teenager and not be robbed of that part of her life. There was still much to ponder, Janet could visualise the days ahead as being full of challenge and requiring all the wisdom she could muster. Little did she know how many times there would be challenges and what shape they would take.

The days slipped imperceptibly into each other and normal day to day farm tasks continued to occupy their time. Melissa had enjoyed each day with Andy checking on the stock. David continued to work at his milking skills and usually under the watchful eye of Emma, a time which they both enjoyed immensely. Jordan and Melissa had now taken over the task of feeding the lambs who were not far away from being weaned. This could not have been a better holiday in every possible way, a thought they both embraced and acknowledged simultaneously.

It was now approaching the time when they had to be planning to return to England and there was already a sense of sadness about their impending departure. The solemn mood was evident after the evening meal was over. Things had changed, and everyone recognized that the holiday was coming to an end, and what an amazing time it had been for both families. There had been a deepening of bonds, but it went deeper. There was an unconscious connection that went beyond families. There had developed this sharing of thoughts and feelings without there being any formal speech. It was evident this had grown amongst the young people and it was becoming more evident to their parents. There was much to ponder.

Melissa woke next morning with only one thought on her mind, she so wanted to see Sally again before they flew home to England. Melissa had already rung before breakfast. They had made their plans now they just needed their parents to support the plan.

Melissa literally bounded into the kitchen asking her mum if it was okay for Sally to come for an overnight stay. Janet was all for it reminding herself how important it would be for Melissa to experience normal things which most teenagers manage in their everyday life. Jake had agreed to bring Sally to Stawell, but someone needed to go into Stawell to pick her up and that would probably be Uncle Ken or even Andy. Some discussion took place and it was decided that Andy and Melissa would go, and even Jordan might like to come.

It was only twenty minutes into town and there was Sally literally beaming all over her face, as she recognized the family car. Melissa was out in a second and her arms firmly around Sally. It was obvious that they had built a strong bond in just a few encounters. Jake looked on, happiness reflected on his face. He was delighted that his daughter had found a very good friend and that distance would not prevent it from maturing. He knew that they had already exchanged Skype and Face Time details. Sally wanted a good, reliable friend and an interest outside of their small community at the Gap. Jake had taken to Melissa almost immediately as he spoke with her as fire control officer. He sensed that there was something special about her but wasn't sure he could put his finger on it, but he sensed it was good.

Introductions were made and then Sally's eyes met Jordan. For a moment she was quite transfixed, as Jordan seemed better than Melissa's description. Jordan acknowledged her gaze and stretched forth his hand with a warm "Hi." Sally could hardly contain her enthusiasm and reciprocated the handshake.

After a quick visit to the supermarket for some cooked chooks and salads, they were heading home. On the way home the two girls hardly drew breath. Melissa was busy telling Sally about the encounter with Lucy and her twin at the shopping mall. Sally's eyes grew wider by the moment, she was speechless and was thinking to herself that Melissa was her special friend. Sally was overcome by a myriad of different emotions, confusion and bewilderment about what transpired at the hospital. How could it be that she had such a clever friend who was taking such an interest in her? Her vacant look stopped Melissa for a moment, she paused for a second and then checked with Sally as to what was going on? Sally had gathered her thoughts by now and was ready to share her feelings. When Sally disclosed all her feelings, Melissa was gob smacked momentarily, and then reached out to her friend, taking her hands in her own and squeezing them fondly and firmly. In the midst of all of this chatter, Sally continued to throw a glance at Jordan and smiled warmly. Melissa smiled and continued their animated discussion. Jordan had hardly managed a word in edgeways, and Sally had not even said a word to him, but the furtive and warm glances said enough. They arrived at the farm and it was well after morning tea-time, so they made their way to the kitchen taking with them the purchase from the supermarket. Nancy was impressed as they had got everything, she had put on the list including the red onions and cos lettuce. She smiled at Melissa and Jordan and said kindly,

"I will send you shopping any day of the week," they both nodded and Sally noticed Jordan again and realized she felt an instant attraction. She gazed at him for a full minute, feeling this incredible energy, like a magnetic pull towards him. Jordan threw a very quick glance in Sally's direction which took her totally by surprise and suddenly she felt her face flush. She quickly looked away attempting to hide her blush. Jordan didn't bat an eyelid nor was he aware of what was going on. Melissa had a little chuckle to herself and thought of her previous conversations with Sally out at the Gap. Melissa was aware that all this had gone over Jordan's head and was happy to keep it that way. This was going to be his journey and he needed to make his own mistakes and learn about girls in his own way. Melissa would always help him of course.

Despite Sally's feelings of compulsion nothing, happened for the remainder of her stay and Sally went home unable to make any headway with Jordan. There was a highpoint as she was able to set up a Facebook contact with Jordan. He was a little surprised by the request as he felt sure she was Melissa's friend, but being the gentleman he was, he was more than happy to oblige. He was also quite chuffed. Sally and Melissa spent much of the day talking and looking around the farm, it was apparent that this was going to be an important friendship for many years.

The next morning arrived all too quickly and it was time to say goodbye and both girls hugged for a long time and tears flowed freely, Jordan looked and realized just how important Melissa friendship was to Sally. They stopped and Sally moved towards the car and then suddenly turned to Jordan put her arms around him and gave him a big kiss on the cheek, for a moment Jordan was caught off guard and momentarily stood motionless and then responded and hugged her back. He couldn't believe how good it felt. Sally then ran to the car and was away in an instant. As she disappeared out of the farm gate Melissa and Jordan stood waving, uncertain when they may see her again.

Heaviness was everywhere around the farm now, not just about Sally, but their impending departure and the thought of leaving their cousins created this deep sadness for them all. Jordan looked deeply into the eyes of Melissa and could already feel her pain. Nothing was said but Jordan instinctively reached out and just held his sister, she relaxed in his arms and her breathing gradually slowed and subsided. Words were unnecessary.

Tea was subdued and everybody was sensing the departure which would begin early tomorrow morning. Packing needed to be completed before bed, so the Thomas family were quite preoccupied with everything that needed to be done. All bags were duly placed at the front door ready to be loaded into the vehicle. Bed was a welcome sight for everyone, and the house slipped into a level of unconsciousness associated with deep and restful sleep.

The morning arrived all too soon, but the mood had lifted, and breakfast was a cheery experience as lots of happy moments were shared, laughter filled the air and stories abounded and more laughter.

Breakfast over, the Thomas's were soon into the people mover and their bags. This time Ken was driving them down and the rest of the family would stay on the farm. Emma was chatting quietly to David and saying a very personal goodbye, she was whispering.

"What a pity we are cousins I could fancy you." David nodded affirming the truth of what he was hearing.

"I have really enjoyed your company all through this holiday and I know we will keep in touch, I am sad because I don't know when I will see you again," he ventured but Emma knew it would be soon. She knew that their alien friends would be in contact soon and the mission would begin in earnest. David still hadn't been for a ride and had no concept of the speed of the travel or its dexterity.

Goodbyes were all said, and the vehicle began its journey to Melbourne and more especially, Tullamarine Airport. Ken was more than happy with the outcome of the crop and gratefully expressed to George just how much he had appreciated the fantastic role the whole family had played in getting the work done and the crop in.

"We should get a rise then". joked David. Everybody laughed except Ken.

"Well I do have a little gift for you all and I hope you will enjoy it." Both Janet and George protested immediately, and David made it clear he was only joking. Ken acknowledged all their viewpoints and casually said, "Nancy and I spoke about this and we have had such a very good year so we are happy to make this gift possible, but you won't know what it is until you board the plane, and that is my final word." Ken said quite firmly. The family sat quietly for a moment and then Jordan began to say,

"I know you put something in our bags whilst they were waiting to be loaded in the car." Ken simply smiled and Jordan felt sure he was right.

The trip was uneventful, and the family enjoyed some more of Nancy's home-made cakes. It was well after lunch time when they arrived at the airport. Ken parked the vehicle and luggage was loaded on three trolleys and they were soon waiting in line. Ken bade them goodbye and promised that it was their turn to come to England for a visit, but there was not much conviction in his voice as he hated big cities and especially cold weather.

When it came their turn at the check point, then came the surprise. They presented their tickets only to be told they were in the wrong queue and they had been upgraded to business class. Janet protested that there had been a mistake and they only had economy tickets. The desk clerk made it very clear that no mistake had been made and showed her the new tickets on his screen. George whispered in her ear.

"I think this is Ken's surprise." Janet squealed in delight,

"Oh, aren't they just something else what a lovely surprise." They both agreed the thought of travelling all the way in economy was never appealing at any time now it would be delightful in business class.

Their seats were amazing, and they could stretch out fully and sleep would be so much better to say nothing of the food. Take off was very smooth and they were all relaxing enjoying the comfort of their surroundings. Melissa and Jordan sat together, and it was then that Melissa began to sow the seed of Sally's affection for her brother. He said nothing for some time and then realized Melissa was right. How could he be so blind? He lay back smiling all over his face, he recognized how much he liked her long dark hair and her olive skin. "Yes," he said to himself, "She is quite a stunner. How come he didn't notice her before?" Just as he was basking in all these lovely thoughts, Melissa chipped in,

"Of course, I have told her all your faults and shortcomings." Jordan came down to earth with a thud,

"You can't be serious. How could you? He questioned sharply."

"Well I figure that we are like sisters now and we must stick together," she responded solemnly. Melissa could see Jordan was now becoming increasingly upset and beginning to raise his voice in protest. Then she looked at him with a huge smile and said nonchalantly,

"Gee I really got you going." Jordan paused for a moment and took a deep breath, "You sure know how to wind me up."

Melissa just nodded and said how funny it was. Finally, Jordan could see the funny side of it.

She took his hand and gave it a big squeeze and said,

"Anyway, you don't really have too many bad habits, you're quite a catch." Jordan smiled and no more words were exchanged.

The trip home was largely uneventful and so much more pleasant in business class. At one- point Jordan was sure that he was listening to a communication from their alien friends. It was as though they were just outside. He called over the stewardess and asked if he could possibly go to the cockpit and speak with the Captain. She was about to say that it is not usually done when Melissa spoke up.

"I sense your right shoulder is quite sore," Melissa offered. Amy the stewardess was momentarily taken aback by this comment and said,

"Well yes it has been strained now for some days, but how did you know?" Melissa continued, "I thought I saw you favouring it as you were serving."

"My you are a really observant young lady." At that point Jordan chipped in,

"Not only that but she can offer you some relief." Now Amy was taken aback for a moment and was caught completely off guard.

"I don't think that will be necessary," Amy responded having caught her breath now. Melissa smiled and simply raised her hand as if to acknowledge that she had heard Amy's request. Amy stopped for a split second as though suspended in thought, a wave of warm tingling emotion passed through her shoulder and she felt instant relief.

"What just happened?" she asked. Melissa was a little nonplussed as she had sought to respect Amy's request. Melissa apologized profusely.

"I just don't know what happened I hadn't meant for anything to happen." Amy stood there completely stunned for the moment and then a look of total relief enveloped her face,

"No don't apologize, I feel wonderful, I can't believe what just happened," she exclaimed. Amy kept rotating her shoulder without flinching it felt so wonderful she couldn't stop smiling. Jordan was still wanting to press his request and began to ask the favour, when Amy promptly said,

"Leave it with me and I will see what I can do." Just a few minutes had elapsed, and Amy was back with a smile. "The Captain will see you now." Jordan needed no second invitation; he was out of seat in a flash. The cockpit was opened for him on arrival and he was welcomed in.

"Now where would you like to start?" Jordan needed no further encouragement.

"Captain have you seen any alien craft on this trip." That was the last thing on the Captain's mind and caught him by surprise. Jordan went on to describe what their craft looked like in explicit detail. The Captain shot a sideways glance at his first officer. Well young man what I am going to say is absolutely off the record and I will deny it all if you ever breath a word to anyone else. Jordan's eyes grew wider by the second. The Captain continued "Yes we have seen this craft and it journeyed with us for the first fifteen minutes of our flight and then it was off, and we never saw it again."

"How did you come to see it?" Jordan paused for a long moment to consider his words carefully.

"Well it was just there as I looked out of my window, it stayed for what seemed ages, but it was only seconds because I had just looked at my watch and then again when it flew off." It sounded authentic but in fact none of it was true and Jordan felt nervous should they pursue the matter any further.

"Your description and attention to detail was quite amazing," commented the Captain. Jordan nodded nervously. "Well, captain you have answered my question and I am very grateful for your honesty and yes your secret is safe with me." Jordan offered and with that he was ready to leave, the Captain followed him out and just gently caught his arm.

"Young man I have the feeling that there is something you are not telling me?" Jordan looked at him thoughtfully and began,

"You are right but if I told you what I know I doubt you would believe me anyway, so maybe its best kept to myself at this time." The Captain felt relieved with the outcome and knew that nothing more would be said.

Jordan made his way back to his seat deep in thought. The question still unresolved, how could they communicate with him when they were so far away. Scarcely had he raised the question when he heard them speaking in his mind. He was startled for a moment and then reassured by what he was hearing.

"Of course, distance is not a problem for this kind of communication, and you will know that we are never far away. However not everyone is as receptive as you and Melissa, and we have noticed that you are developing well in this area." Jordan was so reassured by all of this and felt that there was nothing that he couldn't achieve in the future. By now he was back in his seat and brimming with confidence. Melissa couldn't help noticing his smile, "What are you feeling so pleased about?" her voice was very cheery. "I have just made a brilliant discovery," his excitement was obvious,

"They have been contacting me throughout this journey and I couldn't see how they could be doing that." He then related the conversation he'd had with the Captain and what had transpired in his walk back to his seat. Melissa's eyes widened considerably, and she could feel herself filling with excitement as she too had been privy to all the telepathic conversation. It really did feel like a Star Wars experience and yes, the Force was with them. Just at that moment Amy came back and crouched down by Melissa's seat,

"Young lady you are a very special human being with an incredible gift and thank you so much for sharing it with me." Melissa graciously accepted the compliment and said she was pleased that it had worked out to everyone's benefit.

Melissa and Jordan had always known that there was contact and conversation but had never realized that it could span such distance. Their alien friends were seemingly light years away, but it was as though they were right next to them with their telepathic conversation. Once again, they heard more communication from them.

"At last you're getting it; we have known all along but we needed you to learn this and it just had to be this way. We are really pleased with your growth and you have begun to accept your mission with such wisdom. We always knew that it would be so."

They looked at each other with joy and a peace flooded throughout their bodies allowing them to rest in a way they had never quite experienced before.

The next thing they knew they were being awakened to the sound of plates and trays and yes it was breakfast already and natural light was flooding into the plane. Jordan was soon sitting up and preparing for his food, it looked so much better than economy class, but not nearly up to their Aunt Nancy's standard.

They spent the day chatting and watching movies and playing games and time slipped by very easily. It was hard to believe that their holiday was coming to an end it was now a matter of hours before they would be landing to change planes. However this time it was at Dubai and not Singapore.

The plane touched down and the family was ready to brave more hot weather, after so much sun in Australia they were getting used to this. They were well prepared, but it was air- conditioned, so they didn't experience the extreme heat and were soon disembarking. Amy was there as was the Captain, and Melissa got another warm hug from her as she left. The captain shook Jordan's hand firmly and wished him well and said he would be welcome to fly any time in the future and he would always see what he could do for business class. Jordan was quite overcome with his warmth but didn't dare say that the next time they flew it wouldn't take hours but minutes to reach their destination.

As they arrived into the airport, they could see the heat dancing in waves off the sand in the distance. It seemed quite incongruous to feel so cool whilst witnessing the heat outside. Now they had a considerable wait for the next part of the journey and some discussion took place as to how they might spend the time. However, shopping was not on the agenda and it would be more about walking and exploring although that didn't seem that appealing anyway. For the very first time on their journey they could see themselves just filling in time. Jordan decided that he would find a quiet spot and play on his iPad whereas David and Melissa wondered off together. At David's suggestion they found a quiet corner where they could sit and chat it became an opportunity for Melissa to check in with David. "How much did you enjoy the holiday?" David paused for a considerable time and chose his words with great care.

"I felt very close to Emma and I tell this, if she wasn't my cousin, I would be seriously considering dating her." He continued, "As far as the farm experience, I couldn't have dreamed it would be such a blast. I can't remember when I had such a fabulous time and well the encounter with your alien friends has given me a whole different direction in life. I am still trying to take it all in. But you know probably the most important thing that I have come away with is the fact I am part of an absolutely amazing family and I feel so grateful to be a part of it." He then looked at Melissa quite directly, pausing for a moment and then began to say, "I can't begin to understand the gifts that lie within you. Your ability to read people's energy is quite amazing, and then I watched you with Lucy and I was completely blown away and you did it with such humility." He went on quietly, "This is why I consider it such an honour to be part of this family and the support that we received from each other, and I guess I saw that quality so readily in Emma." At that moment Melissa stood up quite deliberately, walked around to where David was sitting and invited him to stand and just held him ever so gently. David admitted to himself that this felt really good and almost on cue Melissa said, "You realize that when we hug each other without any agenda we are effectively healing the body and our emotions," she continued, "You may not be aware that there is a science around hugging and that we humans need at least four hugs to keep us healthy." David responded,

"You never cease to amaze me and there is so much for me to learn, but do tell me about the colours that you see around Emma?" A smile danced across Melissa's face,

"I wondered how long it would be before you would ask that question?" David then blushed slightly, recognizing the wisdom inherent in his younger sister. Melissa finally responded,

"I watched her every time you came into the room or were in her view and there was always an immediate intensifying and lightning of the colours, so yes there is absolutely no doubt that there is a very strong attraction between the two of you."

David and Melissa continued to chat further and much of the conversation centred on the connection with their alien friends.

"How long now as it been since your first contact?" David asked. Melissa paused and thought for a moment trying to remember the very first night when it landed in their garden,

She mused to herself and then out loud. "It would over twelve months. So much had happened in that short time."

"Little wonder you have built up such a bond of trust, but I don't get that somewhere in your genetic makeup there is some alien DNA?" David queried. "I'm not sure that I do either, but I am confident that in the future it will become clear and I am more than content to sit with that," Melissa replied.

It was now time for some liquid refreshment and David had bought each of them an orange juice. They continued to sit recognizing that they had been chatting for well over two hours and in a moment they would need to make their way to the lounge where they would board their next flight. Jordan was already there waiting and still quite focused on his iPad. He continued his research on global warming and was wondering just how these oil-rich Arab countries would respond to reduction in oil production. And of course, it was only one of the many questions raised by the issue of global warming.

The next five minutes saw all the family assembled at the lounge and within minutes the boarding call was made for the flight from Dubai to Gatwick. It was now early afternoon and the take-off was smooth and without incident. Melissa leaned over to David and smiled.

"If we were travelling with our alien friends, we'd be there by now." David responded, "Well if the night you all went back to the woods when we were at the farm, I can believe what you say. I guess that it's going to be a new experience for me when we get back home."

The trip from Dubai to Gatwick was quite uneventful and they arrived in the wee small hours.

David had already contacted his friend in the taxi business, and he was already on his way to the airport. They had spoken briefly, and he couldn't wait to hear all the news of Australia. David was just as eager to tell him of the awesome time they had and just how good the holiday was. The thirty-minute drive passed without a hitch and it was not long before they were opening the front door to their home, unpacking cases, and putting stuff away. Janet was putting the kettle on, but they only had long-life milk which was never a favourite among the family. They had brought some Australian biscuits back and David was first to open a packet of double chock Tim-Tams. Two days later life would return to normal; George would go back to work. David to university and Jordan and Melissa back to school and Janet would resume her part time job and the holiday would be a distant memory.

Melissa had checked the time and it was lunch time in Australia and definitely okay to ring, so she lost no time in calling Emma.

"We are already missing you guys," they both said it at the same time, reminding them of their very strong connection. David looked at Melissa making gestures that he would like a word and he spoke to Emma for some time admitting something he'd never done before. "Gee I miss you and I wish you were here," Emma replied "I miss you too, but I would prefer it if you were here. It's too cold where you are," they laughed together and eventually the conversation came to an end.

Janet needed to do some shopping and to think about breakfast. Next there would be the midday and an evening meal. Meanwhile everybody else packed away clothes, organized washing and checked that everything was as they left it. They had been away nearly five weeks.

CHAPTER 7

LEOPARDS DO CHANGE THEIR SPOTS

THE NEW WEEK came around all too soon and the family was soon back into routine. George had already left for work and David had almost completed his breakfast when Melissa and Jordan came down. Melissa was excited about returning to school and catching up with all her friends. She had so much to share about their stay on the farm, and all the other activities. Breakfast over, they were off to school and in no time were making their way to the school gates. Just then Jordan took her arm and cautioned her. He was immediately arrested by what he witnessed. There was Alistair standing talking to Terry Cross just inside the entrance. Melissa had also seen the two of them and they both stood motionless. Just at that moment Alistair looked up and espied them and was then quickly walking towards them with this huge smile. He held out his hand in friendship to Jordan and then Melissa, they both reciprocated and were obviously curious about his conversation with Terry. Alistair began,

"Well, have I got news for you. Terry has given up the gang and they seemed glad to get rid of him though they are no longer a force to be reckoned with." Alistair continued, "I went to visit him in hospital, and he thought I was still a gang member. Then I told him that I had quit the gang and I was just checking to see how he was. During our conversation I shared how you were instrumental in getting me to hospital. You were able to recognize I was in danger of losing my life and that the doctors had confirmed just that." Alistair continued, "Terry lay there for a full minute without saying a word. Then, he related what you had said to him before he left the café. "I then told him what a really good friendship had developed between our families and he went very quiet indeed." Terry didn't say anything more and he just asked me to leave. Then he asked if I would come back to see him the next day? I nodded and agreed that would be okay. The very next day as I was making my way to his room, I met this nurse and she said, 'Well, young man I don't know what you said to Terry, but he is in a much better mood than he's been all the time he has been in hospital.'

"I was curious to see Terry this time and he greeted me with a warm smile, something he hadn't done all the time I had been a member of his gang."

He looked at me and then began to speak,

"Not one of my gang members has been anywhere near the place and when I saw you, I felt relieved that you were the first and the others would soon come up, but no one came. Then you tell me that you are no longer a member, but you still took the time to come and see me. Then you shared what Melissa had done for you. I have to admit she more than likely saved my life as well and came to see me.

I don't mind admitting I gave her a hard time. No one has ever taken any real interest in me since my mother walked out of our family. Dad has always got to work, and I have to look after my little brother and sister," he paused for a moment, "This Nurse Scott has been on my case ever since I was brought in, what would she know? She is just another woman I thought, but I know she does care about me because I heard her speaking to the doctor."

"I always thought the gang was my family.

They have let me down and they don't really care, and they don't look up to me as a leader. When you left yesterday, I thought a lot about my life and my friends and realized that I don't really have any." At that point I interrupted him and said,

"I was happy to be his friend, but I didn't want any part of the gang." Terry looked at me straight in the eye and said,

"I have decided that I no longer wished to be involved in the gang, so could we be good friends?" Alistair now paused,

"I couldn't believe what I was hearing. You really mean you would give up your gang to be my friend?" Terry then responded,

"Yes," emphatically. "You see after you left Nurse Scott came in and she picked up that something we had talked about yesterday had somehow changed me. Nurse Scott sat with me for more than half an hour sharing how Melissa had come to the hospital and just how much she had cared that I was okay. I tell you it really made me think about who my friends were and here you are back again." Next moment Terry thrust out his hand and shook mine. We shook hands. "Now he wants to know if he can be friends with you guys?" Alistair stopped momentarily anticipating a response from Jordan and Melissa, but they were too gob smacked to respond! Alistair continued,

"Nurse Scott shared with me that Terry had been in a lot of pain since coming to the hospital. It was so bad that he just lay in bed moaning. It was just after midnight she went into his room and said to him. 'Terry how about I get you some painkillers?' He nodded quietly and then volunteered, 'My dad always said, men should be tough enough to manage their own pain.' The nurse then enquired, 'Has that worked for you?' Terry looked at her shaking his head in the negative,

"Ever since my mum left, I felt this ache in the pit of my stomach and it was much worse in the early days," he said. Nurse Scott continued,

"And I'll bet your Dad has been really grumpy since," Terry just looked at her in amazement and she was absolutely right. She then spoke in very hushed tones,

"You know I have watched many people come into this hospital full of fear because they know they are dying and they describe a similar feeling to the way you have just done, I will sit with them and just ask them to talk about their fear and by the time we have finished they invariably say, "I am feeling better and more peace within myself. This gives them an important opportunity to come to terms with their feelings." Terry just lay there taking it all in and saying nothing. Nurse Scott now had his painkillers and said that he would need to take it with a drink and something to eat.

He then asked, "Could he have a cup of hot chocolate and a piece of toast with peanut butter, please?" Nurse Scott responded with just what he had asked for and he thanked her warmly. She checked on him early in the morning before finishing her shift and he reported that he had had the best sleep in a long, long time."

Jordan and Melissa stood speechless for ages, hardly able to take this all in. Then they realized that Alistair was waiting for an answer about befriending Terry. Melissa then blurted out "Yes of course that would be great."

With that settled, the three of them walked over to where Terry was waiting. He had watched the conversation but lacked clarity about its outcome until they moved in his direction without any obvious animosity.

Jordan was the first to extend the hand of friendship, followed by Melissa. Terry felt quite awkward about it all but then the chat was more than amicable. Just at that moment Terry shot a glance at Alistair and under his breath agreed 'that Melissa was quite a looker.' What he didn't realize was that Melissa heard every word and suddenly Alistair felt very embarrassed. Melissa smiled to herself but offered no comment. Melissa had noticed the colours around Terry were now very different and she could now trust her newly acquired skills. She was quietly smiling to herself and had begun to understand just how powerful the impact of her gift was. Now she was noticing some of the changes that were starting to happen, this felt so good and she couldn't help the excitement welling up inside her.

The bell then sounded, and they were immediately off to their various classes.

The day seemed to fly for Jordan and Melissa and at lunch time they sat in the sheltered part of the school with Alistair and Terry. By now Terry was feeling more comfortable around them and couldn't help himself and had to ask how Melissa knew about his brush with death some months ago. Melissa couldn't explain it or perhaps wasn't ready to let Terry in just yet. It would have to wait for another time. It was obvious that Alistair and Terry had compared notes on the matter but neither of them was any the wiser and in the end, Alistair simply said, speaking for them both, that they were so lucky to have her as a friend.

School was over and Jordan and Melissa made their way home, Jordan couldn't wait to tease Melissa about Alistair. He opened the conversation once they were out of earshot of everybody.

"What do you really think of Alistair, do you fancy him as your boyfriend?" he inquired. Melissa was taken by surprise by his direct question and didn't respond straightaway. There was a long pause and then Melissa began with,

"What makes you so sure he's interested in me?" Jordan stopped dead,

"Well you may not have heard him that night in the woods when some of Terry's gang was giving him a set to." but Jordan knew she had heard the comment because at the mention she blushed ever so slightly. "He had made a similar comment this morning and just look at the way he looked at you when he came over the first thing when we arrived at school. He could hardly take his eyes off you," offered Jordan. Now Melissa was quite stunned by Jordan's observation and she knew she wasn't imaging it if her brother had noticed it so readily.

"Well," she began, "He has said nothing to me at this stage and I'm not sure how I feel, so let's drop the subject." Jordan couldn't help himself.

"Well I like who he is becoming, and I was talking to our teacher and mentioned Alistair. She volunteered that he was coming along in leaps and bounds in her classes and she couldn't quite work out what had changed. She noticed a change after his time in hospital." Melissa was now careful to smile on the inside without betraying her feelings, but clearly, she was impressed.

Melissa now deliberately changed the subject and wondered when they might have a visit from their space friends? Jordan quipped "You have taken the words out of mouth," before either of them could say another word, they both knew it would be tonight. They could hardly contain themselves and their joy was evident as they made their way to the front door. Mum was already looking out for them and was totally surprised by their upbeat mood.

"I can't believe that school could be so energising," she said noticing how they came in. They both spoke at once. "Mum you will never guess who has become our friend." For a split second they looked at each other amazed at the unison in which they spoke. Mum interrupted their stare and retorted,

"No, I wouldn't guess so you better tell me!"

"Terry Cross," they chimed together. Janet's jaw dropped visibly, and she repeated his name, "Do you mean that dreadful boy you spoke to at the café and he tried so hard to beat you and Jordan or at least his gang did."

"Yep that's the one but Mum he has really changed, and we spoke to him when we first arrived at school and he and Alistair had lunch with us. We did a lot of talking," offered Melissa. "Well don't think you can bring him round here; Alistair is more than welcome, and we know his mum and she has been through a very tough time but not Terry."

Then Melissa completely disarmed Janet and said, "Well you won't have to worry about meeting Terry's mum because she walked out on their family when Terry was only seven years old, and he spends a lot of his time looking after his little brother and sister. His dad is often late home from work. I guess I would be angry if that had happened to me." Janet looked at her beautiful daughter and smiled,

"Yes, everybody deserves a second chance and I guess Terry more than most." She felt suitably chastised by Melissa's compassion and said it would be fine for him to come at some stage.

Melissa put her hand in her mum's and gave it a big squeeze and smiled. No more words were needed.

The evening meal was now on the table and the family gathered round to enjoy another sumptuous meal cooked by their mum. There was general conversation about the events of the day and Jordan and Melissa were quite keen to share what a taken place at school in regarding Terry. David expressed his surprise as he had already had a few run-ins with Terry. However, he was more than happy to accept his younger brother and sister's reckoning of the situation. Melissa made it very clear that she felt entirely comfortable with their encounter with Terry and said that she had noticed there was a new warmth in the way he had spoken to them both. There was no mention of the gang except to say Terry was very clear that he was no longer a part of that gang and to all intents and purposes the gang had virtually disbanded. Alistair had become a regular visitor at their home and made it extremely clear that he felt very comfortable with Terry.

They had developed a strong friendship in the absence of Jordan and Melissa whilst they were in Australia.

The animated conversation had abated as the task of washing the dishes lay before the family and each member moved to their assigned jobs. Janet and George had retired to the living room and they were happily resting with their feet up and sharing the day's news. George made mention of the fact that those men who he believed had come from the Ministry had visited them again checking their work. There were more curious questions about the progress they were making. He turned to Janet and said in quite hushed tones,

"I don't really trust any of them and I feel as though they're like Big Brother watching us." Janet looked at him quizzically,

"Do you really think that someone from the Ministry could really be interested in your work?" George nodded gently,

"I am sure that something is going on and I feel it in my gut." That was quite the first time George had ever appealed to his intuition and Janet was taken by surprise, she looked at his face and sensed an unrest in his spirit that she had not experienced before. Suddenly there was a little shiver that went down her spine. In the future she would ponder this conversation again and again.

CHAPTER 8

THE MISSION INTENSIFIES

THE DISHES WERE all done now, and David, Jordan and Melissa were heading up to their rooms. Jordan suggested that they meet in his room so they could discuss the plans for the night. It was clear to all of them now that it was time to meet with their Extra-Terrestrial friends and so much of their conversation revolved around when they would leave the house with the minimum of noise. Melissa had already indicated that she had mind conversation with their friends. It only remained for them to arrange to meet them at the usual rendezvous, the timing however, would be important. They would need for the Mum and Dad to be well asleep. The house was once again enveloped in darkness as was the entire street. There were no streetlights which was most unusual. Melissa was the first to stir and at the prearranged signal her brothers responded accordingly. They moved stealthily down the stairs into the living room and out of the kitchen door. No sound was heard and the door that usually creaked as it opened had finally been oiled. They paused momentarily to gaze at the house and each one wondered what in fact the night would bring, then making their way down the garden path they closed the garden gate behind them and made off to the woods. They knew the path so well that they hardly needed their flashlights. The night was very cool so vastly different from the nights on the farm in Australia.

This was going to be David's first real encounter with travel and there was a certain air of excitement, mixed with some hesitancy as they made their way to the woods. Jordan and Melissa had done this many times before, but their excitement was still clear, and they were discussing just what might happen as they journeyed into the clearing in the woods. By now the clearing was in full view and all they needed to do was to wait patiently. The time began to tick by and Melissa looked anxiously at Jordan and wondered had she got it wrong. Maybe they weren't meant to meet tonight and just as she was thinking those thoughts the message came through loud and clear. "You are absolutely in the right place and this is absolutely the right time." She looked knowingly at Jordan and he knew exactly what was going on and within seconds the craft landed before their very eyes and without any further ado they boarded.

David looked around in sheer amazement, the lines in the craft were so perfectly symmetrical it almost left him speechless. He wondered about the technology and the engineering; it was so aerodynamically perfect. He'd never seen anything quite like this in all his reading and research. Even before he could register another thought he witnessed the experience of his two siblings, the answers were flooding into his mind. He was aware of the conversation taking place, he gasped audibly, and Melissa and Jordan looked on and smiled knowingly and happily. David was now able to relax and was absolutely stunned by the speed at which this craft moved. It seemed as though they had hardly been in the atmosphere when they were touching down at the farm where they had spent the most exciting holiday of their life.

As the door the craft opened, they could see from the inside that Andy and Emma were waiting for them. The three made to leave the craft but found themselves restrained and the message was conveyed that there was too little time and the others would join them. Emma boarded first followed by Andy and it was obvious that Emma had some important news and immediately sat down alongside David her face was positively shinning.

"Wow I have I got some news for you," she volunteered almost beside herself with excitement.

David looked puzzled. By this time Andy was firmly in place and the craft door closed and they were almost off as quickly as they arrived.

"What kind of news?" queried David eagerly. Emma could hardly contain herself and she just blurted out, "We are not really related." It took several moments before David could really take in what she was saying, and his look of bewilderment said it all.

"What do you mean?" He asked quizzically.

"Well," began Emma, "You know how our mums are sisters, well it turns out they're not blood sisters and you must have noticed when you were here that they look very different. I just had to ask Mum how come you're different from your sister in England?" "Mum then explained that she was adopted and to all intents and purposes she was your mum's sister but no blood relative."

The enormity of what Emma had shared suddenly struck David and with that Emma gave him a great big kiss and then said,

"I have been waiting to do that since I found out." and David had no hesitation in responding accordingly. Next moment he took Emma by both hands and said quite gently and lovingly,

"This means that we can be an item," and the only thing that stopped them from continuing their newly celebrated romance was the insistence that they needed to be seated and strapped in, and their hosts had allowed them this special moment. Melissa, Andy and Jordan clapped loudly with warm congratulations. The excited chatter continued everybody was blown away by Emma's news and of course it all made perfect sense, when they looked at their two mums and saw how different they were. They also shared so much of what had happened for them at school and Emma and Andy also shared what was happening on the farm and in their community.

Before they knew it were touching down and for them this was a brand-new location they weren't at all sure where they were. They knew that they had to pick up Lucy and Lynn and the assumption was that they were somewhere near the Sunshine Coast. The craft came to a gentle halt and they looked outside eagerly as the door opened and sure enough Lynn and Lucy were standing there, beside themselves with excitement at being reunited with their friends. They were all finally on-board and now the real adventure was to begin. Lucy and Lynn had their own story to tell and even though they lived just outside the little township of Maleny, they had found a very important contact further up the coast. Mary was a counsellor who supported people who had experienced Extra-Terrestrial contact and she had shared some exciting stories regarding her experiences. She helps them make sense of their encounter and some are more difficult and traumatic than others. Many of the people that she worked with are young people and they came from so many different countries and many of them had truly amazing stories to tell of their encounter with people from another world. The group listened with bated breath as Lucy and Lynn related some of the stories that Mary had shared with them. What was very exciting was that they were not alone in the tasks that lay ahead.

By now the craft was deep into space and they knew that they were going to board an entirely different craft and much bigger and in minutes they were docking into this larger craft. There was an air of mystery as the craft door opened, and just a tinge of apprehension from them all as they were going to meet some of their alien friends.

The figures came to greet them, and they moved gracefully and quietly as they reached out with a hand of friendship. This was their very first face to face encounter and all the members of the group were quite captivated. Their complexion was quite pale, and their 'skin' appeared to be quite translucent. It was then that the group realized the internal conversation which was taking place with their hosts. "We know and sense that we must appear quite different to any form of life that you have experienced so far in your short lives. We assure we are aware of the wide range and variety of human emotion and so it is no accident that we have chosen you to begin this very important work." Both pride and humility flowed from the essence of their beings and with it a growing sense of mission which none of them had ever experienced before. In that moment a bond between the two groups strengthened considerably, the energy was so powerful and the alien people just exuded a sense of peacefulness and compassion. Upon reflection this group of young people had not experienced such peacefulness and they noticed that as this experience continued to deepen something else was happening. This was quite remarkable, and they became aware there was a wholeness developing in them in such a way that they learned a whole new dimension to the meaning of integrity. It was later when they talked about this that they realized that their mind and body and spirit were so integrated that they functioned in a very different way and it gave them a new sense of power. This wasn't power in the sense of control of others, but the clarity of purpose and direction and it felt so good. This new dimension of being allowed them to engage with their alien friends at a much deeper level and the synergy of spirit between them only served to make the bond stronger and more compassionate. Although they couldn't see clearly the expression on their faces, they knew that the energy surrounding them was one of acceptance. They followed quietly and patiently as they were led around this huge spacecraft. They had to stop now as the sheer majesty of this craft unfolded before their very eyes, they had never seen anything so elegant and majestic. They gazed in wonderment and everything that they could see, which was by no means the whole craft. They could hear their space friends clearly saying to them now was not the time to have a guided tour that would have to wait as there were more pressing and important matters to consider. "After all this was the very reason you have been brought to this bigger craft." What was about to happen was so profound and none of the group were really prepared for. It was now up to the hosts to prepare them for this next life changing event. They were all invited to sit and be comfortable. They began, "All of you are aware of the giftedness of Melissa and some of you have experienced it firsthand. Melissa was chosen for this role primarily because of her receptivity, she demonstrated and an openness, a balance and humility not possessed by many of her peers. Melissa also came from a loving and supportive family and of course some of her DNA belonged to our planet. During the next step of our program we are inviting you into these special rooms, where you will have downloaded into your person material which will enhance your gifts. We stress this is an invitation only and you are free to withdraw. David as an example should you agree, your skills and strength will be greatly improved and with it your awareness of impending danger. We do not plan to outline for each of you what your gifts will be and how they will be enhanced. Of course, we simply wish that you are willing to trust us but clearly this is an invitation and no force will be used." The group nodded, acknowledging the invitation whilst reflecting on the impact. There were the normal kinds of questions arising, as to how this was possible and was there danger involved, but then they were encouraged to consider the impact on Melissa. It was at this point a consensus was achieved and each in his or her own way indicated their willingness to continue.

They were taken into a room with lots of strange equipment. There was little apprehension and anxiety for even though they were uncertain of the process they believed they were in very safe hands. They were now looking forward to what was to take place in their own minds, realizing that this event was going to change their lives in a way they could scarcely imagine. They were getting a picture from their friends that they were going to work in specialized areas when they returned to the Earth. Each one would have a special area of his or her own. They were then led to individual cubicles where they would lie down in readiness for the transfer of information. There seemed to be no special apparatus, but the cubicles were sealed and there could be no way for outside interference. The cubicles were most comfortable and the energy within them enabled them to relax and feel entirely at peace. It was in fact so peaceful that all of them experienced momentarily sleep which seemed a very deep and natural because as they awakened, they felt really energized.

Once awake the cubicles opened, and they all assembled on the deck of the ship and once again were directed to their smaller craft. They knew intuitively this was not the time for them to explore this new world and this new craft. So much had happened that they could scarcely take in. The enormity of the experience needed to be digested, and their friends knew this only too well and needed to ground them in their own world. They soon boarded their craft and were making their way back to their home planet, or was it really their home planet? (for the first time they felt like they may have dual citizenship) There was awareness among the whole group and one of the things they noticed immediately was their dramatic increase in telepathic awareness,

they kept tuning into each other's thoughts, but quite respectfully.

David and Emma couldn't stop smiling at each other and the others were chuckling to themselves at the conversations taking place between the two of them. The subject now changed, and they spoke excitedly about what had happened and the consensus was they felt that they belonged somewhere else, including David.

Now they were reflecting on the experience that each one had had in the cubicle and they all confessed a similar experience of an explosion of knowledge in a special field that they had not necessarily been aware of before. It was as though they had downloaded into their mind a whole world of knowledge that they could now access, and such knowledge wasn't known to them before.

They had all become very quiet now realizing that something quite special had taken place and now they needed time to reflect and digest just what had happened. This was going to take considerable time for them, not just to access the information but also to make sense of it. They had yet to see how it would impact in their own lives and influence decisions they would make in the world. This time for reflection would be important for them. Melissa had already done so much in her earlier days as she too came to terms with her own giftedness.

Once on board the craft they travelled quickly through the outer reaches of space and then the craft stopped momentarily. For Jordan and Melissa, it reminded them of their first experience of looking at their planet and seeing how much sadness consumed its people and just how poignantly that moment was. The effect was immediate on the rest of the group for they tuned in to what Melissa and Jordan had seen. There was a long pause and then with one voice they committed themselves to changing this planet. This was indeed a most solemn moment Silence consumed the group; it was though each member was transfixed and the weight of the air was heavy. No one spoke, as the enormity of their pledge began to seep into their souls. Each was deep in thought, what indeed they had promised was huge and were they up to the challenge? Only time would tell. Quietness continued to reign as the craft took them to Lyn and Lucy's property just outside Melany. Just at that moment Jordan raised the question which had been in every body's mind,

"Where do we begin?"

Whereupon the twins answered with a single voice. "We spoke about Mary earlier; she works only with people who have been contacted by alien beings. She is a counsellor and speaks to people and often young people from all over the world."

"Wow that seems pretty cool," proffered Jordan, "I wonder how many contacts she has?"

Lucy then suggested that they spend some time discussing how they might proceed, and they made their way to Lucy and Lyn's little cottage quite away from the main homestead. Lucy had suggested that they move there to give everybody more space. This suggestion was enthusiastically agreed upon by their parents, even so they still usually ate together at the end of each day.

The cottage was ideal, and it gave them a safe space to allow the group to think and plan without disturbing the family. It now seemed a perfect opportunity for them to plan the very next move.

Lucy reminded them that the counsellor could never break confidentiality so they would need to work around that in a way that protected all parties.

Melissa then suggested that the way forward might be for the counsellor to ask the people concerned whether they might like to be linked to their group. Belonging to the group would simply mean that they would specify a city or troubled spot and work with this area in a meditative manner. Melissa was now introducing the 'Maharishi Effect' to this wider community. This will be a way of sending positive energy to the specific community. That immediately met with the group's approval for they could see that the respect and confidentiality would be maintained and allow a greater sense of participation from around the world. It would be then up to the individual whether they would disclose their identity.

It only remained for someone to be nominated to speak to the counsellor whose full name had been withheld up until this point. It was Lucy who volunteered as she had originally contacted Mary and had enjoyed a very fruitful conversation with her less than a week ago. That being decided the remainder of the group made their way back to the craft, but not before some very long hugs took place with some tears of joy and sadness at the parting of their ways.

It seemed only moments before they were settling down in the yellow grassy undergrowth of the Glenorchy property. Now there was a real wrench coming for David and Emma, as it had become obvious that their relationship had gone to another level. Melissa had never seen her big brother shed tears so for her and for David it was going to be a new experience. They held each other very tightly and their warm embrace could only mean love. They all gave each other big hugs and the compassion and affection between them continued to cement a bond which would never be broken.

It seemed only a few moments before the craft landed in the familiar territory of the woods and now the remaining three alighted and said their goodbyes to their alien friends. Slowly they made their way from the woods to their home. It seemed only just a few moments ago that they had left to go on to what had been a most memorable journey. Now the message had burned deeply in their souls, minds and bodies. For the very first time in their lives they sensed a purpose that would continue to consume almost all of their waking moments. It was still very dark, and the house was eerily silhouetted against a very pale moon. They entered quietly through the back door Mum and Dad were still sound asleep and they quietly made their way to their respective bedrooms. Melissa was totally awake and wanted to share some aspects of special briefing, and that being decided, they went to her bedroom.

Melissa began,

"I know that you thought about the larger mission, but have you reflected on the impact of your own giftedness?"

"Not especially," they both responded together. Melissa continued,

"Jordan you watched me struggle as I began to understand and use my gift and at times it felt more like a curse. It has taken some twelve months to become comfortable with it." Jordan nodded; he was beginning to see Melissa's point. "Just how much time you will need is not clear, but it is not going to happen overnight." It was yet another sobering thought and would occupy their attention in the days and weeks to come. It was time for them to return to their own bedrooms.

David then invited Jordan into his bedroom just to ponder the earlier events and what it might mean for them both. The immediate impact was upon their own relationship and the bond between them had deepened substantially. Jordan could begin to see things in the world of quantum mechanics that had previously been obscure and the excitement on his face was evident. David in contrast felt an entirely new awareness in his body which gave him a sense of oneness. He felt at any one time he could ask amazing feats on endurance and strength and his body would respond positively. Now he realized there was more yet to be recognized in his mind alone. They chatted for a few more minutes before turning in, knowing that tomorrow would soon be upon them.

They were both still trying to come to terms with what they had observed on the main craft and how incredibly quickly it could travel through space without it seemingly to affect their own equilibrium. As they pondered this matter, they could hear the communication from their alien friends. They were indicating that it would be a matter of time before all this would not only become apparent, but also second nature and it would become their preferred means of travel. While David felt comforted by this information Jordan was harder to please and he still wanted to know just how it all worked and what relationship it bore to quantum mechanics. He could hear them saying. "Patience my young friend all will be revealed in due time." It was now time for bed and a soft serenity blanketed the Thomas household.

David and Jordan awoke simultaneously and moments later Jordan was in David's bedroom picking up the conversation where they had left it the previous night. They were both excited by Lucy and Lynn's suggestion and the possibility of meeting new young people who may be shared their vision and commitment to a new order and a new world. The language barrier would no longer prove a problem. All the new technology that was now available made it possible for them to have serious and intelligent conversations no matter what part of the world these people would come from. It was clear from the twins that Mary had access to many of these "alien infused people" and they could sense that their contribution was going to be invaluable. The other area of excitement was to realize just which alien culture they may have come from because it was becoming clearer that there was more than one alien life force that had infiltrated the planet Earth. The potential for growth seemed endless and the broadening of horizons could know no bounds. Here they were at the cutting edge and wondering with both awe and excitement just what the future might hold. Then suddenly they remembered the contact they had made at Sovereign Hill and they knew now that they needed to follow-up on that as soon as possible. Jordan followed up with a text message to Dennis. They had now stopped long enough to recognize there was quietness in Melissa's room.

Melissa for her part would have been consumed by such dramatic events, but her sleep had been entirely restful, and it felt quite magical that she could exercise control over her body with such ease. It gave her a strong sense of her own personal power. This was something she had always desired. As she continued to lay in bed she thought more deeply about those earlier times in space and the pain she had seen emanating from the planet she called home. It began to feel quite depressing until she remembered her own contribution to change. Lucy immediately sprang to mind and now she was a really solid team member and had given them a way forward through Mary. She just thrilled at the thought of tapping into all these other people who would most likely come on board. Next her mind turned to Alistair and what a huge turn around had taken place in his life and she knew it wouldn't be long before he would become a valuable team member. Finally, there was Terry and who would have believed that he would made the progress he had, and all of it starting with her!

She lay there for a few moments feeling her confidence rising and realizing how powerful this process had been to rejuvenate her spirit and encourage her the more and just how this could and would impact on the group. Melissa then arose and made her way to the bathroom and was soon bright eyed and bushy tailed making her way down to the kitchen and this time ahead of her brothers. She had indeed picked up on their animated conversation.

Jordan heard the familiar sound emerging from the kitchen below as he made his way back to his bedroom. He glanced quickly around the room making sure that his school satchel was packed, he was now more than half dressed as he became aware of just how hungry he was. He was adjusting his school tie as he made his way down for breakfast.

There was nothing quite like the smell of freshly cooked bacon and he immediately came up behind his mum giving her a hug and kiss on the cheek. She softened to his touch as she recognized the warmth and tenderness he had continued to develop towards the family. For some reason Jordan had never gone through that difficult passage that most boys go through from the age of twelve through to seventeen. Sure, he'd had his moments but nothing quite like so many other boys of that age and Janet had always had this truly wonderful relationship with her middle child. Thereupon she turned facing him looking him right in the eyes and held him closely whispering quietly, "I love you." Jordan's smile said it all. He then looked at the table and greeted his dad and Melissa with another big smile. George looked at him and jested, "All that smooching will not get you any more breakfast." at which point Jordan re-joined, with equal good humour,

"Oh, I don't know it's always worth a try." Janet then interrupted their banter suggesting that Jordan may now like to put some toast on.

He needed no second bidding and just at that moment David appeared in the doorway and nodded to the whole family, and especially to Jordan indicating he too would like a slice. It was not long before they were all sitting down with a breakfast in front of them fuelling up for the day. By now Dad had finished his breakfast and was packing his lunch in his briefcase ready for work. Jordan had always been interested in his dad's work and asked him inquiringly,

"What does your day day look like?" This time George was far more forthcoming declaring, "Well today we are planning the final trials of our work and we believe that we have not only built the smallest battery but also the most efficient in the world, but of course this is definitely not for publication, you may not share this with anyone." Then he quipped,

"Otherwise I will have to kill you." They all laughed, and if on cue, Jordan, Melissa and David said,

"It's okay dad your secret is safe with us." Both George and Janet looked at each other with surprise written all over their face. How was it possible for the three of them to display such synchronicity? Only the future would give them that answer.

They then began to discuss their father's earlier comment about his work, they had never really understood his work as such. This was mainly because it was never discussed but suddenly Dad was turning out to be the Quiet Achiever and there was an unspoken respect and trust for the work he was accomplishing. They began to admire their father and were seeing him a new light; Janet of course listened with interest and then made her own comment.

"Well you didn't think that I would marry just anyone to be the father of my three beautiful children." That stopped the conversation in its tracks momentarily, but it made all three recognize just what a talented dad they had.

Janet watched with interest as the three of them discussed their father's work. She was struck by their enthusiasm and their obvious pride in what he was doing. Furthermore, she couldn't help noticing how well they supported each other and the obvious bond of both respect and trust that was developing in them as siblings. David's attitude to Melissa had taken her by surprise and as she watched them interact her heart warmed immensely. Janet recognized what a beautiful family that she and George had been gifted with, and it filled with her joy and gratitude.

It was David's turn for the dishes and without being asked he was immediately at the sink, water running dishwashing liquid and dishes being washed carefully and systematically. They did have a dishwasher but the habit of washing the breakfast dishes had persisted and always gave them an opportunity to talk about the plans for the day. David of course was off to university and Jordan and Melissa to school. Janet announced that she would be going to continue her research and the house would be steeped in quietness.

School continued to occupy a major part of Jordan and Melissa's life. There had been a significant change in their attitude and approach to their school. They had both taken roles of leadership and continued to win the respect and trust of much of the school community. Melissa's impact on Alistair and Terry had not gone unnoticed and the ripple effect on the rest of the school was warmly welcomed by the staff.

Jordan for his part had been elected a prefect and then took on further responsibility of being head boy due to the incumbent moving schools. George and Janet had been invited to his induction and they felt very proud at his acceptance speech. He seemed a different young man to the eighteen months ago, when had struggled to fit in.

They both continued to develop their telepathic skills, not just with their immediate group, but even with their peers at school. It became such an important tool with which they could bridge the gap with many of their peers and earn their trust and respect. They did of course have their detractors, usually people who were unhappy in themselves. Interestingly Melissa could usually pick them and would sabotage their best efforts to undermine the well-being of her peers. She recounted one such incident regarding Catherine.

Catherine approached her one day with a most cutting comment,

"Why are you such a goody two-shoes all the time?" Melissa paused and looked her straight in the eyes and replied with a question.

"Catherine tell me how it benefits you to continually focus on the negative, how does it feel inside to be so critical?" The question was the last thing that Catherine anticipated, and it was asked with such compassion. It was many months later when Catherine ventured to engage with Melissa again. This time it was different. Melissa could see the animosity had subsided, Catherine then spoke,

"You asked me those questions and they haunted me ever since, and I had to find the answers. I just wanted to thank you for the questions and the way you delivered them. I am beginning to find the answers and my life is turning around. I am so glad you are Miss Goody Two Shoes," with an obvious twinkle in her eyes. There was mutual respect and the two went their separate ways, but a bridge had been built.

Meanwhile David continued to be most diligent with his studies. His long hours had paid off handsomely with some quite outstanding results. His lecturers had taken the unusual step of ringing his parents, commending him on his work ethic. At another level David was a regular member at the gym and hardly a day went by when he was not working out. It now looked as though he had finished his growth spurt, and he stood at just a tad under two metres in height. Now his body was filling out and he had become a proverbial 'man mountain'. The family had commented encouragingly on his increased physical stature.

It was now coming into June and everybody realized that for Jordan it would be his final exam, and where to from there. Melissa would have another year and it would be expected that she would continue at the school she had come to love and respect. Little did anyone know just what the future held for the Thomas family.

There had been little contact with their friends from space during these months and what contact there had been was more to encourage their continual development and growth. This had been appreciated greatly from the whole group and what had developed beyond their wildest imaginings was their telepathic communication level. Melissa could readily and easily tune in to Lynn and Lucy at any time providing they weren't asleep. David and Emma continued to speak to each other at this level all the time but ever conscious that others could also listen in to their conversation. Therefore, mobiles and FaceTime were still important channels. Emma had been smitten from the very start, but the latest pictures clinched it for her. She proudly displayed her man on her phone. Not only was he handsome and incredibly well built but he was also smart, and she wasn't about to let him go. Nancy and Ken had watched their relationship develop and whilst they were very happy, they knew it was still early days.

It's had now become a habit for David, Jordan and Melissa to meet in one of their bedrooms at the end of the day. This usually took the form of a re-cap, what had been learned and what experiences they'd had. Sometimes it was quite short, and others gave opportunity for serious debriefing. What had really excited them all in the last couple of weeks was the expansion of the group and the focus of using the 'Maharishi effect'. They had chosen a prison located in Queensland. The intention was to focus on peacefulness, creativity and positive attitudinal changes. Lucy and Lynn had direct contact with the authorities as they both had social work backgrounds which involved them in some of the prison programs. There was some progress, and there were encouraging signs, and the governor of the prison had indicated he would support a meditation program for all the prisoners.

Melissa was quite delighted with this as she knew from her own experience that you can engage people who have lost their way and they can be turned around and the evidence from the studies only served to convince her more.

David was the first to leave as his lectures started right at nine o'clock and he needed more time to get there. However, before leaving he walked up to his mum and gave her a big kiss on the cheek, she was not only surprised by this action but delighted, and instinctively began to wonder what else was going on in his life. Melissa and Jordan could read the enquiry written on her face, both in unison responded,

"It's okay mum we will tell you about it later." This comment only reinforced the lovely bond that was emerging between their three adult children.

Within an instant the house was quiet, and Janet was left to reflect on the continuing growth of her family. It was now time for her to be off to work and it was often her practice to reflect on the family. She was especially curious about the change in David, his warmth towards her, and the respect he was so readily demonstrating to Melissa. He had always been much harder inside, seldom letting his guard down and never showing his true feelings. She wondered whether this was due to their initial style of parenting, or whether it was simply because David was the firstborn and somehow had taken on the role of protecting his brother and sister. It was a very challenging time for Janet as a young mum and trying to impress in her workplace. She always knew that it was more difficult for women to make their mark and she devoted much more energy there than maybe towards David. As she reflected on those earlier days, she felt some pangs of guilt, recognizing that she may not have been as emotionally present as she was with Jordan and Melissa. She caught herself **beating** up **on her performance. Her mind retreated** into her guilt and she became aware that this was a pattern developed over some years. The next revelation was recognizing that what triggered this, was her memory of David and especially those early days. Her next challenge was how to deal with this new insight? Her first step was to embrace the feeling of guilt, so often she had changed the pattern of her thoughts and avoided the pattern in her mind. Her next step was to discover what was driving that guilt? What was the key emotion underneath all this?

It was time to reflect and maybe use her journal to write it down. This would mean she would come back to it later. She knew instinctively forgiveness was the key, but why was it so difficult to forgive oneself? It had always been a struggle. Then she remembered that pencils have erasers! Again, it was something to ponder and her journal would prove beneficial. It was okay to get it wrong because there was always forgiveness. Yes, it was true 'To err is human but to forgive is divine' Now she returned to David aware that he had really evolved into a beautiful human being, one she could be justly proud of. It had been a good time of reflection for Janet and she couldn't believe that it had been four months since their holiday in Australia and her young adult family had all moved into another school year. This was Jordan's final year, how quickly time had gone.

By now Jordan and Melissa had reached the school gates and Alistair was there waiting for them. On their way to school Melissa had shared with Jordan that she felt Alistair could be made aware of their encounter with their friends from another world. Melissa then reflected that maybe it could wait awhile. However, Jordan was more than open to the idea as he could recognize that over the months absolute trust had been demonstrated. Even David remarked he noticed a real growth in Alistair. They spoke briefly with Alistair about the possibility of him coming home with them after school. Alistair was delighted because this friendship had meant so much to him and he knew that it had really helped his mum feel at home as well.

David's day at university was full of pressure and he hardly had time to think about all that they had discussed the previous night. However, he found time to text Emma and was absolutely overjoyed to get an almost immediate response because he knew it would still be very late in the day when he sent it. It took him all his time to concentrate on the lecture and he found himself at their familiar landing spot when it dawned on him that they could be an item. The day passed without further event and by 4.30 in the afternoon he was on the bus making his way home. It happened this time that he was first home and immediately raided the fridge, some things never change, he made himself what had become known to all the family and beyond, 'a Dagwood special' consisting of cold meat, lettuce, tomato, cheese, mayo, and beetroot all between two modest slices of bread. He was sitting at the table happily devouring his handiwork when Melissa and Jordan burst in, with Alistair in tow. Jordan looked longingly at the Dagwood, but David was not about to surrender any of his handiwork and suggested that Jordan should make his own. He needed no second invitation and looked at Alistair who immediately nodded in acknowledgement that he could happily eat a horse and maybe the rider too. They all laughed. Melissa was not fazed by any of this she looked in the fridge but then closed it, feeling quite satisfied within. She would be more than happy to wait for the evening meal.

It was now five thirty pm and any moment now mum would be walking through the door and as if on cue the front door opened, and their Mum appeared. She immediately noticed Alistair and greeted him warmly and then said,

"Will you be staying for tea?"

"I would love to," he replied, "But I will need to check with my mum." A brief conversation followed on his mobile and he was happy to confirm there would be okay for him to share an evening meal. Melissa turned to her mum asking her if she needed some help with the meal. Of course, Janet was more than happy to have some more hands in the preparation.

It was now after six pm and George came into the kitchen where Melissa and Janet were busy preparing the evening meal. He looked quite exhausted and there was a look of frustration across his face. Janet had seen that look many times before and knew that the day had not gone according to plan. She asked the customary question as to how his day was. He looked at her and began to describe the events of the day.

"Well you wouldn't believe it, but we had another visit from those people in high places, it is as though they actually don't want this project to succeed. Instead of giving us support and encouragement they keep introducing new guidelines new requirements and they make absolutely no sense at all, and one of them actually hinted that any future government funding may be withheld altogether." Janet's response was immediate,

"Do you think they have another agenda entirely?" this was something that George had never considered suddenly it began to make some sense. Why else would they keep visiting this project and putting so many barriers in the way. There is no doubt with the introduction of these batteries, power supplies in the world would necessarily become more redundant and of course the impact could be catastrophic in the workforce of these countries.

Just at that moment Jordan and David came in on the conversation and became interested. Jordan paused for a moment, and you could see his mind ticking over trying to find the right words to ask the question he needed to.

"You would think that these people in high places would be only too pleased to welcome technology that is going to help the planet," Jordan said hesitantly. George looked fondly at his younger son and smiled faintly.

"Yes, one would hope so," re-joined his dad, "But I get the feeling that there is more to this than meets the eye and that governments all over the world are not ready to shift the economy in a new direction." At this point David bought into the conversation.

"Dad, am I hearing you right that you actually believe that our government is getting involved because they are afraid that this new technology will threaten the economic viability of countries all over the world?" "Well it is certainly something like that," offered George hesitantly. Jordan immediately thought back to his hero Nikola Tesla and just how he had been silenced. He knew that the moment Tesla had died his flat was raided by the government of the day and the material never saw the light of day again. It then dawned on Jordan that his beloved dad may well be in the firing line of people who would want to do him harm, but he kept all of this to himself. Jordan had a passion for a clean planet that was well in advance of his years and just at that moment he walked over to his dad and said in a very clear strong voice,

"Dad I'm so proud of the work that you are doing and we as a family need to do all we can to support you, so whatever you need just say the word," Jordan's voice was full of conviction and there was a murmur from the whole family in agreement with the sentiments that Jordan had expressed. George looked at his son warmly and he said straightaway,

"Just the way you have spoken right now gives me all the encouragement I need, and I feel so very lucky to have such a supportive family."

Janet and Melissa had now dished up and Alistair had been called from the living room to take his place at the family table. The chatter now stopped as everyone appeared to be hungry after a full day. It was only as the meal was coming to an end that conversation again began to erupt. Nothing more was said about George's work as much of that was still highly confidential and nobody wanted to make his life any more difficult than it already was. It was now becoming quite late and the dishes had all been done and put away and one by one the family members began to retire. Melissa and Jordan went into Jordan's bedroom and Alistair was also invited. The two of them then began to explain to Alistair the many encounters with beings from another planet. It was obvious that Alistair was totally blown away by what he was hearing. A look of incredulity continued to haunt his face. He knew these two very dear friends were serious. There could be no doubt in his mind of the truth of their shared understanding of what had happened to them over the many months.

They impressed upon him the absolute need for confidentiality that he could share this with no one not even his mother and he was bound by the bonds of their friendship to offer that confidentiality. They spoke to him of their mission and watched his face intently as they shared the work that they had committed themselves to during the last space encounter. He could scarcely take it in and felt hugely honoured and humbled by their invitation for him to become a member of their group. It was now time for him to leave and make his way home. He was both excited and afraid, but he felt so privileged to be part of such a mission and he looked ruefully at Melissa and Jordan musing,

"This is certainly a far cry from being a member of Terry's gang." They both laughed in agreement and saw Alistair to the front door but not before he'd stuck his head in the lounge and said good night and thank you to George and Janet for what could only be described as the most momentous three hours of his life. He knew that his life would never be the same.

In the meantime, Jordan and Melissa had gone upstairs to their bedrooms and were thinking of turning in when David appeared.

"What happened regarding the contact with Dennis who we met at Sovereign Hill?" David inquired. Jordan hadn't checked his text messages and went downstairs to get his mobile.

Alistair was familiar with the trip home and knew exactly which bus to catch and where to get off. As for sleep that was not an option this night for Alistair. His mind was running at a million miles an hour and he kept thinking of all the questions he wanted to ask but there wasn't enough time. Tomorrow would be another day at school and maybe there would be opportunity for him to satisfy his curiosity. He eventually arrived home and his mum was still up waiting for him and ensuring he was safe. She could see by the look on his face that there was a different air about him, and she just asked him very gently how his night was. He looked at her with such a firm gaze and volunteered that it was probably the best night of his life. He looked very tired despite the abundance of energy and without further ado he gave his mum big hug and was off to his bedroom.

Sheila smiled to herself inwardly as she reflected on the changes she had witnessed in Alistair since he had befriended this family. This gave her a warm glow to know that her boy had not only settled down in his schoolwork but that he was content and at peace with himself. Now had some real direction in his life. Little did she know of his involvement in the mission, but even if she had there is no doubt, they would have been the very real sense of pride in his aspirations. It was now her turn to take off to bed and her sleep was going to be deep and peaceful, whereas Alistair's sleep was fitful and wakeful and sometimes pinching himself to see if it was all real.

Morning came around all too suddenly and Alistair awoke within an instant. He dressed quickly and made his way to the kitchen where his mum had already prepared his breakfast.

"My we are in a hurry this morning, I don't think I have ever seen you so eager to go to school. There must be something really exciting for you to be this keen," mused his mum thoughtfully. He smiled broadly but gave nothing away.

"Well I guess I'm not going to be told what it is that it's firing your spirit at this moment," said his mum as nonchalantly as possible. He looked up from his bowl of cereal which he had almost consumed and winked cheekily at his mum. There were no further questions and in his customary manner now he gave his mum a big long hug. She whispered quietly,

"I do love you very much and I'm very proud of you." Alistair re-joined,

"I love you too Mum, and I'm so glad that you are my mum." Then without another word he was gone out of the door and on his way to school. He had now worked out some of the questions which most intrigued him, and sure enough Melissa and Jordan were already there at the school gates waiting for him, but then so was Terry and he knew that his questions would have to wait. The day passed with little opportunity for Alistair to field his questions and it was only on the way home that he had further time to have his curiosity satisfied. Of course, he wanted to know how they first met and then he wanted to know where they had been in the galaxy. He also wanted to know how in fact they made contact and was quite intrigued with the notion that they didn't use voice connection but could speak directly to the mind and communicate that way. He finally conceded that they were far more advanced than we were and was looking forward to his first meeting. Before he could finish that thought he had his first message from the alien culture. His eyes were as wide as saucers and he looked at both Melissa and Jordan and said to them,

"Did you hear that?" They both nodded in the affirmative and assured him this was just the beginning of a whole new world for him.

"When do you think our next meeting will be?" There was both a hint of impatience and curiosity in his voice, which of course was it quite understandable given all that he'd experienced in the last twenty-four hours. The message came through loud and clear it would be in the next forty-eight hours, however, it would most certainly be dependent on the weather as they would like some cloud cover in such a built-up area. It would be clear, and the message would be sent, and they would need to be ready within the hour of notification. Alistair could hardly contain himself he was jumping all over the place like the proverbial Jack-in-the-Box whilst Jordan and Melissa looked on with a great deal of mirth at his antics.

It was now time for them to go their separate ways and Alistair caught his usual bus, whereas Jordan and Melissa could walk home and enjoy their time together. It wasn't long before they reached the front gate of their home and they were pleasantly surprised to find that David was already home. Jordan and Melissa had both come to respect and value their older and bigger brother. It was clear that David had bulked up considerably since his last journey in the spacecraft and his constant working at the gym made him quite a formidable figure. He was now taller than his dad measuring just over 200 cm. They always felt safe when David was around and had come to value his protection as well as his friendship and support. David was now standing at the front door and decided to wait for them, for he too had got the message that they would meet in the next 48 hours. They all burst in the same time and made straight for the kitchen and as usual Mum had food laid out on the table as both Jordan and David had huge appetites and needed no second bidding to tuck in. David spoke briefly about his day at university and particularly of his new interest of aerodynamics and space travel. His mum looked at him quizzically,

"Well that's very different coming from you and here was me thinking that your focus was entirely on chemistry and physics." David nodded in acknowledgement of his mum's comment but re-joined saying,

"Both aerodynamics and space travel are very much part of the world of physics. It is my belief that we need to find another way of propelling a craft through space without using rocket fuel." Janet was a great mum and was able to accommodate all her children's interest without fear or favour, she was more than supportive of David's new interest and they continued to exchange views on what the future may hold in such areas. David felt very reassured by his mother's support and made comment how much he valued not just her support but the insightfulness in relation to his interest. By now Melissa and Jordan had satisfied themselves with chocolate cake and some Eccles cakes and were now heading up to their bedrooms, but not before acknowledging how good it was to come home to such a lovely spread. David quickly retired to his room, where Melissa and Jordan joined him. Jordan then saw Dennis's name and clicked on 'open.' He read it out slowly.

"I am Dennis's mum and he asked me to tell you that he's very sick, we are sitting by his bedside in hospital and not at all sure he is going to make it!" All three looked at each other, Melissa then took the initiative and said, "I'm sure that I can turn this around," and before going to her room she asked Jordan, to ask the family to keep in touch. It was likely that this happened at 5 pm in England when Jordan had opened the text and it was probably between 1am and two am in Queensland. Jordan texted back requesting that they keep in touch. In the meantime, Melissa had gone into her room and quietly sent healing to someone she had never even met. David looked at Jordan and said simply,

"If anyone can turn this situation around it will be Melissa." Jordan nodded affirmatively.

David was now ready to return to his room where he immediately began his assignment which was due by next Monday. There was lots of research and he needed to go to the library to at least resource some of the texts. He then made a snap decision that he would take himself off to the library right away. He slipped downstairs and told his mum that he would be out at the library for at least the next hour, but he hoped to be home for dinner, round about six o'clock. Janet nodded in acknowledgement and said gently, "Be careful on the roads they can be quite busy and cyclists for the most part aren't always acknowledged." David knew only too well that Mum was right, and he agreed that he would be incredibly careful.

Melissa and Jordan were already seated at the dinner table when David walked in, he quickly went straight to the bathroom to wash his hands in preparation for the evening meal, only to be met by his dad who was just coming out of that same bathroom. They nodded a greeting to each other and within minutes they were all sitting around the table as Mum dished up quite their favourite meal. Jordan and Melissa had some news regarding Dennis, but it would have to wait until the meal was over and they could share it in one of their bedrooms. Tonight, it was pork belly, applesauce with roast veggies, broccoli and Brussel sprouts. It was Melissa's turn to offer a blessing and once completed there was no further conversation as everybody loved Mum's pork belly roast.

The meal was concluded, and the two boys looked at their mum longingly checking to see what was in the desert offering. They couldn't believe their luck, it was apple pie and ice cream with cream, and they were there only ones who had enough room to fit it all in and fit in they did.

Everybody wanted to know how George had fared at work, and yet again they had had a visit from the 'men in suits' as George described them. This time they not only came to the office but wandered out onto the factory floor checking on the progress and generally being complimentary and supportive.

George was now senior management and was quite surprised by what he noticed with what he considered a change in attitude and he had spoken to his senior colleagues about his observation. They concluded that there had been an apparent change in attitude, but notwithstanding they still had a healthy scepticism about their visit and felt sure they couldn't really be trusted. Jordan voiced his indignation at their continued interference into such important work. Whilst David agreed he was quite sure that the men in suits, as they had become known, had far more sinister motives, which as it happened his father agreed with. Janet and Melissa could only be baffled by such behaviour and clearly wondered what could be gained by their continued checking of the entire operation.

Tonight, was the night of the new dishwasher and it being Jordan's opportunity to stack it which he had carried out very deftly and then it was up to bed. George and Janet retired to the lounge room where they watched a little of the late news and then turned over to watch Britain's Got Talent. They enjoyed the variety of talent presented with each program.

The rest of the family had met in Jordan's bedroom to share the news regarding Dennis. Jordan was able to report that there had been marked improvement in his condition and now he was sitting up taking in food which he hadn't done in over a week. The change came within minutes of Melissa going into her room and sending him healing. His parents were completely surprised and nonplussed by the sudden turn around even as were the medical staff.

It was clear that they had received notification that they were to meet at the usual rendezvous with their friends who came from beyond Andromeda. They were busily rugging up as the night air had a severe chill.

CHAPTER 9

A NIGHT TO REMEMBER

I T WAS JUST nine thirty pm and by now the house was in darkness as the trio made their way into the woods. There was an air of expectation and this was going to be Alistair's first encounter in experiencing their mission. They talked excitedly as they made their way to the now familiar location, Melissa reached over to Jordan and put her hand on his forearm as if to caution him, it was as though she had sensed something, they paused for a second but nothing seemed untoward and they continued to their destination. David was more hesitant, he was sensing danger! He was hanging back, his sensitivity more developed since their last trip into space.

They now had clear view of the clearing and could hear the unmistakable humming sound of the alien craft. Suddenly as if from nowhere lights flooded the whole area and within a split- second confusion broke out everywhere. Jordan noticed immediately that the craft disappeared as quickly as he had ever seen it move. They were men dressed in camouflage clothing seemingly coming from all directions. Jordan had noticed a large net, which on reflection had been an attempt to thwart the escape of the alien craft, but to no avail. The men quickly moved on the two capturing both Melissa and Jordan readily, however, it was not so easy with David. His training immediately kicked in at the sight of threat and his first assailant lay motionlessly on the ground and now he turned to the second would-be assailant and dealt with him accordingly. This continued until there were five men partially paralysed. However, he was outnumbered, and it was only seconds that one of his captors produced a taser gun and stunned him to the point of helplessness.

In the meantime, Alistair who had been inadvertently held up watched all this at a safe distance. He had witnessed the whole thing and was totally perplexed by these events. It was fortunate that his mum had made an unusual request just as he was ready to leave, and he would never deny her. It now became apparent to him that her request had been quite fortuitous in saving him. He continued to watch their operation and observed what he believed was quite a lot of sophisticated equipment to monitor and record the whole event. He could scarcely breathe, leaning forward all the time to see if he could pick up precisely what was going on. It became obvious this group of armed men had carefully and strategically placed themselves in anticipation of the space craft. It was becoming clearer that they intended to intercept and capture the craft. Just how they could have known was not immediately apparent. It would become a question which they needed to find the answer.

Meanwhile the trio were bundled into the back of three vans, which had all the hallmarks of a security vehicle meant for dangerous criminals. They would be treated as dangerous as each of them was handcuffed with their hands behind their back. They were shocked and confused and they just sat in silence. The vehicles now moved slowly through the bushland and onto the nearby road, and by now David was coming around. Another aspect of his development was ability to withstand such assaults on his person. He was dazed and felt quite afraid but again his skills and training kicked in and he gradually regained complete composure by focusing on his breath. He knew that he could break the handcuffs with some deft hand movements and a fine wire. It wasn't long before his hands were free, and he stood up and looked out the back of the wagon.

After what seemed an age the vehicles came to a standstill. David's vehicle was opened first and he had the element of surprise. In less than seconds he had captured the two guards and held them hostage. He motioned to another to unlock the other two vehicles and let his brother and sister go which they did. This was to no avail as more reinforcements had arrived and they were surrounded. They were ushered into a building that they had not seen before. It turned out to be the headquarters of MI6, but they had no idea that this was the case. They had all been receiving the same message from their alien visitors which basically encouraged them to deny any knowledge of encounters with them. They were to make up a story about going to a late-night movie and were simply taking a shortcut through the woods. They also learned that their visitors had been caught totally off guard and had no option but to abort their meeting and preserve their anonymity and freedom.

Meanwhile Alistair continued to observe the equipment around the site while noticing that guards had been posted strategically to keep the site safe. Eventually and stealthily he made his retreat and headed towards home, feeling a mixture of being perplexed and concerned for his friends. He slipped in through the back door ever so quietly and made his way up to his bedroom and did something for him which was quite unusual. He took out a brand-new exercise book and he wrote down all the details of the events of that night and did a drawing of where he had seen the equipment. This was indeed going to be very important in the hours that lay ahead.

By now Melissa, Jordan and David had each been separated and placed in a room by themselves. It wasn't long before the door opened and two men appeared in suits reminiscent of the men who visited their dad's factory, and this certainly wasn't lost on Jordan. They began with a barrage of questions, "How often have you met these people in this place?" Jordan looked them fairly in the face and eyeballed them and began,

"Am I not entitled to have a lawyer present? this seems to me to be totally inappropriate and unfair," The two men were caught on the back foot because Jordan was correct, and they were governed by the same protocols that existed in the Metropolitan Police. The interview was suspended there and then. Melissa's defence was similar as she was entitled to a parent and a social worker, she like Jordan had put them right on the back foot. For David it was the same and he insisted on his rights that he be allowed the services of a lawyer. The whole interviewing process had now come to a grinding halt for the moment and the men at MI6 had to play a waiting game.

It was not long before two men arrived at the home of Janet and George and were banging loudly on the front door. Eventually lights came on and George opened the door to be confronted by the men in suits. The first man had never met George and explained that they were from MI6. He then announced that their children were at MI6 headquarters about to be interrogated. George stood there lost for words.

"We have evidence that suggests they are in contact with alien life!" By now Janet had come down, robed in her dressing gown and had just caught the tail end of the conversation. They were eventually invited in and it was then that George recognized the second man. He was indeed one of those who visited the factory on a regular basis and from George's viewpoint there was no love lost between them and the feeling was mutual. The second man was quite a bit smaller looked at George and said,

"I might have guessed that somehow you would be involved and that your family is involved in subversive activity." George could feel his heart beating and his blood pressure rising, not only was he a proud man but when it came to his family, he would defend them to the death. He took a step forward and looked down on this little man getting right into his face and challenged him.

"How dare you accuse my children of subversive activity, and frankly that's rich coming from you who does nothing but white-ant our entire operation at the factory." By now the little man was warming to the challenge and looking straight into George's face and eyeballing him,

"We caught them red-handed meeting with an alien culture and believe me we are going to nail them. You probably won't see them for a very long time, unless of course you are involved which wouldn't surprise me in the least. It is just the kind of thing I would imagine from you. I knew from the first time I saw you, that you couldn't be trusted."

This was too much for George and he raised his arm with clear intention of striking this jumped-up little upstart, but he had scarcely raised his arm when his whole body became rigid and he fell backwards with a sickening thud. Janet recognized the signs all too well and immediately checking for a pulse and finding it ever so slight. She looked at the men who were both stunned. She shrieked at them to call an ambulance. Janet then proceeded to give him mouth to mouth and kept working tirelessly and feverishly, attempting to bring life into now what was becoming a lifeless body. She continued for what seemed an eternity until the ambulance officers arrived. They had him on a stretcher in no time and in a moment the ambulance was heading to the Emergency Department at the nearest hospital.

They had immediately applied the paddles but there had been no encouraging signs and Janet could feel her anxiety going through the roof. She looked on helplessly from the front seat of the ambulance while the two medics continued to work on George. Once the ambulance arrived at the hospital, they whisked him straight into the ICU, whilst Janet stood impatiently by the door watching everything. She knew all the signs and could feel her heart sinking. This couldn't be happening, her mind kept on racing, she needed her family and with that she turned and faced the two men who had come separately.

"I need my family and I need them now and you two get your sorry arses out here and bring them pronto," she was livid beyond belief and very scary! There was no argument from them and the smaller man who seemed to be in charge responded immediately and said,

"They will be here just as soon as we can get them to you."

He quickly called headquarters and they assured him that the family should arrive in the next ten to twenty minutes, whereupon he relayed that message to Janet who was now completely overcome with grief. The door to the ICU opened noiselessly and the doctor leading the team looked at Janet confirming that George had gone. He took her to a private room and her sat down asking her if she would like a cup of tea, but she was too overtaken with grief and her tears knew no bounds. He then explained to Janet that her husband had gone into cardiac arrest and that they had been unable to revive him and even their best efforts had failed. The doctor then took Janet by both hands and expressed deepest sorrow to her and the family. He then became aware that Janet was on her own and he asked,

"Is there anyone I can call for you?' To which she replied,

"Thank you but my family is on its way and I am expecting them soon." The doctor then said to Janet,

"We will need a few minutes to prepare your husband and am assuming you are wanting a viewing for yourself and the family." Janet nodded without speaking and squeezed his hands and thanked him. No more words were exchanged. Janet sat down quietly; she now had the unenviable task of telling three children just what had happened. She took several deep breaths and composed herself as well as she knew how to, she knew that she had to be strong for the sake of her family. She dried her eyes and looked down and for the first time realized that she was still in her dressing gown She then became aware that events had completely overtaken her, and she had become even more vulnerable. It was at that precise moment that her children burst in the room and they immediately surrounded and held her and for the very first time she felt safe and drew from their strength. She then sat them down and related all the events of that evening and that their beautiful father had passed into another world.

The response of their children was predictable, Melissa's tears began to flow because in her heart of hearts she knew had she been there, the outcome may have been quite different and she may have been able to restore him through the gift that she had received. Both Jordan and David were so angry they could only focus their attention on the men in suits. David was quite ready to go into the corridor and lay them out. He was more aware that his training was never used for that reason and right now his mum needed him more than ever, not just to be present for her, but to be responsible as well. David was surprised by his own mature response and twelve months ago there would have been an entirely different outcome.

The doctor came to the door indicating that they may go into the ward to see their dad. Melissa was still crying in fact she was sobbing, and it seemed that nothing anyone could do could console her. She looked at her dad lying there and threw herself on him and held him so tightly. Janet reached out and stroked her hand gently and it was as though she was stroking energy into her body and for a moment Melissa relaxed. She then expressed that she was feeling quite faint and the boys made sure that she was comfortable and warm. She closed her eyes and it seemed as though she had drifted off, but in that moment something quite remarkable took place. Melissa began to leave her own body she was looking down at herself in the room and to her surprise she was aware that she was not alone. She blinked and looked again, incredulous at what she saw. Could it really be her dad? Then he spoke. It was so totally reassuring, and she saw him being so much younger and fitter, there was so much he had to say to her. "I am so very proud of all my family," He was now aware of their incredibly important mission and that he would be with them each step of the way, looking out for them and protecting them whenever he could. He went on to speak about his courting days with Janet. Melissa smiled with complete confidence and peace of mind and knew that it was time to come back. She found herself sitting bolt upright in the chair, eyes now wide open and her whole disposition changed. The boys were still holding onto their mum and she was buoyed by their strength. Melissa then stood up and embraced her family and whispered,

"It is going to be okay; you may find this hard to believe but Dad is in this room but in an entirely different form." The boys looked at each other and then they looked at their mum who was obviously taken aback by Melissa's comments. They knew their sister only too well and that her comment would be based on experience and well considered. Janet continued to stand by the bedside holding George's hand for it was still warm and reassuring. The boys had now found a seat and were sitting down with their attention directed to Melissa.

Melissa then briefly described her out of body experience and whilst Janet had not ever experienced such an event, she had certainly read many different stories by people who had. They listened intently as Melissa described the young version of her dad. She described the blue suit with the shirt and the blue bow tie that only Janet could possibly have known about. It brought back a flood of memories of their life before the children were born. She talked about her dad being aware of their mission and without going into any detail of the mission she indicated that he would be there for them always. Janet was still preoccupied with the early memory of George, her beau. It was indeed a beautiful memory and one that was offering her some balm for her grieving spirit. She could feel herself smiling both inside and out and felt as though she could move on in some small way. It was now time for them to leave the hospital and head home, they entered the corridor only to be met this by the little man who had originally goaded George. He put up his hand as if to motion them that the children were still in custody.

At this point David stepped forward in complete control and said definitively, "You and your stupid little interviews will have to wait, we need to be together as a family. We need to grieve and support each other and then we will deal with you."

Just at that moment his colleague came carrying two cups of coffee and said to the family that not only were they a free to go, but he had organized a car to take them home.

It was now very late, and the car pulled up in front of the house. Their attention was immediately arrested by two events. There was a white van, completely enclosed, parked adjacent to their front gate and there were two men stationed right at the front gate. David motioned to Jordan and Melissa pointing to the van and the two men and whispered one word 'surveillance'.

They all piled out of the car and made their way to the gate whereupon the two men in plain clothes went to walk them down to the house. Immediately Janet put up her hand and stopped them.

"I am quite sure we are able to find our way to our own front door," she said crisply. The pair retreated to their post and just as they got to the front door David whispered,

"I wouldn't mind betting that they have been in every room in this house and bugged them." They entered without breathing a word and David immediately went to his room and found paper and pen so that they may communicate without being heard. Melissa and Jordan became immediately aware of another visitor only this time they were obviously friendly and completely trustworthy. They now knew that it was time to share with their mum something of the mission and of course something of their friendship with an alien culture. In the meantime, David had gone back to his room to be greeted by one of the visitors who literally slipped into his hand a small device which would enable them as a family to silence all the bugs in the house. David bounded down the stairs feeling very pleased and very relieved. He went around the room holding this very small device and as he got to each listening device the lights on the sensor lit up and then faded. The bug had been silenced. David went systematically through every room in the house until every bug had been silenced. Then and only then did he feel comfortable. This caused much consternation in the surveillance van outside for they had heard nothing from the family and now they could no longer listen and couldn't understand how each device had failed.

Curiosity had certainly got the better of them and they were very soon marching down the path and knocking on the door. Now they just couldn't barge in and ask how it was possible for all the listening devices to be shut down. So, when the door opened, and they simply wanted to check that everything was in order. Since David had opened the door, he was more than happy to welcome them in, and he had the clear communication that this little machine could not only erase bugging devices but also memories and he was about to try it out. The gentlemen were invited to sit, and David positioned himself quite neatly behind each of them at different times and just simply pressed the button. The men were happily engaged in some conversation and were even offered a cup of tea and were quite oblivious to what had just taken place. They enjoyed their cup of tea and looked at each other blankly thinking that it was time they went. They arose and left, and the surveillance vehicle drove off because they could see no reason why they should remain in this location. All memory of their mission had been erased. Nevertheless, the two men at the gate remained, as for them nothing had changed, and they still needed to see and check just who came and went. It was now that time when the family needed to share the events of the last twelve months. Melissa and Jordan felt it was their responsibility to tell their mum just how all this came about. They started with that very first eventful night when they had both gone out to find the alien craft and they continued to share what had happened including the events at the hospital concerning Alistair, the events at the shopping mall in Ballarat concerning Lyn and Lucy and the amazing healing that took place and David's eventual introduction and meeting. During the whole of the explanation they watched Janet's anxiety literally dissipate in front of their eyes. She took it all in and from time to time questioned certain aspects of their story but never once doubting the veracity of what they were sharing. Janet had known for a long time that there was something special by way the of bond between her three children and she had seen them grow in a manner which belied their age and experience. At least now she had an explanation as to just how quickly and beautifully they had matured and realized that with people like her three, and obviously others there was great hope for the world.

They continued to sit around and chat for now they needed to start letting family know of George's passing. David certainly volunteered to ring the family in Australia, and it would give him a chance to speak with Emma which he always looked forward to, even in these circumstances. The mobile certainly had its uses and they all had an opportunity to speak to Ken and Nancy. They were shocked and very saddened to learn of George's sudden and untimely death and they promised they would be on the first aero plane to England and hoped they would arrive in time for the funeral. Next, they had to make arrangements for the service and contact the funeral home. They would also need to plan the service and make a list of all the people who would want to celebrate George's life.

It was just then as dawn was breaking there was a knock at the door. David instinctively arose and went to the door and there stood Alistair. David was surprised as there was no way Alistair could have known about George's death. He was immediately invited in and explained that he had felt some compulsion to come. They looked at him and shared the news that everybody in the family knew about their mission and that Alistair was a part of the mission.

Alistair was dumbfounded by the news of their dad's passing and immediately expressed his deep sorrow to the family. He was visibly overcome because he'd got to the stage of looking at George as maybe as surrogate dad and he shared that very thought with the family. They were very warmed by his honesty and his respect for their dad.

Alistair then said that he needed to come to the point for he felt the communication he had from their alien friends that he needed to go back to the site in the woods and to erase the memory banks of those machines and those of the men involved in the operation. They all agreed that Alistair would be the right person because he was not known to any of the people in MI6. He hadn't been detected at the site and David knew that this was very important for those details to be removed and never see the light of day again. David quickly slipped the device into Alistair's pocket and accompanied him to the gate where the two men were keeping guard and whilst David engaged them Alistair happily used the machine to erase the whole matter and the memory of their task.

There were still many things that needed to be addressed and David lead the way with his first important question,

"Mum just how long will we survive financially given that Dad will no longer bring in a regular pay packet?"

"Well I do know that your dad was very thoughtful with this part of his life, and I know that he had a very substantial insurance policy in the event of anything happening. We need to find that and check just how much that will provide. I also know that where he worked, he had an extremely good superannuation scheme and that also will now become available." David spoke again,

"Do you have even a ballpark figure of what assets we might have, then?" Janet was taken aback for a moment and couldn't quite understand David's preoccupation with money. He could see that the questions were uncomfortable, but then explained,

"It is possible that we may need to leave this country because there is no doubt that MI6 will be after us, and it would be nice to know that we could relocate somewhere where we would be relatively free from their clutches."

Suddenly this all started to make sense to Janet for she could see that MI6 would not be that happy to let this go especially now with the friendship with beings outside of this world.

Alistair had now reached the woods and was extremely cautious as he approached the clearing. He could now hear voices clearly and to his amazement the equipment was being loaded and taken away. He was now too late it seemed, he inched ever closer remembering all the details he had noted when he got home the of the previous night. He could now see men busy moving trucks into position to load on the equipment and there was but one man watching the equipment. Just at that moment as he moved forward a twig snapped under his foot and he was immediately observed by the one guard. He marched straight over to Alistair and pulled him up by the shirt asking him what he thought he was doing; this was a protected site. Alistair blurted,

"I didn't see any signs and I saw this equipment and was curious," and with that pointed to the nearest piece of equipment and asked, "What does that do?" The soldier instinctively turned around and looked. In that instant Alistair had the machine out and on him. He turned around and looked at Alistair with a blank look and wondered why this student should be here. He then walked over to the others who were preparing the truck and removing the covers and questioned what on earth they were doing out in the bush at this time of the day. That was Alistair's opportunity and he took it with both hands. Within seconds his machine had erased all the stored data. The drivers by now were more concerned with loading the equipment than with this intrusion, they needed to get on with it and in that moment, Alistair disappeared into the woods again and nobody thought any more about him. His mission was now accomplished, and he could go home feeling very relieved. He received a very warm encouraging message from his friends from outer space which lifted his spirits no end.

By now the events of the last twelve hours had caught up with Alistair and suddenly he felt quite tired and weary. Eventually home was in sight and he made his way up to the front door put his key in and opened it quietly. It was now early morning and in fact time for school. As he came into the kitchen his mum was waiting and looked at him quizzically. He began to explain the events of the last twelve hours with his focus on the loss suffered by David, Jordan and Melissa and of course, their mum.

Sheila was positively distraught at the news and immediately wanted to call the family and express her sorrow and sadness at their loss. Alistair dissuaded her for the moment and suggested that it would be more appropriate if she were to go around and visit them at some time during the day. Sheila certainly felt that was good counsel but still wanted to ring to let them know she was thinking of them. After that very brief phone contact the two of them sat down and talked about what the day might look like. Alistair felt it was just too much to put in a full day at school and they decided it would be better if he stayed home and caught up with much needed sleep. This was agreed and he sat down and as any young man of sixteen years, tucked into a hearty breakfast and an exceptionally hot mug of tea. This finished he took himself to his bedroom where he showered and retired for much needed rest. His brain still couldn't switch off from all the events of the last twenty-four hours, eventually he dozed and went into a very deep sleep.

Sheila decided to call work and explain that she needed to see her friends who had just lost their father and her husband. She then made her way the bus station and waited patiently, by now it was mid-morning and the air was still quite brisk. She had waited but ten minutes as the bus glided quietly to a standstill. She waited momentarily as several passengers alighted, punched her ticket and sat herself down. The day was quite cloudy but there was green everywhere and she was happy to sit and reflect and take in the scenery as the bus meandered through both country and village streets alike. Some thirty minutes had elapsed and by now she was nearing her stop, she pressed the bell and made her way to the exit and then another ten minutes of walking she would be at her destination. The street seemed eerily deserted as she opened their front gate and walked quietly and nervously to the front door.

She had been quietly rehearsing what she would say once inside. Sheila then pressed the button and the sounds of the chimes reverberated through the house. The door opened slowly, and David was there to greet her, initially he reached out his hand which Sheila took in her hands and instinctively let go and put her arms around this towering man. David paused momentarily and then feeling the warmth and compassion of her embrace relented whilst feeling some of his pain dissipate. He was taken by surprise for a moment, but his gratitude quietly overcame his surprise. He could feel himself really warming to Sheila like a very dear friend and it did feel so good. David then showed her to a seat in the lounge and within moments Janet and the rest of the family had assembled and there were hugs all round and it felt the words were superfluous. By now Melissa had put the kettle on and was preparing to make a cup of tea for everybody. Meanwhile David had gone into the kitchen and looked for whatever he could find by way of biscuits and cake and soon returned armed with two plates full.

Janet then began to share the events of the last thirty-six hours, including Melissa's awareness of George's presence at the hospital. Sheila could scarcely take it in, though she knew only too well from Alistair's experience that this young woman had some extraordinary gifts. It was obvious from the look which flitted across Sheila's face there was doubt of the reality of what Melissa had experienced. The two women were sitting together on the couch and Janet took Sheila's hand very gently and very lovingly and acknowledged her doubt. Of course, it's okay to doubt, this is not your everyday experience but what made it absolutely convincing for me was Melissa's description of George in a suit that Melissa had never seen. She began to smile, the suit had special memories for her because George wore it on the very first night that he took me out on a date and Melissa could not possibly have known nor could she have ever seen it as by the time the children came along it had long since gone to the charity shop. Melissa had described it in detail as it was quite unusual suit but at the time it made George look quite the man about town. By now the doubt was evaporating from Sheila's face and more importantly she felt strangely encouraged by the knowledge that this life was only part of the journey.

Suddenly Melissa spoke up again,

"Mum there is something more Dad shared, and it was that same night as he stood outside your front door saying goodnight." "This should be interesting," chipped in David. Janet could hardly hide her amusement, her smile continued to broaden. Melissa now continued,

You said to Dad,

"Will I see you again?" and Dad replied,

"You better believe it! What about tomorrow night?"

Sheila was watching Janet's face throughout the whole conversation and now there could be no doubt as to the veracity of these words. There were tears streaming down Janet's face as she relived what was a very special moment. She turned to Melissa instinctively reached out to her daughter and embraced her wholeheartedly, she then whispered in Melissa's ear,

"I am so blessed that you are our daughter," It was a special moment and one that would find its way into the treasury of high points in both their lives.

There was a loud knock at the door which brought David to attention immediately, he sprang from his seat and opened the door slowly. The family was startled by his sudden movement but even more so when two men pushed passed David forcibly knocking him to the floor. The family immediately recognized these two men as those who had tried to bully them at the hospital. There was a strong belief in Janet's mind they caused the stress in George's life which had led to his demise. By now David had got to his feet and stood squarely toe to toe the biggest of the two from MI6. The man went to push David and within a flash David taking his arm and moved to right up his back and brought him instantly to his knees.

"You realize young man that there is a penalty for assaulting an officer of the law." "Not when the officer makes the first aggressive move," responded David.

By now Janet had risen to her feet and encouraged David to release the distressed officer, which he did instantly. Somewhat shaken the man arose composed himself and began addressing Janet. He had hardly got halfway through his sentence when Janet cut him off in midsentence.

"How dare you intrude on this family in the midst of our grief, which has been caused in no small measure by your complete insensitivity and belligerent manner." "Furthermore, we were assured of privacy until at least we had been able to bury George and grieve properly."

He was immediately taken aback by the sheer forcefulness of the authority in Janet's voice. In the meantime, Jordan had been busy in his own way and was quickly making a phone call. Jordan's ingenuity with the computer knew no bounds and he had located the most senior official at MI6 and was patiently waiting for response. The connection was made, and Jordan briefly described the events from the time the two officers had arrived, whereupon the senior officer requested to speak with those two men. Jordan moved to the bigger of the two men and said rather nonchalantly,

"I think your boss would like a word with you right now." Jordan had now handed him the phone and the following conversation which wasn't entirely audible left the family in no doubt that their intruders had grossly overstepped the mark and were required to report back to head office without delay. Both men retreated hastily to the front door which David had already opened and beckoned them through. Notwithstanding the self-appointed leader looked at the family and questioned,

"How did you manage to convince all the officers stationed at your house to leave?" He was met by a solid wall of blank faces conveying beyond any doubt that they had no idea to what he was referring. He was determined to have the last word.

"I promise you I will get to the bottom of this, even if it kills me." By now David had become even more exasperated by his belligerent attitude and looked him in the face and retorted,

"That can be arranged." By now the door was closed, and the whole family breathed an audible sigh of relief.

Janet was visibly shaken by the whole saga and reflected,

"What an entirely objectionable human being." There were nods of agreement from each member of the family including Sheila who had witnessed the whole event. Normally Janet would not have encouraged David to be so forceful but on this occasion, she commended him for his forthright defence of the family. By now David was standing by his mother's side with his arm firmly around her shoulders and giving her the support. This would normally have come from George when she had been subjected to such intrusive and offensive behaviour. In the meantime,

Jordan had rung back the senior officer at MI6 and reported the whole conversation at the door, including David's last comment, whilst the mobile loudspeaker was turned on. What followed stunned everyone.

"Young man I was very patient with you and removed my officers forthwith, please let this be an end to the matter and do not contact me on this number again."

Janet had now gained her composure and motioned to Jordan to hand her his phone. At this point she launched into a well-ordered tirade of the whole event.

"I do not take kindly to the intrusive belligerent attitude of your officers, nor am I impressed with the forcible way they entered my home and least of all will I be treated like some common criminal, which is precisely what it felt like by your senior man. It is my considered opinion that my husband's death was brought about in no small measure by such an attitude initially and this stupid man has learned nothing from his initial entry into our home. His final words as he left were still full of venom and you sir need to take full responsibility for his behaviour. Believe me when I tell you this matter is not going to end here and be really clear I am not entirely without influence." There was a stony silence for some moments and eventually the man indicated quite brusquely that his officer was conducting an investigation of a most serious matter and that the children were right at the centre of that investigation. "I am deeply saddened by the loss of your husband and you have my word that there will be no further intrusions into your privacy before the funeral service."

The call ended and Janet sank slowly into her favourite armchair with a long deep sigh. The family knew all too well just how straightforward and grounded their mother was and it had always been a source of inspiration for them to follow in their dealings with people.

Sheila had sat there quietly taking it all in and feeling very grateful that she had such strong and responsible friends, and felt even more encouraged to think that Alistair had been welcomed by these three quite special young people knowing that they would encourage the essential qualities which she passionately believed were part of the real Alistair.

Now came the unenviable task of arranging George's funeral. Just two undertakers had been contacted and they were to get back to Janet with details of the hearse, the mourning car and the cost of the casket. The family sat around discussing the format the funeral would take, and at that point Sheila rose to leave. Janet motioned her to sit down persuasively saying that she had become quite part of the family and would appreciate her presence and contribution if she felt so inclined. Sheila resumed her seat and nodded affirmatively that she would be more than happy to offer any help she could, and in her heart, she felt quite honoured.

Timing was going to be important as they had contacted Janet's sister in Victoria. The latest information was that they were on their way to the airport and would be leaving that very night. It would be at least twenty-four hours before they arrived in London at Gatwick airport, and of course after flying for such a long time they would be in no shape to attend a funeral straightaway. It was decided that the funeral would take place in five days' time giving the Australian family time to overcome jetlag and lack of sleep.

That being decided the next thing would be to decide where the service of celebration would take place and of course that would largely depend on the two undertakers. The family agreed that it would be good to have the service at the funeral home. Janet reached for the phone and call the first of the two. After the two phone calls it was quite close in terms of which funeral home they went with. However, Janet was warmed by her engagement with the second funeral home. They seemed to be very much on the same page as the family and the facilities would more than adequately house all the mourners.

The mood had noticeably changed and the reality that George's death was starting to sink in for everyone. The colour in Janet's face had evaporated and she no longer seemed the strong confident woman who had spoken so firmly to the most senior officer at MI6. There was considerable silence as David, Jordan and Melissa were painfully aware there would be no more Dad eating breakfast, coming home later in the day, the emptiness of this reality was overshadowing the family. They sat together and realizing what important role Dad had played in all their lives even though very often it was almost a silent role. Dad had been so reliable and punctual in his work. He was enthusiastic about his research and all of that had now finished. Melissa was now feeling this keenly as she understood how much her dad had loved her and how encouraging he had been in her growth, maturing into a young woman. She pondered quietly; she could feel the tears streaming down her cheek. Yes, indeed she had encountered him in the world of spirit, but this was never going to be the same as him sitting at the breakfast table or coming home and sitting at the head of the table, happily engaging with his family. Janet had now moved next to Melissa on the couch and ever so gently had put her arm around her beautiful daughter and assured her that her tears were okay.

David especially responded very differently and could feel his anger rising. Just when he and his dad were not just getting on but were sharing some lovely things in common. Now in the midst this blossoming relationship between them, George had been taken away. He felt cheated and he looked for someone to blame. His thoughts immediately turned to the officer in charge who had originally directed his aggression to his dad. It would take time for David to come to terms with his anger and what it was that was really fuelling it, but he would get there and be both richer and wiser for that part of his journey.

CHAPTER 10

A FOND FAREWELL TO A QUIET ACHIEVER

THE DAY HAD passed without further upheaval, and Sheila supported the family with appropriate cups of tea, and small offerings of food, but no one seemed hungry, losing their dad had more than taken the edge of their appetite.

The finer details had all been worked through and the celebratory service would be on the Friday, giving the Australian family opportunity to rest and catch their breath. It was arranged that David would pick them up from Gatwick and bring them straight home, though sleeping arrangements had not been finalised. Sheila kindly offered to house some of the family at her home, but she did understand that it would be better for all the family to be together, for which David was quietly thankful. Andy would most certainly sleep in David's room as it had more space and Emma happily ensconced in Melissa's room with an extra bed. It only remained for Ken and Nancy to be housed and it was thought that Janet might use the spare room and Ken and Nancy would have her queen bed.

The sombre mood continued to prevail and nobody not even David fancied any food. A light meal had been prepared by the hand of Sheila with support from Melissa. The family sat down together, and it was so noticeable there was no George. There was no animated chatter but clearly a feeling of gloom over the whole meal table. It was then that Janet spoke up,

"Would George want us to be remembering him in this way, I think not, so let each one of us recall something that reminds us of his loving contribution to this family. Yes, it may bring sadness, but it will also bring us joy because he was such a strong person in his own quiet way." There was nodding assent from everybody who sat around the table and it was Jordan who began reminiscing about his dad. "You know I really appreciated the encouragement he gave to me when I spoke to him about Nikola Tesla, I so admire the fact that he didn't poor cold water on my enthusiasm. Rather he encouraged me to believe that such enthusiasm would take me a great deal further in life than cynicism which so often overpowers a young mind." Again, the whole family nodded their assent and recognized the true worth of their father's contribution. Melissa then confirmed Jordan's comments and shared her special bond between her and her father. She recounted the time on the farm after the snake incident and he had come to her recalling some of those important times when her skills came to the fore. She recounted the incident with Terry Cross and he then told her that the school had rung him in relation to her insistent behaviour on behalf on Alistair. He then pointed to the snake incident reminding her that there was something special that she had within her being.

"I looked at him in surprise having no notion he had taken so keen an interest in my life. He then put his arm around me and reminded me that I probably had some of my Irish grandmother's gift of fey, only more well developed." Suddenly there were tears flowing gently down Melissa's face and even the boys were blinking at her comments.

"This was my beautiful father affirming me in a way that I could only dream about." It wasn't long before the mood around the table had changed dramatically. Janet then reflected,

"I am so sure that our lovely man would now be celebrating his family from the other side and he would be so proud of the way each one of you is developing. I bet there is nothing that would make his heart sing more than our present conversation." David paused for a moment and cleared his throat,

"What really makes me sad and so very angry is the fact that in the last six months I felt I really got to know my dad on a different level. It felt as though we were becoming real mates and that bond was only getting deeper. I so appreciated his sharing of his own failures but that he used them to advantage and reminded me that failing was an important part of learning. I guess those moments are pure gold for me now and I feel so grateful that he was our dad." There were tears of sadness and joy trickling down Janet's face as her awareness of what a beautiful man she had married and now lost, but that his very essence would live on through his children and her heart was filled with gratitude. It was now getting quite late and Sheila needed go home. She suddenly realized that Alistair had been at home all day on his own, not that that worried her as she knew he was very responsible when left to his own devices. Sheila made her way to the door but not before saying a big thank you for allowing her to be part of the family. And of course, the family warmly embraced her before she left. David had offered to take her to the bus stop, but she felt that the walk would do her good and had respectfully declined.

The Australian family would arrive at approximately four thirty am on the Wednesday morning, so David needed to have everything in readiness the night before. This gave him a completely full day to make sure that the car and its accessories were in full functioning order. Jordan had been enlisted to help David checking all the lights were working. The oil and water needed to be checked. They would begin their task tomorrow morning. It now felt that every contingency had been taken care of and that nothing had been left to chance.

Janet had decided to dress George herself in preparation for the viewing in his casket. Melissa had agreed that she would help her mum with the selection of clothes with which she would dress him. The one thing that remained was the decision as to who would speak on behalf of the family, and it seemed that David would be that person, and that Janet would write her few of her own thoughts to be read out by her firstborn.

The family continued to sit and reminisce. There were more lovely stories shared, but Janet was in no doubt that their holiday to Australia was certainly one of the highlights for George. He had loved the open spaces on the farm and especially the bond that had developed between himself and Ken. They had found much to talk about whilst taking on the challenge of driving the big header whilst taking of the crop. They all agreed that that holiday had been the very best that they had enjoyed as a family and not only had they enjoyed their Australian cousins but as a family they had grown stronger and closer. It was certainly a very bright note on which to finish the evening, and it was clear that everyone was weighed down with the emotional stress. Janet wanted to acknowledge her family and so she embraced both David and Jordan on either side and then invited Melissa to do likewise so they formed a circle and just held each other for a long moment and Janet quietly gave thanks for her children who now where young adults in their own right so very mature and responsible. That being acknowledged, each of them made their way to their bedrooms knowing that tomorrow would bring its own set of challenges.

How gently the dawn began breaking through the windows of the Thomas household. It seemed to know that this family needed some gentleness from the elements, and for a moment the sun's rays were shrouded in misty cloud which conveyed its own sense of softness and comfort. Slowly the family arose to be very clear that their gentle warrior was no longer with them in body but was certainly with them in spirit and would be constantly watching over them. This time there was no bounding out of bed and there was no bustle at all in the kitchen and no smell of cooking food as the family made its way down to the dining area. There were of course warm hugs exchanged by all the family and a heartfelt good morning as well. It would be a simple breakfast that morning just cereal, fresh fruit and of course a cup of tea and toast. The mood at the breakfast table was quiet and restrained and was in only interrupted by the telephone. David immediately arose and took the call only to realize that it was his mum who needed to take the call. The caller immediately identified himself as the manager where George had worked for so long. He simply wanted to ask that he be given some time to speak at the funeral at which all his colleagues and workers wanted to attend. He spoke for a few minutes to Janet painting a picture of George that had not appeared on her landscape. That was not entirely surprising as he had spoken little about the people with whom he worked or the nature of his work. It was only latterly when prompted primarily by Melissa and Jordan that he had opened up a little more about the confidential nature of his work. Janet was again buoyed by his comments and was really looking forward to hearing from this man who had been his boss but also his esteemed colleague. Of course, he could speak, and she would look forward as would the rest of the family as to seeing a side of George which had hitherto been hidden.

By the time Janet had returned to the breakfast table most of the breakfast dishes had been put on the sink and the washing up was already in progress. Janet quietly finished her breakfast and shared with her family the upshot of the conversation with George's manager.

It was early Autumn, and the crispness of the air was evident as each breath issued in the stream of steam. By now David and Jordan had taken the car out of the garage and were systematically beginning their checks. Tyre pressures were first and only one tyre required attention. Then the spare tyre also needed to be checked and as one might expect it had not been used in a long time and the compressor was once again brought into life. Jordan then got into the driver's seat and began switching on the various light settings and David for his part checked to see whether any globes needed to be replaced. It was clear that the right-hand indicator rear was not functioning, and they needed to replace the globe. Only one more globe needed to be replaced and that one was very important as it was a stoplight. George was always very thorough and invariably kept spare parts for his motorcar but on this occasion no amount of searching provided them with the necessary replacements. David decided that he would get on his bike and go to the nearest auto shop where he could purchase the necessary globes. It took him all of ten minutes to purchase what was necessary and in the meantime, Jordan had been busy making sure both water and oil were at their required level. Brake fluid was checked and found to be okay, handbrake was fine and so the only remaining tasks to be done were the vacuuming and ensuring the boot was empty in readiness for luggage. The windscreen and rear window had been cleaned and the driving mirrors set up accordingly for David. They had needed to be adjusted as David was taller than his dad and sat higher in the car. One last job that needed to be done was to ensure that the lights on the high and low beam were in sync. That was done with the car facing into the garage so that the lights could be adjusted if need be. There was nothing further to be done and the car was then reversed into the garage ready just to drive straight out in the wee small hours of the morning. David and Jordan then made their way into the house to see if there was anything more they could help their mother with in preparation for George's funeral.

Janet and Melissa had everything in hand and the only thing they required was for David to take them to the funeral home where they could dress George accordingly. By the time they left the funeral home George had been dressed ever so smartly it was just past lunch time as they once again reversed the car into the garage ready again for the morning trip to Gatwick.

The family now gathered around the kitchen table and after a light lunch David shared there were two things that needed their immediate attention. The first would be the assets of the family and just how great the financial resources were. Janet had located the insurance policy and had spoken to them earlier that day and it was confirmed that there would be payout of some £850,000. The next question would be to look at George's superfund where he worked and again Janet had had the foresight to ask that question when she spoke to his manager earlier in the day. He had indicated that he would ring back later in the day and almost on cue the phone rang. However, it was not the manager but the senior officer from MI6 indicating that they would like to begin interrogating the family as soon as the service had concluded. Janet was somewhat taken aback by the request and wanted the family to have time to speak with the other mourners when there would be light refreshments served. It was agreed, but Janet asked just what was so important that they needed to have the family at their headquarters. The officer responded curtly "I think your young people would best be able to tell you what this is about," and left it at that. The receiver was put down and Janet looked quite pale. Her young family watched her face and guessed most of the conversation. David then nominated the second and perhaps more pressing issue of just how they planned to deal with the interrogation of MI6. It was more than clear that those two men who had initially confronted George were not about to let this go. It was at this point that Melissa raised the question regarding their alien friends and that on this occasion the family would be looking for some guidance and insight as to how to proceed. All of them had been thinking just how they might deal with this when the time eventually arrived for them to revisit MI6 headquarters. Now was the time to pool their collective wisdom. "Well we can be clear that the records that they thought they had in the woods are non-existent. Alistair was very clear that the device had worked a treat and they would know by now that they have no evidence." David continued,

"It seems to me that our original story of heading off to a late-night movie is still valid and we had all said that on the night before we went to the hospital." There were nods of agreement from the other two. It would be good to ask them to show us the evidence, however, our individual responses would need to be most convincing. There was clear agreement from all three, and Janet who had always encouraged her family to be truthful began to recognize that the stakes were incredibly high. It was at this point that the communication from their friends from space began in earnest.

"Yes, the plan could work, but you need n to consider every contingency, because discovery at this point would put the whole mission in jeopardy and in the event of exposure, we would need to abort." At this stage Janet was not party to this telepathic form of communication but simply watched with interest the responses of her children. They looked at each other and realized the gravity of the situation. They could think of nothing more they could effect from their perspective. Janet looked on curiously as she was aware plans were being made of which she had no consciousness and the visitors drew this to the attention of the young family. They immediately filled in Janet as to the initial plan and the gravity of the situation and said simply, "We will await further communication from our friends."

"There are immediately two possibilities, firstly we need to erase the memory banks of those two officers, one of whom you have found I think the word you used was obnoxious. That in itself might prove difficult to effect and there is a distinct possibility that because this level of emotional intensity is so strong, we may not be able to remove it completely. We shall just have to wait and see, and you can be sure that those two men will certainly be present at the service on Friday." David had made that the mental note that Alistair needed to return the device as soon as possible and a phone call would be made just as soon as these matters have been resolved. "The second option is a last resort and it would mean our direct intervention into your lives. Melissa you would remember the first night in your bedroom when you saw one of us leave your room by simply walking through the walls. If needs be, we would remove you at the most opportune time and relocate you to our distant craft where you have already visited. This poses serious problems because you would appear to have disappeared without trace and it would likely create more problems than it would solve and eventually you would need to return to your home and to your mother. There is one final solution and it is one that we are very loath to use." A faint smile flitted across David's face and yes, he had guessed it. "If by some misadventure our obnoxious friend's life came to an end, then most certainly our problems would be at an end." David's smile broadened considerably as he warmed to the idea by the minute but was initially at loss to see what kind of misadventure could possibly befall him. "We need to let you digest all that we have spoken of and then we will communicate further."

David continued his role as spokesperson for Jordan and Melissa and briefly outlined the options that were before them. Janet could scarcely take it in, she just sat in silence almost pinching herself to ensure that this was indeed the reality. She pondered the faces of all her family and saw the solemnity of the occasion but still had little idea of what was at stake. One thing she did know was that this group of adventurers would choose the wisest action and would work from there. It was agreed that they would go with option one and simply try hopefully to erase the memory of the last two witnesses.

With that decision having been made David immediately went to the phone and called Alistair and suggested that they meet as soon as possible so that the device could be returned to David in readiness for the service to be held on the Friday. They discussed long and hard where they should meet, and it was felt in the interests of safety that Alistair would come to the home as he had been a regular visitor. One of the things that had sharpened for David was an energy vibration that allowed him not only to sense imminent danger, but also a sense that he had been singled out for constant attention, which in fact proved to be the case.

The phone continued to ring and eventually George's boss returned the call giving Janet information that she needed. She was very pleasantly surprised with the figure simply because the company itself had matched George's contribution with the two for one, which meant a total payout of just over £900,000. Janet thanked him profusely and expressed her gratitude of the wisdom of the group in providing for their workforce. This had taken a huge load off her shoulders, for it would mean she could pay off the small mortgage and if needs be, sell the house and maybe, as David had indicated relocate to another country. Of course, it was clear in David's mind which country he would want to be relocating to, but they had not come to that bridge and therefore they did not need to make that decision.

Janet then sat the family down yet again and discussed what would be available to them in the immediate future and that it would be a family decision as to what would happen if indeed, they were to move and of course whether they would stay in England. The events of the next three days would no doubt determine their future, but no one could anticipate the outcome of the service on Friday.

It wasn't long before the doorbell rang and David in his customary caretaking role went to answer and anticipated that in fact it would be Alistair. As he opened the door, he was greeted by Alistair's enormous grin who was more than delighted to be visiting his 'extended family'. He ventured a comment that he had seen a solitary gentleman standing at the end of the street and guessed that it was yet another plain clothes detective. David had right to be suspicious and felt sure that this guy was there primarily for his benefit just to check on his coming and going. Alistair's was warmly welcomed by the family and it was in fact time for a cup of tea, so they all sat down while this time Melissa did the honours. Alistair shared the news of the man at the end of the street with the family and David simply reconsidered the notion that it was probably more for his benefit than anybody else's. However, David was not about to let this one go, and suggested a plan that least might flush him out. The plan would be for Melissa and Jordan to go and casually enquire that he seemed new to these parts and to ask him if was he waiting for someone? Then Jordan would straight out confront him and just say to him that he looked like a detective and Melissa would then watch his face and read him accordingly and know beyond any doubt that this expression would confirm or deny his role.

"The lovely thing is he would be none the wiser." Melissa smiled,

"Wow this is going to be like taking candy from a baby," for she knew all too easily how to read body language in a most unobtrusive way. The cup of tea was drunk, and then Alistair was on his way. the only thing was he wanted to stay around to see if in fact he was a policeman, but he needed to get home and spend some time with his mum. Within five minutes of Alistair's departure, Melissa and Jordan casually made their way to the end of the street and observed the man in clear view leaning on the fence. They were making the pretence of walking around the entire block and as they approached, they had their questions ready. "We couldn't help noticing that you are waiting, are you waiting for someone in particular?" "No not really," replied the man. Jordan then volunteered.

"I have not seen you around these parts before." there was a stony silence and the look on his face showed even more discomfort. Melissa then took an entirely different tack to that which had been agreed upon. She began,

"Should we be concerned about your presence, we are constantly warned of men like you loitering in our neighbourhood, Jordan I think we should call the police and report this man."

This threw him completely off guard and he opened his coat and flashed his warrant card and before he put it away both Jordan and Melissa had looked at its authenticity for which they had every right. With that Jordan turned to Melissa and said,

"It's really nice to know that our friendly police service is looking out for us in our neighbourhood." And with that they both offered their hand of friendship and shook his warmly as it was reciprocated and continued their evening walk. They continued their walk laughing and joking and when they were well out of earshot, they gave each other high fives celebrating their mission had been accomplished. Within fifteen minutes they were back home sharing the event and just how all it all unfolded. David looked at Melissa with a coy smile and simply acknowledged,

"I should have just trusted you anyway you were quite brilliant."

David reflected that he was right to get Alistair to come, rather than for him to venture abroad. It was obvious that he was a marked man and that this was largely due to his run-in with that of obnoxious man who had been so aggressive with their dad. It was time for an early night as David was aware that 3 am tomorrow would come around all too quickly, so he quickly showered and made off to bed. It had been a full day for all the family and they too were not long in following him.

The high-pitched beeping momentarily startled David from a very restful sleep, he switched on the light and made quickly for the bathroom. He returned to his room and dressed quickly ready for the drive to the airport. He made his way down to the kitchen and to his surprise there was his mum preparing a light breakfast for the journey. He was particularly grateful and enjoyed the brief conversation before he headed out the door and down the road. Janet listened for the car until its sound no longer disturbed the night air and then quietly and calmly, she took herself back to bed thinking about what needed to be done when her Australian family arrived later that morning.

It was usually about a thirty to thirty-five-minute drive but on this occasion, it would be less as the traffic was minimal at this hour of the morning. David had mixed feelings certainly the sadness of losing his dad when their relationship was just really taking off and of course the thrill of seeing his uncle and aunt and more especially Emma who no doubt had stolen his heart. He couldn't conceal the tinge of excitement that he was feeling. He was playing one of his now favourite CDs, and as a result of his martial arts training, he had looked for music that would help him with his inner control. He pondered the gentle melody of Canon in D by Pachelbel. He began to wonder whether it might be suitable as a wedding march for when he and Emma were to be married, and then he stopped himself thinking that he might just be jumping the gun, while smiling at the same time. He continued to listen to more of the composers of that era noticing how soothing the music was. This was certainly not his first choice of music, but as he continued to work with his martial arts instructor, he had talked about the kind of music that would encourage a meditative state.

David was only a about seven minutes from the car park at Gatwick and they were standing at the baggage claim and were in the process of loading their luggage when he heard his mobile phone ringing demanding his attention. He pulled over quickly and retrieved his phone and listened, sure enough it was Emma and he could hear her squeals of delight as he said "Hello." She very quickly let him know that they had landed, and they were at the baggage claim and in the process of loading their bags onto to airport trolleys. Emma didn't think there would be any hold- ups in customs. David knew his timing could not have been better and he said he would be there in the next ten minutes to pick them up. He drove quietly up to the arrival bay and could see the family waiting by the curb side, the car drew gently to a standstill and he instinctively pulled the boot lock. David was out in a flash and warmly greeting his uncle, aunt, Andy and of course he saved the best till last with a totally consuming embrace of Emma as well is giving her a big smooch. David was happy enough to load the luggage and managed to get it all into the boot, save one overnight bag which could be easily managed across the back seat. Ken sat in the front, Andy and the rest of the family sat in the back with Nancy in the middle and Emma sitting directly behind David. The chatter was non-stop, but the main focus had been on Janet and just how she was coping with such a sudden loss. David was keen to share some of the family conferencing that had taken place over the last two days and indeed paid attention to the difference his dad's empty chair had made to all the family. He shared how Janet had changed the course of the afternoon when she reminded them that this was the last thing that George would have wanted, and she had invited each one of them to share their most memorable experiences of their relationship of their dad. He continued to elucidate what a change had come over the family and how that one act changed the mood in the house entirely. The family was quiet for a moment and then Nancy remarked,

"That sounds just the kind of thing Janet would do, she is so insightful, and it certainly had the desired outcome. Well done to your mum, David." David nodded in agreement,

"There is no doubt we have had wonderful parents for role models," and then he threw a glance at Nancy and said,

"You and uncle have done very much the same." This time Andy and Emma nodded affirmatively, and they took their mum's hand and gave it a big squeeze. David couldn't believe that they were only two minutes from home as he turned into the street and believe it or not there was the plain clothes detective still on duty. David gave him a courteous wave as they turned the corner which immediately raised questions from the rest of the family. David said. "When we get inside, I will explain everything, and I will let Melissa tell you in her own words how she sussed him out." It was now moving passed five a.m. as Janet opened the front door and literally threw her arms around her sister.

"I can't tell you how good it is to see you all and how absolutely thrilled I am that you are here to be with us and to celebrate George's life." They were all lifted by Janet's whole demure and once inside there were long hugs from each member of the family. In the meantime, David had been busy along with Andy unloading the luggage and taking it to the various rooms. By now Melissa and Jordan were partially dressed and had come down to welcome their Australian family. Melissa took Emma by the hand and led her to her bedroom which she would be sharing for the next week at least,

"We have so much to share with you," Melissa said ruefully. Emma immediately replied,

"We know about the dilemma you face and yes we are absolutely here to support you in every possible way we can." Melissa was neither surprised by Emma's admission of knowing or by her unfailing support. However, Emma was intrigued by the plain clothes detective at the end of the street, so in the next few moments Melissa filled her in on how conspicuous they made him look.

Emma chuckled to herself "I bet he felt a right prat and so he should. I am amazed that he is still at his post and now my guess is that he is reporting back to headquarters that we have arrived." Melissa nodded in agreement and then suggested that after a cup of tea the family might like to catch up on some much needed sleep. The two of them had already begun making their way down to the kitchen and they were closely followed by David and Andy. Happily, all the sleeping arrangements had been covered then after quite the briefest cup of tea the Talbot's made their way to their beds.

By now the morning had well and truly dawned, David Jordan and Melissa were in no mind to go back to bed so they sat with their mum in the lounge planning what they might do for the day. David still hadn't worked out what he finally wanted to say at his dad's farewell. He felt it needed some more refinement and since there was no activity in the kitchen, he took himself off there with his laptop. He continued to change and add to the eulogy until he felt how it needed to be. He then came back into the lounge and asked if the family would like to hear it so as to check really represented the whole family. There was immediate assent and so David read it out to them. The family eulogy had really summed up the essence of their dad, it was to the point and not to flowery. David felt pleased with the feedback and was now content that he had really summed up his dad as a 'Quiet Achiever.'

They day was interspersed with many visitors who had come to pay their respects to the family. Janet had made it clear in her notices in the paper that rather than flowers for George they would make a donation to the Heart Foundation. What had taken the family by surprise was the number of men who had worked with George over all those years had come into the home and just broken down, many of them with tears streaming down their faces. It was Janet who was able to console them and certainly not the other way around. Many of them had left feeling uplifted by the energy that pervaded the whole family.

It was late in the afternoon and darkness was beginning to envelop the street, there was a stirring from upstairs and one by one the family made their way down to the kitchen. Andy was the first to reappear followed closely by Emma, and she did look quite a sight with her hair still tousled and all over her face. Nevertheless, it didn't faze David one bit and he reached out and embraced her and was about to give her another big kiss when Janet gently chided him about the time and the place. However, Emma had no such parental oversight and so she firmly took David's face in her hands and gave him a lovely long, good morning kiss that would last him a lifetime just thinking about it. Janet paused for a moment and smiled because it took her back to that very first flush of love that she and George had experienced in those early days. It wasn't long before Ken and Nancy appeared feeling much more relaxed yet knowing that their body clock would still take some time to make the necessary adjustment. Jordan, Melissa, Emma and Andy busied themselves in the kitchen and were happy enough in the preparation of a light supper. There was chicken in gravy, creamed mashed potatoes and green peas. The adults had sat in the lounge room sharing the events of the last few days. David for his part had spoken of his role in delivering the family eulogy and Ken asked if he might be allowed a few words in paying tribute to George. They then all gathered for supper and the conversations continued. For David it been a very long day and he was more than happy to make his way up to his bedroom and even though the family had slept handsomely for the greater part of the day they were still happy enough to retire early and tomorrow would be another day. The lights went out one by one and the house was bathed in its customary silence and darkness, but still lurking under the streetlight was a single valiant detective keeping watch on who might be coming and going.

The morning was gentle and the sun had continued to persist in breaking through the cloud cover but with little success, there was an occasional shaft of light reminding everyone that Autumn was upon them, the trees were looking quite bare as they swayed gently in the breeze marking the change in the season. It was so different in Australia as the gum trees never really lost their leaves even in the bleakest of winters. Andy looked out of the window to be greeted by an array of fleecy white clouds as they meandered across the sky. He didn't dare open the window recognizing that as gentle as the breeze would be it would also be very cold. He was extremely grateful that he had packed his fur-lined duffel coat, however, for the moment an all wool jumper would be sufficient to keep out the cold. They made their way down to the kitchen only to find the rest of the family was assembled at the breakfast table. On this occasion a light breakfast was in order and an array of breakfast cereals adorned the table. By now everybody was helping themselves and Janet had managed to pull out some stewed fruit from the freezer thus giving a further adjunct to breakfast. Most of the conversation centred around how everybody had slept, and that there was consensus that it had been a good night and that everybody had begun to feel normal again despite the jetlag.

There had been nothing planned for the day except maybe a walk to the woods and beyond just so that everybody could get their bearings. They discussed this at length and wondered what their plain clothes detective would make of the family going in different directions. They would need to ensure that he was aware of those different directions and maybe giving him a challenge as to who he might follow if indeed he chose to follow anyone. They did make a joke of it all but underneath all of this they knew there was a very serious element underlying his presence. They realized that after tomorrow when the funeral had concluded they knew that they would have to front up at MI6. It was interesting that they spoke of this with Melissa who seemed the least perturbed. She had demonstrated incredible insight when dealing with things that confronted her on the spur of the moment. In contrast David and Jordan needed time to prepare themselves, and some of the day was spent rehearsing the plans they had put in place.

The day unfolded at a leisurely pace and about mid-morning the whole family ventured out and much to their surprise when they reached the end of the street there was no plain clothes detective. They knew the lady in the corner house very well and as she came out to put her wheelie bin out, they asked her if she had seen a man who had been occupying his post now for several days. She smiled and with a deliberate flicking of the eyes indicated that he was inside her house. She ventured she had taken pity on him being out in the cold and it offered him a cup of tea and a piece of toast, which he gladly accepted. Just at that moment he appeared in the doorway and straight away walked down the pathway to resume his post. Nobody said anything to him but simply acknowledged his presence with a smile, and then as planned the family split up into three groups and went in different directions. There was a little consternation on his face and moments later he was on his mobile phone obviously reporting, however, he couldn't possibly tail all three. Melissa and Emma headed in the direction the woods whilst David, Andy and Jordan continued around the block and the adults crossed the road and continued down the street. He made no immediate move to follow but it was obvious that he was intrigued by the girls' decision to head off in the direction of the woods. He waited some time before making his move and watched them carefully from a distance. What he hadn't noticed was that the boys themselves had hidden in one of the gardens where they knew they would be safe They knew that their cover would not be blown and then they in turn decided to follow him. Melissa knew this part of the woods particularly well as she had traversed them with both Jordan and David many, many, times. The girls talked and laughed together they stopped and looked at plants and particularly looked for squirrels who played noisily amongst the trees. They were more than aware that their friendly detective was keeping a respectful distance, so they decided it was time for some more fun. Melissa had primed Emma as to the very best hiding place in all the woods. Without a sound, the two girls slipped noiselessly out of view and waited. It wasn't long before he ventured past with a look of complete consternation on his face. He couldn't believe these two had so effectively given him the slip and he began to panic racing off deeper into the woods.

About ten minutes had passed and the girls knew it would be safe to make a hasty retreat which they did. It wasn't long before they teamed up with the boys and made their way back home. As they got to the corner of their street, they were surprised to find another and a different detective on duty. They smiled pleasantly and Melissa as cool as you like suggested that he might like to go and find his mate was probably quite hopelessly lost in the woods. The man didn't know which way to look and felt silence was certainly the better option on this occasion. By now the young people had reached home and were laughing and joking about the fun they had at the expense of the police service. They burst through the front door chatting and laughing and were greeted by their parents. They spoke at length about the whole incident continuing to laugh about how they led this poor man a right merry dance. The adults listened with interest and couldn't but be impressed by the cunning behaviour of the girls. Ken then remarked,

"Isn't it great when you can play them at their own game and beat them so convincingly. I have to say young Melissa, I am totally impressed with your presence of mind". Melissa smiled quietly and her mum supported the comment with alacrity. Jordan then raised the possibility of contacting the local press as he had made some connections over the last twelve months. It was decided that this would only rub salt into the wound, and it was decided to let it go. The boys then decided that they may just make another brief trip around the block and headed out the door. They reached the end of the street in no time and were surprised to find a couple of men chatting quite amiably. Jordan immediately recognized one of them as one of his contacts in the press and was curious as to why he had stopped and what had grabbed his attention. The detective was very keen to move the boys on and suggested they do so without delay, but Jordan had already asked the question whether the lost detective had been found? The detective was becoming visibly agitated and suggested that if they didn't move on quickly, he would charge them with making a public nuisance. They happily moved on but of course that threat to this group of young men only aroused the curiosity of the press man further. He continued to ask questions, before long he too was given short shift. They continued to make their way around the block chatting about what had just taken place. Then something quite strange happened. As they passed this house Jordan and David always noticed that dog came bounding up to the gate and barked ferociously, but on this occasion the dog bounded up to the gate and wagged its tail profusely at the presence of Andy. Both Jordan and David remarked about Andy's affinity with animals, he stopped momentarily to pat the dog and the dog jumped up at the gate licking him profusely.

"It's funny you should mention this, but I noticed this change in chemistry after our last visit to the larger spacecraft. I suspect that what they loaded into my DNA has in fact impacted on my relationship to animals. It's been a real blessing to work with all the animals on the farm but especially the dogs. They have responded amazingly and herding in sheep which was always a challenge is now an absolute breeze because not only do the sheep respond better but the dogs likewise." Jordan and David nodded in assent and they described what just happened with this very aggressive dog as being a minor miracle. They said,

"Whenever we go this way, we are always careful to either be very quiet or to make sure the gate is firmly closed." The owners usually made sure that the gate was firmly closed and locked because if it caused any damage to anybody the animal would be immediately put down and they certainly didn't want to lose their good guard dog. The rest of the journey home passed without incident or comment except that Jordan couldn't help wondering how come that press guy was there on the corner speaking to the detective, nevertheless it was very serendipitous.

It was now mid-afternoon, and the boys shared their story and the coincidence of the press guy speaking with the detective. Janet looked immediately at Jordan and before she could mouth the question, he emphatically denied having called him, believing that it was better to let sleeping dogs lie. The whole family had another good round of mirth at the expense of the police service, which they believed was working closely with the MI6. Ken and Nancy had been filled in on the details surrounding Melissa, Jordan and David and both could not contain their incredulity. Ken had gone as far as to say,

"I suppose there was no mention of little green men." No doubt, and the adults had taken it all largely with a pinch of salt, and Janet had played along with it all the time but knowing that all these young people had a very special connections from outer space. Just at that moment the doorbell rang and David as usual stepped up to his new role. He looked cautiously through the peephole and saw that it was Jordan's press friend and motioned to Jordan that he might like to come and speak with him. Jordan immediately threw a glance towards his mother and with a casual nod of her head suggested that he might as well finish the story now.

Alec as he was known to Jordan wanted more information and at the same time had one eye cocked to the corner of the street making sure that he wasn't observed. Jordan took him around by the side of the garage and told him of the whole fanciful story, about the three of them travelling deep in the woods at night to meet an alien spacecraft. At that point Alec lost interest but had to admit that the behaviour of the police seemed quite strange and out of character. However, he decided he would take it to his editor and maybe they would run a story spoofing the whole idea. Alec left discreetly making sure that he wasn't observed and hopefully that would be an end to all the goings-on.

The remainder of the afternoon passed without incident as the family sat around chatting about old times. The evening was already closing in and Jordan and Melissa had ventured outside looking carefully at what little of the night sky they could see. The clouds engulfed most of the night sky and the moon was high overhead, it was as Alfred Noyes had written so long ago "The moon was a ghostly galleon tossed upon cloudy seas." it was quite eerie to be watching the vastness and the majesty of the heavens and both of them had experienced the thrill of seeing it from an entirely different vantage point.

"If only our aunt and uncle knew the truth about us, it would blow their socks off," mused Jordan. Melissa nodded in assent but was quite sure that one day they too would become aware of Andy and Emma's role in the future of the planet. They both shivered in unison and they knew it was time to go in and it was also time for bed. Tomorrow was the big day, and everybody would be ready to say a fond farewell to George's body. The family was acutely aware that his spirit and his presence would overshadow them the rest of their lives.

Amazingly the clouds had cleared in the night and the sun was lightly kissing the raindrops as its hues descended upon all in its path. The family was awoken by the sheer brilliance of the day and each one felt the warmth of the sun reaching into their own heart. Ken almost bounded down the stairs and went straight to the front door opened and in walked outside as if to make sure it wasn't a dream. He came back in rubbing his hands with glee and feeling totally alive. It was only a matter of minutes before all the family arrived and Janet as usual was busy in the kitchen, only this time she was ably assisted by Nancy.

Breakfast again was light, and everybody served themselves and there was much animated conversation. Nevertheless, underneath all this there was a heaviness, it wasn't to do with George's farewell but very clearly it would be the young family's return to MI6. Melissa was more upbeat about it than either David and Jordan, but she also aware of the gravity of the situation and needed to have all her perceptive factors functioning at their highest order.

None of the family had wanted to go to the viewing, they had all said the same thing, they wanted to remember George as he had been and for Ken that had been on the farm out of Glenorchy sitting in the driver's seat of their big header, enjoying every moment in air conditioned comfort and the challenge of handling such a big machine.

The service was scheduled to commence at 1 p.m. and the family needed to leave at twelve thirty a.m. They had ordered two funeral cars and the only thing that needed to be done was for the family to be dressed and ready at the scheduled time. They had all taken great care in their selection of dress for the day and so after breakfast had finished and dishes cleared away, the time had had reached ten thirty am. It seemed everybody wanted to use the shower at once and eventually the bathrooms were quiet and everyone was busy ensuring that there was nothing out of place by way of the clothing on their person. They had agreed earlier that when they were ready, they would assemble in the lounge room downstairs and slowly but surely the entire family presented just after noon. David had ensured that his speech was ready and that he had the device which hopefully would erase all the memories of the two MI6 officers. He had had several conversations with Andy as to how to use it and where he might keep it. It was essential that this device never find its way into the hands of MI6, as it would certainly give them all the ammunition, they needed to implicate the three of them. Andy understood this only too well and of course at that stage there would be suspicion falling on him and that was something he couldn't risk. He spent some considerable time reflecting on the gravity of the matter, knowing that he couldn't afford to make any mistakes.

The mourning cars arrived precisely at twelve thirty the chauffeurs were superb in escorting the family into the vehicles and the drive to the funeral home was both respectful and deliberate. The cars glided to a gentle standstill, whereupon a tall well-built gentleman who obviously had an earpiece in, reached forward and opened the door. As it happened it was David's door that he opened, and he immediately sprang out and requested that he move right away from this area. David was in no doubt that this was another member of MI6 and his intrusion into the family was not welcome in the least. The man immediately retorted, "Excuse me sir but I have a job to do and this is part of my job." At this point and Ken came up alongside David and whispered something in the man's ear, he nodded in acknowledgement and backed away allowing the family to move to the chapel. Janet began to look around and couldn't quite believe the sea of cars that had arrived at the funeral home.

"Wherever are we going to seat all these people?" was her first concern, "I never in my wildest dreams imagined that George had such a large circle of friends, and most of them were families."

They made their way into the chapel and the attendants were scurrying everywhere organizing for extra seating.

Meanwhile David had colluded with Andy, pointing out the most obnoxious man he had ever met from M I6. He was sitting right at the back trying to look inconspicuous and frankly wasn't doing it very well. David immediately went over to him and engaged him face to face. The officer pointed out that there would be no escaping. For his part David indicated, they were more than happy to accompany him to MI 6 headquarters. Meanwhile Andy had come up behind him with his hands in his pocket and aimed at the device fairly at the back of his head. The only difficulty was that he couldn't be sure the device had successfully erased the memories of the two officers. But he did it several times and to both gentlemen who were none the wiser. Andy then took his seat next to David expressing considerable concern that he was uncertain as to how effective he had been. David acknowledged with a nod.

The service was an amazing tribute to this 'Quiet Warrior'. George's boss was the first to speak and what he said revealed a side of George's life of which the family had no idea. He spoke at length about George's total involvement in the families of all who worked at the factory. Then he waved his hand at the assembled people as a testament as to how they had appreciated George's support and compassion over all those years. He simply quoted some of the comments those families had made. Tears trickled down Janet's face and the family became so very proud of their dad. David sitting next to his mum kept squeezing her hand. The gratitude and quiet joy that filled their hearts would carry them through the days ahead.

Ken then arose and spoke so briefly about the family's recent trip to Australia. Ken reiterated the friendship and bond that had developed as they had often sat together in the header at Glenorchy farm, stripping the crop some six months earlier. He spoke about the excitement and the fun Georges had managing such a huge machine and how deftly he had become at manoeuvring it through the paddock.

It was now David's turn; he arose quietly and with measured steps moved to the lectern. He began by mentioning the afternoon when his mum had reminded them to focus on just one of the lovely contributions George had made in their lives. He spoke about the shift in the mood of the family on that afternoon. He went on to highlight just how close he had become to his dad, and that their idealism was similar and that he felt so encouraged by those conversations. His mood then changed, and he spoke of the sadness of losing someone who he felt he was just getting to know. He freely admitted losing his dad had left him feeling angry. He briefly touched on the night of his dad's heart attack and was saddened by such an aggressive intrusion from a serving officer in the police service. There was a quiet stillness that descended upon the whole assembly as David uttered those words, but he wasn't backing away from them and he concluded that his dad had been an amazing role model for all his family and an amazing husband and deserved entirely his title the 'Quiet Warrior.'

The service concluded well over time but as it happened there were no other services scheduled and mourners were encouraged to take their time and enjoy light refreshments. Janet was literally overcome by so many of the families that George had touched in his workplace. She knew only too well that not only was he thorough in the way that he worked but at heart he was gentle and caring and would always go out of his way to support someone who needed support.

David and Andy had chatted, and the upshot of that conversation was that the device which was still in Andy's care should be used on David, Jordan, Melissa and Janet in the event of a polygraph test. Janet would no doubt accompany the children and Ken had agreed to go with her in support. That was all achieved quietly and respectfully, and Janet was made aware of the plan.

Andy was intrigued by the little man who had sat at the back trying to look inconspicuous. The sun was still shining in a cloudless sky as he walked out onto the patio and espied the M I6 officers. He made his way over to the men and began the conversation checking when precisely they would be taking his cousin to headquarters. It wouldn't be long now as some of the mourners were starting to leave the chapel, and the lounge room where the food had been served. The officer had been leaning against the concrete balustrade when he stood up and went to bypass Andy. Andy just gently held up his hand and said,

"I am really curious what makes you think our cousins could possibly be involved with people from another planet?" He was obviously frustrated by this question but was prepared to say just a little. At that very moment Andy caught a glimpse from the corner of his eye a huge German Shepherd bounding towards him. He realized that he was the attraction and was in no mind to have this huge dog leap on his chest, and with split second timing he just turned aside and the dog's paws glanced off him and firmly into the chest of the officer. The force of the leap sent the officer flying backwards and his head crashed heavily into the concrete balustrade and within seconds blood was pouring from an open wound at the back of his head. Some of the people who were standing nearby saw it all happen. Melissa witnessed it as well. She instinctively reached for her mobile and dialled emergency and requested an ambulance straightaway to the funeral home. The staff were immediately on hand and were assisting with first aid and Melissa stood watching, cognizant that the colours around him were fading rapidly. He was perilously close to death and she was faced with the dilemma of intervening and possibly healing or letting him slip into another world. By this time Jordan and David was standing by her side and they both took her hand and whispered,

"If he is going to go, you need to let him go." it seemed to be the right decision and that would solve so many problems. Momentarily she turned away, her dilemma was real, but she wasn't sure how she could effect healing in an instance like this. Her mind turned to her dad and the fact she couldn't be there for him and anger began to well up inside her. For some moments she responded to that and by that time she turned back to where the man was lying his colours had completely disappeared.

His colleague had now made his way to his side and a few more staff had done as much as they could, and he went to reach for his phone to call emergency services and was surprised when he heard the distinct yet distant wail of the ambulance.

"Thank heavens someone has reacted quickly!" he said quite audibly. Melissa was still holding her mobile phone, and, in that instant, he realized that it was she who had called for an ambulance. He came over to her and thanked her saying "You may well have saved his life." But he could not see what Melissa could see and she knew that he was not long for this world. The ambulance duly arrived, and the paramedics wasted no time in getting him onto the trolley and into the ambulance. They immediately took his pulse and looked at his colleague, and the look left them in little doubt as to his future.

There were still two officers from MI6 who now instructed the three young family members, Janet and Ken to make their way to the waiting vehicle. Nancy would return to the family home with Andy and Emma. Andy was so completely surprised by the turn of events and could never have imagined the outcome. Within seconds of the Shepherd's impact he was patting the dog and settling him down. The owner was quite bewildered by the dog's behaviour and when he saw Andy he apologised profusely. "He is normally extremely shy, and when I let him off the lead, he always stays close to me." "Frankly I was gob smacked when he took off because in the three years that I have had him he's never displayed behaviour like that." Andy confessed to him that he had an unusual affinity to all animals but most especially to dogs and he couldn't explain it beyond that. The Shepherd was still nuzzling Andy's hand as this conversation closed and again the owner was at a loss to explain the attraction.

CHAPTER 11

MUCH ADO ABOUT NOTHING

THEY ARRIVED AT the headquarters of MI6 and were quickly escorted to three separate interview rooms. David and Jordan were no longer minors and therefore needed no parental oversight and their interrogation started right away. They were given the offer of legal representation which they took, and the interviews began. David was asked as to why he would be in the woods at that hour of the night with his brother and sister to which he replied.

"We were off to see a late-night movie." "Which movie had you chosen?"

"We hadn't finally decided but we had narrowed it down to two." Which two?

"The Last Jedi or Goodbye Mr. Chips, which of course is an old movie but certainly one of our favourites." The lawyer interjected,

"Just how relevant is this?"

The officer waved his hand dismissing the intrusion and the interrogation continued.

"How is it that you chose a more dangerous route than the pavements which would have been lit by streetlamps?" David re-joined,

"We know the woods like the back of our hands and for us there is very little danger, and both Jordan and Melissa feel particularly safe with me because of my training in the martial arts." The officer replied,

"Yes, we know about your martial arts training and that it nearly landed to you with an assault charge." David could feel the anger rising and he took a deep breath, "I believe it is an assault if I had initiated the aggression, however, it was your officers who displayed all the aggression, which seems to be the only language they know." Once again, the interrogating officer waved his hand in an act of dismissal, and countered nonchalantly,

"It was always going to be your word against theirs and I know who they would believe in a court of law." David instinctively looked at his lawyer who had leaned over and whispered, "This is one battle you won't win, and it doesn't matter anyway." David acknowledged and took several deep breaths in order to stay focused. The attempt to rile David had failed and he now needed to see if he could exploit another weakness of this young man. The next question came right out of left field, and the officer referred to a possible relationship with Emma, his cousin from Australia. His lawyer needed no second bidding and challenged the appropriateness of such a matter in the interview. The officer readily recognized that he had overstepped the boundary and turned to the tape and noted that the matter be deleted from the record. The only emotion that David displayed was that of complete surprise and of the lawyer's early intervention had prevented him from showing relief, which of course the officer was looking for. He then returned to the previous line of questioning and rather dryly said to David,

"We will of course be checking out your story with your brother and sister." David responded, "I am more than happy for you to ask those questions because it's a decision that we had made as a family, and there were certainly no signs of discomfort in David's posture.

"You do realize that we have record of the whole event in the woods." The officer volunteered. At that point David leaned forward and looked straight into the eyes of the officer and said ever so calmly,

"I would like to see the record as I'm sure it would prove our point." The response was curt and to the point,

"All in good time." The lawyer had watched for some time and now was about to prove his worth.

"If you have evidence that will clearly link my client to this event then we need to see it now, otherwise you have no business in holding my client any longer." The officer responded, "We are experiencing some technical problems, but the technicians believe they can retrieve the records."

The expression on David's face remained completely calm and it seemed from the officer's is point of view that nothing could faze him. David then seized the initiative and quietly asked,

"How is your officer doing who was taken by ambulance to the hospital?" It was now David's turn to watch his face, David's training in the martial arts had always taught him to look at the eyes because it was from there, he would read the next movement. For just a fleeting second his eyes told David that his colleague had passed away. David continued to seize the moment,

"I can't say that I was particularly fond of him, especially when I think that in no small part he precipitated my late father's heart attack, but I am sorry that he is no longer with us as I imagine he has family and no doubt they will miss him." The officer tried to engage David with his eyes and David was up for the challenge, but the officer found it difficult to maintain his focus and he challenged David with these words,

"What makes you so sure that he has passed away?" David's response was swift and to the point,

"Your eyes tell me just that." And for the first time in the officer was completely on the back foot and he knew that this interview had not gone as he had planned. The only two avenues that were now open to him was the possibility of conflict between their stories and the introduction of the polygraph which he was able to subject David to.

The lawyer sensed it was now time to raise the matter of the recording and check how much more time was required. The interrogating officer noted for the tape that he was leaving the room in order to check with the technical staff in another part of the building. He returned a few minutes later and it was obvious the frustration was getting to him and he indicated that they had made little progress if any. The lawyer then put it to the officer,

"There could be no possible reason to detain my client further."

The officer looked thoughtful for a moment and indicated he would require some more time out. Again, the tape was addressed indicating that he would need to be gone for at least five minutes. He then consulted with his other two colleagues who had also been interrogating Melissa and Jordan. To their absolute dismay their stories correlated and confirmed David's record of events and it was becoming obvious that there could be no reason to detain them. He returned to the interview room where David was being held and decided to play his last card. He advised David that he would be hooked up to the polygraph machine and asked a series of questions. The whole exercise proved futile and the result indicated and supported David's truthfulness regarding the whole matter. The lawyer continued to press his claim that they could be no legitimate reason for David to be held and reluctantly the officer in charge indicated that he was free to go.

They were about to make their way to the entrance when one of the officers indicated that they were still one last roll of the dice and he was suggesting that both Janet and Ken could be subjected to a polygraph test. It was agreed amidst large protestations by Ken and he suggested that not only was it a waste of police time but a waste of taxpayers' money, nevertheless, he was to humour them. Janet looked quite anxious as she sat down for this would be a totally new experience and it was duly noted by the operator that her condition presented as quite anxious. Notwithstanding, she came through with flying colours but not before the operator went through the process twice. Ken looked on in complete bewilderment and wondered how much longer the farce would continue and both officers consulted and decided that it would be a waste of time to check Ken. They all assembled in the foyer of MI6 headquarters and a car was called which would return them to their home. It was dark and the crisp night air reminded Ken that he was very much on the other side of the world. They all managed to squeeze in, and the journey home was almost in complete silence as they turned into the street. They noticed that their detective in plain clothes had gone and each one gave an in sigh of relief.

They all piled out of the car and as they reached the front door Nancy had opened it wide and was there to greet them. She knew pretty well by the smiles on their faces that everything had been resolved and Andy couldn't conceal his joy at the outcome. When the other four were together he said under his breath "That will teach them to mess with us." David was a little more subdued and he looked at the group and said quite solemnly,

"This was just round one, I know that there will be many greater challenges as we continue with our mission." There were high fives all round and the recognition that the going would only get tougher and more testing and that they absolutely needed to be very vigilant in the future. By now they had all washed up and found themselves sitting in the kitchen around the table looking hungrily at Nancy's preparation. Only Melissa was missing, and she went upstairs saying something about needing some time out. Nancy was certainly at her best when preparing food and her big family looked hungrily at the ginormous shepherd's pie as it sat in the oven It had been an exhausting day for all concerned and the mood around the table was certainly one of relief. The conversation was measured as they reflected on the service to celebrate George's passing. Melissa had taken some time out for her own personal meditation. Once again, she had found herself drifting into another world and to her surprise and delight, she had engaged with the spirit of her dad. She felt the warmth of his compassion as well is the acknowledgement of a memorable celebration. She could see his warm smile and felt immensely strengthened by his supportive love. There were tears of joy trickling down her cheek as he disappeared into the ether and within a moment or two, she had come back into her body. Just at that moment Emma had burst into their bedroom and saw the dampness on her cheeks. Before Emma was able to say a word, Melissa put up her hand indicating that she was fine and her broad smile confirmed her body language. Melissa then shared her encounter with her dad and then Emma sat momentarily transfixed while listening to her cousin. She thought to herself, "Is there nothing that Melissa cannot do?" She seemed to push the boundaries in almost every area of their lives. "I will share this with the family later, but I can hear mum calling us for tea and we need to be there." They were down the steps two at a time and soon joined the others. None of them were church people but Janet paused for a moment and invited everybody to bow their heads in gratitude for the events of the day, for the family from Australia and for the food before them. There was a resounding Amen from everybody. The food was delicious, and it seemed that everybody was savouring each mouthful and reflecting on all the events of the day. Finally, everyone had finished, and David really wanted to check the house out to make sure there were no bugging devices still alive. He went systematically through each room and invited all the family to think of ingenious places that MI6 could possibly think of. The family followed David from room to room whilst Nancy and Ken looked at each other quite bewildered as to what was really going on, Andy and Emma explained that initially MI6 had raided the house and left listening devices throughout in order to implicate David Jordan and Melissa in what they believed was selling out their country. Nothing more was uncovered and Ken who had been watching intently had become interested with the device that David had been using. He admitted that he'd never seen anything quite like that before. He assumed that it was an entirely new device that had not long hit the market. All the young people looked at each other and smiled and even Janet herself allowed herself a wee smile. Ken looked puzzled and said,

"Am I missing something here?" By now everybody was in the lounge room sitting wherever they could find space. Janet then looked at all the faces and said it is time to put all the cards on the table. There was unanimous response of assent from all the young people. There had been clear telepathic communication from their friends in space, and it was clear that Ken and Nancy needed to be informed.

Janet began to retell the whole story from beginning to end and she made it very clear that all their offspring were deeply involved in changing the direction of planet and that their alien friends had built a strong secure and respectful relationship with all of them and even some others. Ken and Nancy could hardly contain themselves as the story continued to unfold, Ken then paused for a moment and reflected,

"That really was serious business back at MI6 and David Melissa and Jordan could have been charged with conspiring against the government of Great Britain and its people." David nodded in assent and pointed out that it was so important for you Uncle Ken not to know anything should they have pursued a polygraph test on you. He nodded realizing that he had dismissed the whole notion as entirely fanciful, but he was quick to ask how it was possible for David, Jordan, Janet and Melissa to come out clearly telling the truth. David was still holding the device and he said quite simply, "It is this little machine that has saved our bacon throughout the whole operation. We have used it to completely erase the memory banks of all the agents who were involved from MI6, so it was easy for Andy to use it on mum, Jordan, Melissa and myself, so in that time lapse we were completely oblivious to our involvement with an alien culture. However, since then our friends have continued to download information directly to our memory banks and restore all the information that had been erased. Ken and Nancy were reeling with all the information that had been given to them in such a short time. Emma looked at her mum and dad and gently reassured them both that they had never planned to deceive them or to keep them from the truth and they were assured that the time would come when the truth would be out in the open. Janet took Nancy by the hand and looked at them both,

"Do you have any questions before we turn in for the night?" This time Nancy responded,

"I guess we have a thousand questions but right now we need to digest this. It has indeed been a huge shock and that my guess is that it will take some getting used to. I mean, all our family are going to be involved in a perilous mission"

Everybody was now thinking about bed time and Melissa said that she had something to share with all the family. Emma was sitting next to her on the couch and took her by the hand giving her support, Melissa smiled gratefully and said,

"When I went up to my room after arriving home from MI6 I went into a deep meditation and engaged with our dad and I just wanted to share, how proud he was of all of you and how moved he was by the entire service of celebration and he knew that his time here had been very well spent." There were no dry eyes and the joy on their faces said it all. On that happy note, it was off to bed for everyone.

CHAPTER 12

ESCAPE TO THE COUNTRY

A NEW DAY DAWNED, and the family had meandered down to the kitchen for breakfast. Yesterday had been a huge day and some family members had taken the opportunity to sleep in. There wasn't a lot of chatter at the breakfast table and both Andy and Emma noticed that their dad was particularly quiet, that was usually a sign that he had something on his mind or that he was plain grumpy. They would know if it was the latter by looking at Mum and the signs were, he was grumpy. Emma could usually work her way around Dad, and she leaned over and touched his forearm and enquired how he was. There was a long pause, and he began to share what was on his mind. "Well yesterday certainly put the cat among the pigeons. Here I was thinking that you and your brother were very settled and happy to continue the farm in the Talbot name, now I find that your thinking about shooting off to the other side of who knows where and who will look after the farm?" Andy and Emma looked at each other quite bemused,

"Of course, we will continue to farm in fact we are more committed since we have met our space friends than ever before," Ken looked puzzled and then countered,

"Just how do you plan to do that when you are busy with a mission that takes you to who knows where?"

Andy acknowledged his dad's concern but reminded him that they had already started on their mission and that not only had the farm not suffered but their contact had already had a positive impact on the farm. Ken nodded in acknowledgement of what he was saying but was quite relieved to hear them say very clearly their commitment was rock solid.

Janet then broached the subject of how long the family would be able to stay away from the farm. She indicated it would be great if they were around to share their feelings on the possibility of a new beginning. David, Jordan and Melissa were not surprised that this topic could come up, but just a little surprised that it has come up so quickly. Janet continued,

"It is obvious that we cannot stay in this house and we need to find a much more secluded location if we are to continue this mission." Then Janet left them all quite speechless with what she shared next,

"Our friends from another planet have already been communicating with me and making some suggestions as to where we might relocate. They are more than clear that they need to be out of the sweeping zone of MI 6's radar." There was quite a long moment of silence as everybody around the table took in what Janet had said. Both Ken and Nancy were taken aback by Janet's inclusion of herself in the mission, and whilst the five young people could easily accommodate that idea, they were surprised by the swiftness with which their space friends had moved. Suddenly the quiet mood around the table disintegrated and it seemed everybody had something to say. Janet looked at the whole family and smiled quietly,

"My goodness me that's one way to get things started." The conversation stopped as abruptly as it had started, and it was up to Janet now to guide the direction of just what needed to be decided.

"Our friends have given us three clear locations that they feel would be much safer than here, and I have been busy this morning looking on the real estate pages checking them out. May I suggest that you all look at the locations that I'm about to give you and look at the pros and cons of each." David looked thoughtful for a moment and then looked right at his mum suggesting that maybe they needed to choose another country. Janet smiled wanly,

"How did I know that you were going to make that suggestion and we all know where that other country might be?". Emma's grin broadened considerably and suggested it wasn't really such a bad idea, and the universities in Australia were very high quality. That thought had certainly crossed the minds of our friends but for whatever reason they are suggesting we relocate in our home country. Janet then gave them the locations, and everybody went off to look at the three sites. It was then that Ken and Nancy questioned Janet as to her part in the mission.

"Well these are my children and we are a family and whatever they are involved in involves me as well. Now in the short amount of communication that I have had with our friends they totally agree that I need to be part of the team, and I imagine that they will be speaking to you along the same lines." Ken shook his head for a moment and asked himself out loud.

"Could this be really happening?" Nancy surprised him and said,

"Isn't this rather exciting to think that we have friends from another galaxy." Ken looked at both women in some bewilderment,

"There is no doubting that you too are sisters in spirit and you were certainly brought up in the same household." They both laughed together, and Ken remarked,

"I wouldn't have it any other way." However, Ken still had more questions,

"Have you any idea what it is that you're letting yourself in for?" Janet smiled gently,

"No not really and I can't even imagine what the future holds, but do any of us know about our future and losing George in this last week has taught me that we must take every opportunity to make the world a better place for our being here." Janet responded.

"My sentiments entirely." re-joined Nancy "It seems as though I am outvoted." Ken responded light-heartedly, whilst recognizing the commitment and compassion both women had brought to the table.

Ken and Nancy then took some time out to look at the various sites, whilst Janet busied herself contacting local real estate people. She knew instinctively that their property would be highly sought after as it was in a prime location and for many other reasons. Her enquiries were met with a great deal of enthusiasm from all the companies that she approached, and the agents promised to come around to view the property that same day.

The family gradually assembled again in the kitchen, bringing their iPads and laptops to share their variety of responses. Ken and Nancy were the last to arrive and were quite excited about the selections that had been made. Now followed a most animated discussion, most focused on a property in Cornwall. Its major disadvantage was being a long way from any university which the family would need to access at some time in the future. It was certainly remote enough with only the old farmhouse nearby, and whilst the house was very much old-world, the inside was very modern and looked very warm and inviting. The best thing about this property was that the sale of their existing house would cover the purchase of this property, with a substantial sum left over. They decided to write a list of the pros and cons of the property and then compare notes. Hardly had they finished and that there was a knock at the door. David ever ready to accept his new role strode to the door and checked through the peephole to see if it was anyone, he could recognize. On further checking with his mum and looking more carefully at the gentleman and lady who were standing there he assumed that they were people from the local real estate office. He opened the door and invited them to come in and everybody retired to the lounge room where there was more seating. In Janet's mind this company sounded the most appealing and as the discussion continued that appeal was further confirmed. The agents indicated that they already had people interested in this area and were confident they could effect a sale sooner rather than later.

The discussion now turned to when prospective clients might be able to view the property and just how much time they would need to get the house ready, all of which was really unknown given that they had never moved and there would be huge amount to sort through and recycle. Then added into that mix were all of Georges personal effects, which was a task that Janet was neither prepared for or ready to even tackle. Especially since his funeral was so fresh in all their minds but particularly Janet's. It became obvious to everyone present that Janet was still having an internal struggle and that was to be expected. Melissa sensing this moved right next to her mum and gently put her arm around her and just held her, Janet immediately burst into tears and leaned heavily into her daughter's arms. Grief consumed her and everyone sat silently acknowledging the poignancy of the moment. Janet eventually regained her composure and breathing rhythm and released so much of the tension and pain of the last week. There was a willing acceptance of Janet's tears as everyone present knew in their hearts what an incredible wrench this had been for the survivor of this deeply bonded couple.

It was at that point Rob and Lindy stood up and made towards the door it was now time to take their leave. David obliged without any further conversation until outside, where it was agreed they would return when they had something more definite. By now Nancy had summed up the situation and had the kettle happily singing and was preparing several plates of finger food. She was being ably assisted by Emma, Melissa and Jordan. There was very little conversation now and the atmosphere was very contained with everyone aware of Janet's deep sense of loss, to say nothing of the family's loss as well. The tasks that confronted them were many and it would consume most of their waking moments. This of course would be a good thing for everyone, being busy was always a good foil for taking one's mind off the grief. It was the night-time Janet found the most difficult, when she was left with the emptiness and solitude in her own room then she felt more acutely the loss of her soulmate. Her family had listened plaintively to her tears and restlessness and felt singularly powerless to heal the grief which was so present in the sanctity of her room. Each morning Janet came down for breakfast they witnessed her red puffy eyes and knew that her sleep had been restless and broken. It was a cruel blow for her as a mum and a wife, just when her family needed a dad the most, he was taken from their midst. For Janet one of the challenges would be whether she would have the wisdom to lead and guide these remarkable three young adults. She was more than aware they had developed their own sense of self. She pondered for a moment all that had taken place in the last twelve months They had all grown so much and as she reflected she sensed this overwhelming gratitude not just for the support they had given her, but for their wisdom and insight which was well beyond their years. Now as dark as the nights were, her spirit was buoyed knowing that she, together with George, had played a major role in their development and there was light the end of the tunnel. Her spirit lightened considerably, and her face brightened, and her eyes shone, and everyone knew that she would conquer her grief and come through with greater resilience.

None of this had gone unnoticed by David and being the eldest he felt it was his role to support his mum in whatever way he needed to. At that point Janet stood up and David immediately went over and stood by her side. He suggested that it might be good for them to walk out in the fresh air that would be helpful to his mum right then. For a moment she was surprised but then reflected just how much he developed and how warm he had become. With that she linked her arm in his picked up a scarf on the way out and closed to the front door behind them.

David began to tell his mum just how proud he was of her; he shared his admiration of her work ethic and her science degree and the way she had raised the family and as a mum. "You have always been there for us despite your workload," he continued, "You have been an inspiration to me which is why I eventually chose to go to university. Mum, I really do admire you and when I marry, I would like her to be just as you are." For a full thirty seconds Janet was speechless, he had so blown her out of the water with what he shared. She stopped for that time and turned and faced to David full on and put her arms around him and just held him and whispered,

"They are without doubt some of the most beautiful words I have ever had spoken to me and to come from my firstborn they touched the very core of my being. I am so grateful and so proud that you are my son." David stood there for what seemed an eternity just holding his mum and affirming everything that had passed between them and he realized just how deep was the love that they shared. They continued to walk sharing the possibility of going down into the country or migrating to another part of the world and maybe Australia. Either way it wasn't going to be an easy decision but for the moment it wasn't clear, and the sale of the house would more than likely take some time. They talked about what a lovely time it had been when they were visiting their family in Glenorchy and how much they had enjoyed that rural setting.

Janet couldn't help herself and she enquired as to how strongly he felt about Emma. David was more than happy to oblige, and he began to share how he felt.

"Well," he began, "she is intelligent she is very grounded, has lots of common sense and she's beautiful." Janet nodded in acknowledgement of all that David had said and suggested the time would allow them to make the right decision whatever that may be. David acknowledged his mum's wisdom and felt very comfortable in sharing his real feelings for Emma.

David then turned his attention to Melissa and shared just how important she had been in his encounter with their alien friends. It had been so good to be able to share what had happened on the farm at Glenorchy and how much he'd come to respect Melissa and especially what she offered to the world. "You know I watched her at the shopping mall just lean over Lucy and you could see the immediate impact of her gift on this young woman and it happened so easily without any fuss from Melissa. There was no fanfare, no 'look at me how good am I.' She has wisdom way beyond her years and the great thing is, she's my sister."

"I am no longer surprised by what comes out of your mouth David, and I know Dad would be so proud of you now," Janet mused slowly. They had now reached the front gate of their home and were happily walking arm in arm and Janet's whole countenance had changed and she felt so much better. David reached out to open the door, she took his hand and gave it a big squeeze and smiled warmly. Beyond any shadow of doubt Janet felt very comfortable about what the future may hold so long as her family was together. The aching void was still there but her heart was lighter and her spirit warmer.

Nancy and all her helpers had organized supper and they were sitting in the lounge room chatting about all the possibilities that lay ahead of them.

There was lots of animated conversation at supper, and much of the conversation centred around where the family would move. The consensus was Cornwall and the farmhouse was the preferred location, but its major drawback was accessing university even though much study could be done online. However, no firm plans could be made until the sale of their home and there was still no clarity around that.

The next major event in the life of the family was the return of Nancy, Ken. Andrew and Emma. They had spent considerable time away and the farm always had things that needed to be done. Nancy and Janet had strengthened their already strong bond after George's funeral and Janet was now apprehensive about losing not just the support but the resourcefulness and presence which Nancy had offered so unobtrusively. Janet was in a better space now and so much of this was due to the support, not just of her family but also from Nancy. David of course was already apprehensive about losing that physical contact with Emma, they had spent so much time together sharing their plans and dreams and realizing how much they had in common. Their time together had only strengthened their relationship and both had realized there was a lot more to the relationship than they had first imagined. However, the days ahead would sorely test their resolve on their commitment but for the moment it seemed pure bliss when they were together. They both knew that their studies required from them serious commitment and whilst they had enjoyed this time together, there was still lots of excitement in developing and enriching their own experience and study which is such an important part of the future.

Time seemed the enemy now for the Glenorchy family, the days had slipped quietly by and that chore of packing inevitably confronted them. Clothes were all washed and ironed and were carefully packed away in preparation for the long flight home. It would have been so much quicker and easier to be transported in the 'alien's craft' but of course it could never be as there would be no record of them ever and entering Australia again, and how could they explain that?

Their flight left early in the morning and cases were ready by the door, the taxi had been ordered and now it was time to catch some sleep before the long flight. Sombreness pervaded the whole atmosphere of the house, and there was no escaping the heaviness that surrounded the families. Slowly but surely members retreated to their sleeping quarters and stillness and darkness enveloped the house yet again.

It seemed as though they had hardly been asleep when the clatter of the alarm clock went off and very quickly the whole house was alive with light and activity. Janet and Nancy had already started to prepare breakfast and it wasn't long before the family appeared at the dining room table ready for some sustenance. The mood was a little more upbeat as everyone recognized this was only going to be a temporary separation, they knew that their mission which was about to commence would necessitate regular meetings with the rest of the team. This fact alone was enough to keep their spirits high and to give themselves purpose to the tasks that lay ahead.

David ventured that it was going to be so much easier now that the whole family knew of the mission. There would be no more need for secrets and the most important people in their lives, their parents would not only know but be entirely supportive which only contributed to the confidence of the young team. There was general agreement and approval for what David had offered and it gave resounding encouragement to each and every member of the family. Melissa who had been observing all of this smiled benignly, aware that all the colours and all auras around each family member were both vibrant and healthy, and she made comment to that effect. The rest of the family acknowledged Melissa's gift with an acclamation of hand clapping. Breakfast was consumed with gusto and just as quickly as the clatter of knives and forks had heralded its beginning their silence confirmed its conclusion. The dishes were then stacked in the dishwasher and everybody completed their final bathroom routine. It was now only a few minutes before the taxi would arrive and David had got the family car out and was ready to follow the cab all the way to the airport. The cab eventually arrived at the airport and within moments they were heading to the departure entrance. At this time of the morning traffic was at its minimum and the journey was effected in very good time.

Goodbyes were difficult and there lots of hugs and some tears but there was an overwhelming sense of gratitude from Janet and her three young adults for the part that Nancy, Ken, Andy and Emma had played in that time shortly after George's passing. There was plenty of waving as their Australian cousins made their way to the departure lounge and with the last member, Emma blowing David a kiss, their goodbyes were complete. They then made their way to the car park and as they were doing so the first rays of the new day began dawning and each family member wondered what this day would bring. Little did they anticipate the surprise that would confront them later that day.

The journey home was largely uneventful, and David pulled the car into their street, and turned safely into the garage. The sky was clear, and the air was crisp, with all the promise of a warm day. Janet made her way to the front door turned the key and opened it wide, she was about to call out to George and say 'we are home' but caught herself before the words escaped from her mouth. She still imagined him to be there somewhere and for a moment she stumbled emotionally letting her grief escape, and she remembered the minister's comments realizing that he was still there, but she was unable to see him. By now everybody was inside, and Jordan had put the kettle on and suggested that they now have a cuppa and decide what they might do for the rest of the day.

It wasn't long before the tea was made, and the family sat around the kitchen table talking about the unenviable task of packing. It had now gone past eight o'clock and just at that moment the phone rang, and this time Janet picked it up being the closest. The chatter stopped while she spoke, and they were guessing it was in fact the real estate people from the conversation they could hear. It wasn't long before the call was finished, and Janet moved back to take up her cuppa. Their curiosity couldn't be contained, and she could see by the look on their faces they were eager to hear what the estate agents had to say.

"Well this is all very interesting," announced Janet. "It looks as though we have two prospective buyers and they want to have a second look and they have even gone so far as to put a holding deposit on the house," continued Janet. "They would like us out of the house in six weeks if possible and they would prefer to come around sooner rather than later."

It was then David who suggested that they might go down to Cornwall and have a look at the property and that certainly seemed a sensible suggestion. A picnic lunch was suggested and very soon everything was prepared and packed in the car. They were just about ready to drive out of the driveway when Janet's mobile went off and so David stopped the car allowing his mum to take the call without distraction. They could all see the look of total surprise and the tone in her voice that whatever was being discussed had come out of left field. Janet reiterated that they wouldn't be home all day and they would have to come on another occasion. Janet had hardly finished the conversation when Melissa, Jordan and David chimed in, in perfect unison, "Who was that?"

"Well you're not going to believe it but it was the CEO from MI6 wanting to drop around to give us a present for all the trouble he put us through. However, I told him that it wouldn't be possible as we would be out all day." Melissa and Jordan's response was immediate.

"This feels like another Trojan Horse and one which we need to be wary of." David who had listened to the whole conversation now volunteered,

"We can always check this out with our sensor from our friends." Everyone agreed that this would be the best course of action and they moved onto the next topic.

It would take them at least two hours to reach their destination in Cornwall and much of the time was spent discussing what alterations might be necessary and how accessible university would be.

They spoke at length to the agent after viewing the property extensively. There was no doubting that it needed upgrading in a number of significant areas, and builders and building supplies were discussed even further. The more they talked together the less likely it seemed that this property would be where they would end up. The agent had left them alone to discuss what options lay in front of them and the family decided it was time to have a picnic lunch. They needed to find a nice spot in the sun to enjoy the fresh country air. At the end of their lunch it was decided and Janet rang the agent and let her know that the property wasn't quite what they were looking for. Janet then asked her if there were any other properties that were of a similar nature that they would find attractive, but there was a negative response from the agents who suggested that there were no more properties available for viewing that ticked most of the boxes they had requested.

David slid comfortably behind the wheel, Melissa and Jordan sat in the back and Mum was the co-pilot on the way home. They spent most of the time listing the positives and why they thought they were positive. They journeyed through other towns along the way and checked the real estate boards but without success.

It had been a particularly long day, and everyone was tired as the car turned into their home street. The house was in darkness but in no time at all the lights breathed new life and soon everybody was inside helping to get the evening meal. More chat followed, but no clear direction as to where they would finally settle. It was an early night for everyone and once again a house was bathed in silence and darkness.

Janet was already up busying herself in the kitchen, so it appeared, but in reality, she sat the kitchen table with her head buried in her hands. Melissa had made her way down so quietly that Mum had not witnessed her arrival, she watched her mum through a full ten seconds before asking,

"Mum, you okay?" At that point Mum lifted her head and Melissa could see her tear stained cheeks puffy and soft, "Clearly, no," ventured Melissa answering her own question and she made her way to where Mum was sitting and gently put her arm around her and gave her a hug. Janet looked carefully into her daughter's eyes searching for an answer.

"I still don't know why he had to die so young and I miss him so much. I do think sometimes I took him for granted somehow believing that he would always be around." Suddenly there were more tears and sobs and Melissa who was now quite as tall as her mum lifted her gently from her seat and just held her.

"We do miss him as well but for you it must be so much worse as you have been together so much longer, and you were so close." Janet nodded recognizing the truth of her daughter's comment but at the same time feeling so much better for her support and love.

It was quite late, and Janet knew that the boys would be down soon looking for some breakfast and now she felt better and so after drying her eyes she soon became busy in the kitchen. The industry in the kitchen was interrupted with a very loud banging on the front door and both looked up in surprise wondering who the earth would be wanting to speak to them at this time. Melissa read her mother's eyes and went to the front door and just as she did David came down the steps from his bedroom closely followed by Jordan.

Melissa could hardly believe her eyes as they came to rest on the boss, Adam from MI6. Melissa paused for a second and watching his silhouette in the crisp morning light, her instinct told her this was not a friendly visit. She could see all too clearly that his aura was dark and murky, and she had learned that dark colours usually meant trouble. He stood for a full ten seconds and then asked if they may be permitted to come in as he announced that he had a gift for her mother. Melissa beckoned him to come in and he was followed closely by another man whom she had not seen before. They were ushered into the lounge and invited to sit on the sofa, whereupon Melissa returned to the kitchen announcing their arrival to her mum. Janet arrived in the lounge and began simply by saying,

"Well if I'm honest this is not a pleasant surprise as I thought we had seen the very last of you!" She was still thinking about and feeling the pain of the loss of George and frankly this man was the last person she wanted to see right now. Janet's steely eyes looked straight at him and almost through him. Her children knew that look only too well but they had never seen it quite so intense and for them it was a clear warning to stay out of harm's way or certainly a safe distance. Even Adam was taken aback as he watched her looking into his very soul and with all his training, he stumbled to find the words to address Janet.

Regaining his composure, he produced quite a large box and said gently, "I know this has been a very difficult time for you and your family and I would like you to accept this gift as a peace offering." Then he promised them that they wouldn't hear from him again. Janet looked for a moment and softened visibly as she took the gift with both hands with considerable curiosity and placed it firmly on the table. Just at that moment Melissa made a sudden and pronounced exit to the kitchen closing the door behind her. She sensed the vibrational energy of her father, so sat quietly with measured breathing. She had taken the precaution of locking the door so as not to be disturbed and in just a few seconds it was as though she was transported to another world. She could now make out his outline quite clearly and just watched those facial expressions. He was saying how proud he was of his daughter and incredibly grateful for her access to the world of spirit. She could make out that he was so glad she had been able to give strength to Janet, and at the same time reminding her that he was in a very good space. "You are not to pine for me." and then, as quickly as he appeared, he disappeared, but not before warning Melissa that the man in their lounge room was both devious and dangerous. She sat for a moment in reflection and knew that she would need to share this with her mum and the family.

By the time Melissa had re-entered the lounge room David had disappeared and so too had Leo who was the new second-in-command. Janet looked at Melissa asking her that everything was all right and Melissa simply nodded and said,

"Yes fine." and at that point Janet then offered the guests some tea, which Adam politely declined, indicating that they needed to be at the office and that they would need to leave soon.

Adam, then called after Leo telling him it was time to leave. Whereupon there was an immediate response and the clatter of feet could be heard descending down the stairs amidst animated chatter. They had been exchanging conversation on the martial arts and Leo seemed quite in awe of David's level of competency and was saying as much as they entered the lounge room. Adam readily acknowledged David's skills having witnessed at first hand their impact some of his men. In a moment they were gone, and Melissa was now quite focused on the object which had now been unwrapped. What had caught her attention were the lines of energy that were emanating from the object and the words of her dad were ringing in her ears, 'deceptive and dangerous'. Melissa was now reflecting on how and where she could take the family to highlight the new intrusion into their family. She immediately motioned to Mum to come down to the back garden and decide which plants they needed to dig up and take with them into the country, and at the same time turned to David gesturing that he needed to come as it would be he and Jordan who would be digging up the plants. Melissa couldn't quite get over the bemused look on her mother's face as by now they had all assembled at the bottom of the garden.

Janet began,

"I can't imagine why we had to do this right now?" Melissa responded immediately,

"Well firstly I need to let you know that when I ducked into the kitchen it was because I was sure that Dad was trying to make contact and sure enough it was so." Melissa continued,

"Mum he wanted me to assure you that he was in a really good place and that you were not to worry about him, nor to feel angry towards MI6, but of course he does miss us all hugely." Janet sighed audibly and they could all see the stress gradually leave her face.

Jordan then chimed in,

"Why couldn't you tell us that in our lounge room?"

"Well," replied Melissa "Dad warned me that Adam was both deceptive and dangerous and as I looked at Mum's so-called gift it was emitting a field of energy. This led me to feel that it was some kind of recording device but very high-tech. We need to confirm this before any serious conversations take place in the house again and we need to be extra vigilant about whatever we say." Janet gasped,

"I knew I shouldn't trust that man, he is worse than his colleague who was killed in that accident and certainly a lot more devious." And before anyone could say anything more Janet was marching back to the house and stopped at the garden shed and retrieved a substantially heavy object. By now David had caught up with her and stood immediately in her pathway asking,

"What are you planning to do?"

"Well for starters I think I'm going to destroy his piece of equipment right now!" Janet retorted. At which point David took both of her arms and said "Mum, I think we need to think about this in another way. If we destroy it, would he not wonder whether we had something to hide, whereas if we let it be we can use it to our advantage and maybe completely throw him off the trail." By now Melissa and Jordan had listened to that conversation and were clear about the very good sense which David was speaking. Even Janet who was obviously so hurt and infuriated heard the wisdom in David's counsel. Janet recognized the pragmatism in her firstborn which reminded her so much of George and she smiled and acknowledged the value of his comments.

"We need an outdoor meeting," David and Jordan chimed in together and before they finished the sentence, they looked at each other almost in disbelief, whilst Melissa and Mum stood back and laughed. For Jordan and Melissa that had become commonplace and they soon realized even more the telepathic nature of communication.

Chairs were arranged readily, and conversation began.

"This whole episode this morning has put a very different light on our family, and it seems that we will get no peace when it comes to MI6 intruding in our lives. We cannot go on living here with this kind of intrusion," continued Janet. There was immediate agreement from her three family members.

"So now we need to consider other options," The obvious choice was of course Australia and they were all aware this would have first claim on their allegiance, but there are other options to consider. Canada it seemed came in at number two but after much discussion it was agreed that Australia was everybody's choice. Now came the test of sending a message to MI6 that they were still planning to resettle in the Cornwall area. It was going to be tricky not to have freedom of speech in their own house and they still were not clear just how this recording device worked. It seemed likely that not only did it report conversations but tracked movement in the immediate area of its ambience. David had tried the bug disarming device but Melissa could still see energy emitting from it and their friends confirmed it had not responded that well and so they were stuck with it. This reinforced their determination to use it to their advantage. Initially they decided to place reminders of the dangers of free speech, but it was clear that these signals could only mean something to the members of this family.

The house returned to a kind of normality with constant conversation around the suitability or lack of regarding properties they'd already visited in Cornwall and more conversations were had with the real estate agents checking whether there was anything more to consider.

In the weeks that lay ahead Janet and David worked assiduously, initially with the Australian Embassy and on their application to emigrate. Health checks were completed as was their suitability for employment, and Janet would be welcomed with open arms because of her experience in her field of research. Their financial position clearly gave them a great advantage and there seemed no blocks to prevent them from emigrating.

Janet had raised an interesting question with her family and for herself she had made the decision to return to using her maiden name and after much discussion the family followed suit. The clear intention was to leave the country as surreptitiously as possible and hopefully avoid the watchful eyes of MI6. Janet would use her maiden name of Clarke. Furthermore, they would not go through passport control together, thus giving a different appearance to the family.

School continued for Melissa and Jordan and final exams were completed by both of them. It had been so fortunate their school year would be completed before their anticipated departure. It was not going to be the case for David, his studies were continuing for considerable time. He knew that he would have to make alternative arrangements but could do nothing immediately without raising questions. It was fortunate for them all that term vacations were just beginning.

Janet had now returned to work and had used her time to update her C.V. She had taken the step of requesting leave and cited her need to spend more time with her family during their vacation. It was all coming together now.

Six weeks had now elapsed, and they were still no nearer to making a decision about their house and property in Cornwall. They were considering other country locations. Nevertheless, they had made several trips to the country which had only resulted in more frustration for estate agents as well as the for sellers and the would-be buyers.

On another front the plans to emigrate were now all in place, the tickets had been purchased and the final days were looming. The plan was for them to leave just at dusk with as little noise as possible. Planning it this way would give them at least eight hours head start before anyone might suspect they were no longer in residence. In addition, Jordan had devised a system whereby the next morning the family voices would be heard loudly and clearly at least in the kitchen to give the impression they were still in residence and hopefully give them even more time.

They arrived at the airport and quickly made their way to the ticketing desk. Their bags were weighed and loaded, and the family made its way up into the departure lounge. Nobody but nobody knew of their departure not even the family in Glenorchy were aware of this decision. They had decided that the safest possible strategy would be for no one to be aware of their move. They would not even take the risk of using their mobile phones to alert their Australian family. They had even learned to block out the telepathic process with the help of their friends.

It soon came time to board, and it was obvious that Janet had sat in the lounge anxiously waiting for that call. The preparation for take-off completed, Janet finally felt she could relax but little did she know of the adventure that was to unfold in the next thirty minutes.

The plane had barely reached its travelling altitude when the young man sitting next to David reached under his seat and pulled out what was clearly a knife. David was completely taken off guard and the assailant had done so just in time to capture the passing stewardess. David glanced at the receptacle from which the knife had been taken to recognize that it was made from ice and would have gone undetected through security. The sharpness of the blade needed no verification has he already drawn it across the hand of the stewardess which had now started to bleed lightly. The man was now ushering her forward as if making for the cockpit and David knew that if he was going to do anything to rectify this he would have to act quickly. He knew that he needed to distract the assailant for a split second and that would be enough and so as he stood up just behind them and he called out,

"Hey buddy I think you've forgotten something." He instinctively turned around and in that split-second David chopped his right arm with such deft skill that he dropped the knife and winced in pain at the severity of the blow and fell to the floor. The stewardess had now escaped and gone forward to report the incident to her supervisor. In the meantime, David had taken care of the assailant who was now decidedly looking very sorry for himself and was obviously in a lot of pain.

A few moments later the captain announced that the plane need to return to base to take care of some business that had arisen during the flight. Fortunately, it had all happened so quickly that nobody except those closely involved knew exactly what had taken place. Now the stewardess had made it her business to come and thank David profusely for his speedy intervention. Then not long afterwards the first officer came down to congratulate him on behalf of the captain and crew. An incident report had now been completed by the first officer together with David and the stewardess. Melissa had watched all this unfold and now her eyes widened when she saw the hostess from business class come down as well. Melissa immediately recognized her from their previous flight over nine months ago. She eventually caught her eye and called Amy, there was immediate recognition and Amy came over and they both stood and spontaneously hugged. "Isn't he your brother?" enquired Amy. Melissa nodded to which Amy responded,

"You are quite a family," Melissa simply smiled and acknowledged her comment.

By this time the plane was coming into land and some normality had returned for the staff and passengers alike. Once on the ground, Airport Security were quickly on board and were taking the offender away. David was interviewed along with others who witnessed the incident by Airport Security and a copy of the first officers report was also taken. The stewardess had decided that she was fine to continue but the captain decided otherwise, and she was routinely replaced.

The whole incident had delayed their actual departure by over two hours thirty minutes. By now Janet's anxiety was palpable and nothing Melissa could say to her was able to pacify her in the least. Janet's mind was so frantic even her alien friends couldn't get through to her. Jordan could see the distress on her face and leaned over and said quietly.

"Mum, it is highly unlikely that they know we have left the country because they still believe we are heading down to Cornwall. If they remotely believed otherwise, they would have had their agents at all the airports."

Janet looked at him and smiled and thought maybe he was right and now she could relax. Then Jordan received confirmation from their friends 'out there' that their exit still remained undetected. He shared the news with Janet who immediately felt so much better and finally she stretched out and lay back. Perhaps now she could get some sleep.

Now there was another surprise in store for the family, but this was much more pleasant than the last. Once the plane had reached its travelling altitude Amy came down beaming all over her face. Amy began,

"In recognition for what you have done for the crew both past and present we have decided to upgrade you all to business class." She continued "I have had a word to the captain, who just happens to be my fiancé and he has absolutely approved the recommendation." Melissa couldn't help herself and she just had to have a look at Amy's left hand in order to check out the ring. More hugs and congratulations and best wishes from the family followed and then they moved to business class. The night passed without further incident and that some twelve hours later they touched down in Dubai. Janet had relaxed considerably, and the family had slept so much more easily, largely due their changed circumstances on the flight.

There was very little time once they had disembarked for them to reach their connecting flight, but they all felt relaxed and ready for the next leg of their journey. Janet had not even mentioned what they had left behind. Her entire focus was now getting everybody to the next flight. They arrived with barely ten minutes to spare but happily their seats had already been allocated. Another pleasant surprise awaited them, and it was off to business class, entirely due to the efforts of Amy's fiancé. In no time at all they were comfortably ensconced in their new surroundings and being looked after almost like royalty. Jordan looked over at David and said cheekily,

"I could get used to this." David nodded in agreement and they sat back to enjoy the remainder of the flight. Once in the air David had managed a text message to Emma indicating that they would arrive early the next morning in Melbourne, and wondering by any stretch whether Uncle Ken could meet them? Yes, was the reply over two hours later, and with it the question. "What is really going on? David responded,

"Will tell you when we arrive." Love you xx.

CHAPTER 13

A DAY TO FORGET

IT WAS NOW eighteen hours since the family had left for the airport and Leo whose task it had been to monitor the family's movements was becoming increasingly concerned. The quietness of the house the night they left had not aroused suspicion as they had often gone to bed early after a trip in the country. The next morning voices were heard and confirmed as being those of the family, and whilst there was no clear vision, it didn't unduly concern Leo because the visible recording mechanism had continued to break down, and now the breakdown seemed complete!

What eventually began to raise alarm bells for him was his continued enquiry with all the real estate agents he had contacted over the weeks previously. Each enquiry resulted in a dead end until finally they were all exhausted. By now it was late afternoon, and he raised his concern with Adam. They were soon hurtling to the family home and pulled up outside and strode up to the door knocking loudly. There was no response and perhaps just as well as a response would have had some real explaining to do as to why he had broken his promise. They began checking with the neighbours whom Janet had primed long before. Janet had asked to them say nothing about what they may or may not have seen and they had happily obliged as their friendship went back over twenty years. The next stop would be the Council and to check the CC TV cameras along the street. By now the council officers were closed and nobody was wanting to return to assist them, but they did come back when enough pressure was applied.

Then the search was over before it began as all the CC TV cameras had been disabled. Leo looked at Adam and the situation grew worse by the minute. There were more CC TV cameras, but no one could be clear as to which route the car could have taken even if it had gone. A the brief check through the garage door had revealed no car. Watching so much footage was indeed a time-consuming exercise and time was their enemy. They had to put the departure time of the family at approximately an hour after the voices had finished and that was their first major mistake. Adam had alerted the major airports to look for on the passenger list a Mrs Janet Thomas and the three names David Jordan and Melissa. It was now well after ten pm and every possible lead had been exhausted. They both knew that they had missed something and feeling as tired as they did, they knew that they were not functioning at their best. It was time to call it a day, and it was certainly a day in the chapter of MI6 that they would prefer to forget.

"Well at least they are out of our hair now and we shouldn't be hearing from them again if they have left the country as I suspect." Adam said quietly. Was it indeed the last time he would be hearing about this family, only time would tell!